DEATH
on
WEST END
ROAD

DEATH
on
WEST END
ROAD

A Hamptons Murder Mystery

By

CARRIE DOYLE

DUNEMERE
Books

NEW YORK
SAN FRANCISCO

Published by Dunemere Books

DUNEMERE
Books

ISBN: 978-0-9972701-8-1

DEATH

on

WEST END

ROAD

1

Antonia Bingham sat in the library of her inn and stared in disbelief at the woman across from her. Their conversation was so absurd that Antonia caught herself checking for hidden cameras or, at the very least, a group of friends to pop out from behind the sofa shouting "April Fools!"

She knew it wouldn't happen. First of all, it wasn't April. It was summer in the Hamptons: a beautiful Thursday afternoon in late July, warm but not hot, with a relentless blue sky and nary a cloud. Secondly, Antonia's life had been taking such strange turns lately that her reality was no longer what one would call normal. Just a couple of months ago she had discovered a dead body, which had led to two more dead bodies and the eventual arrest of a serial killer. It was heady stuff, and fairly traumatic, especially since Antonia had been caught in the middle of it all and ended up in Southampton hospital.

Antonia didn't want to think of that now. She had only recently put it behind her in an effort to be "done with murders," a phrase she never imagined she would utter. She was feeling much better, and was finally able to walk without the wobbly assistance of a cane. Now that it was summer—the busiest season at the Windmill Inn, when everyone came out in droves to tan and dine and play in the Hamptons—Antonia needed to focus and manage. Unfortunately, Pauline Framingham had other ideas.

"Well?"

"I guess the obvious question is, why are you coming to me?" asked Antonia.

"Why would I come to you to solve a murder?" asked Pauline. She took a sip of sparkling water before carefully wiping her lips with a linen napkin. Antonia noted that she left no trace of a lipstick stain, though her lips were richly colored. *Pauline either has naturally amazing lips, or she has discovered the world's best lipstick*, Antonia decided.

"Isn't it obvious? You just solved a murder."

Antonia almost smiled. "Yes, but that was accidental. I happened to find a dead body. I almost ended up dead myself."

"But you didn't, did you? And you found the killer. My best friend was killed. Bludgeoned to death with a tennis racket on *my* tennis court, and I want to find out who did it."

Her harsh tone was somewhat unnerving, and Antonia shifted uncomfortably in her seat before responding.

"Why not go back to the police?"

Pauline scoffed. "They didn't solve it the first time, and

twenty-seven years later, they couldn't even figure out who killed Warner Carruthers. *You* did."

Antonia had her own reasons not to like the police, yet still she felt compelled to protest. "That doesn't mean . . ."

"Bottom line is, I was their number one suspect. I was lucky I was seventeen at the time and had the best lawyers in New York City working overtime, because otherwise I'd be sitting in some Pennsylvania ladies' prison with a three-hundred-pound girlfriend who has flabby thighs and split ends. I don't think it would suit me very well."

Antonia couldn't even conjure up the image, and frankly didn't want to. "Well, what about a private detective?"

"We used them back in the day. They were useless. Just took our money and then came back to my father and said it was me. It was always me. Everyone wanted me to be the killer. It was as juicy as a made-for-TV movie. Susie, the blond, preppy 'girl next door.' Me, the dark brunette, the spoiled, rich heiress. Best friends turned enemies. I supposedly found out Susie was fooling around with my boyfriend and killed her in a jealous rage. That story has everything: money, greed, beauty, and evil, but that's just it: it was a *story*. It had everything but the truth. It was, frankly, a load of horse crap. I did not kill Susie. And you can be certain my boyfriend would not have fooled around with *her* behind my back."

Antonia watched Pauline carefully. She was a striking woman of forty-four, with hazel eyes and long silky, dark hair. Antonia guessed Pauline had probably always been called "handsome" rather than "pretty," yet with age her beauty had increased. Perhaps that had a little to do with the fact that she was enormously wealthy—her family was still the largest shareholder in the multibillion-dollar pharmaceutical company her grandfather had founded—and had access to high-quality maintenance. But Antonia didn't really believe that; Pauline didn't look pinched or pulled or overly Botoxed. Instead, Pauline's beauty emanated more from the way she carried herself: she was confident and poised and had superb posture. Not to mention cheekbones that you could slit your wrist on and perfect grooming. Antonia felt the need to sit up a little straighter every time she glanced at her and wished her own dark wavy hair was not quite such a tangled mess.

"You could try a private detective again. I'm sure they're a lot better now than they were twenty-seven years ago."

"I could. But look, I did my homework before I came to you. You may have this nice little façade going of the charming little innkeeper who lives a celibate life baking and cooking at her award-winning restaurant. I can almost see you in thirty years with a bun on the top of your head and kittens nipping at your checkered apron. But I know underneath it all you are one shrewd woman, and you know this town as well as anyone who grew up here. You have your ear to the ground. People come and go at your inn all winter long—locals, summer people, weekenders. You must hear and see things that no one would believe. And people trust you. They like you. You're a local, but you're also an outsider, a Californian. I've even heard that our local movie star came to visit you in the hospital—"

Antonia felt herself blush. How did Pauline know about Nick Darrow?

"That was—"

Pauline didn't wait for her to finish. "I also know from recent events that you are one hell of a dogged snoop. And that is just what I need."

Antonia was both flattered and offended. Basically Pauline was saying that she was nosy, but likably and successfully nosy. Since she had recently turned thirty-six, Antonia had come to terms with the fact that it's important to know one's self, and she couldn't deny that there was truth to what Pauline said. Antonia was . . . curious, as she would prefer to call it. (She had been nicknamed "Snoopy" as a child. Not after the floppy cartoon dog, but for her tendency to eavesdrop.) Was it a crime that she liked to study people and learn as much as she could about them—particularly the guests at the inn? She'd found herself on dozens of occasions playing psychiatrist to various visitors who had come out East in search of something that they hadn't found elsewhere. Antonia liked to help people; it was her nature. Still, her past two successes uncovering murderers had been flukes. Hadn't they?

"Pauline, one thing you have to think about is, are you sure you even want to go there? It happened a long time ago. And I know Susie's death was tragic, but there could be consequences to revisiting it. I hate to say it, but all the clichés come to mind: let sleeping dogs lie; don't open that can of worms . . ."

Pauline glanced distractedly at the plate of coconut macaroons that Antonia had baked moments before her arrival. She hadn't touched them. Neither had Antonia for that matter, and it was taking extreme willpower. That twenty pounds she had promised to lose by summer was still hovering around her middle, as resilient as ever. And the two months when she could barely walk because of her injured knee had certainly not helped her fitness routine. Antonia held up the plate and offered the cookies to Pauline, but Pauline shook her head. With a shrug, Antonia took a small one. *Know thyself*, she murmured inwardly, as if this excused it.

"I just learned that Susie's mother is on her deathbed. She has less than a month to live. It is her dying wish to find out who killed her beloved only child. I would like to bring her some peace . . ." Pauline's voice trailed off.

"That's very sad."

Pauline nodded.

"But . . . do you think the killer can really be caught? After all this time?"

"I think *you* could find him. Or her."

Antonia thought of Susie's mother. As an only child herself, Antonia could only imagine the anguish her mother would have experienced if she had been killed, and so young. It was too awful to think about. Maybe Antonia *could* help find the killer. She couldn't do it alone, though. Perhaps with the help of her friend Joseph, who was a crackerjack researcher, and Larry Lipper, who was a good investigator, she might be able to uncover something.

"You know, you were one of my initial suspects last time,

when I was trying to figure out who killed Warner," Antonia said, taking another small cookie. She couldn't help it; those chewy little drops of heaven beckoned.

Pauline laughed heartily—a husky, masculine laugh. "I'm sure."

"No, really. I knew that he had burned you in his documentary, and I thought of you as a woman who would do what she needed to do to fix things."

"I am," Pauline said evenly. She held Antonia's stare without flinching, and Antonia could sense hardness behind her eyes.

There was a pause. Antonia was warming up to Pauline. She was definitely haughty and a little vain, but she was a straight shooter. There was something refreshing in that. And now that Antonia saw a softer side—one that wanted to find the killer of her best friend in order to bring solace to the victim's mother—that humanized Pauline. But Antonia had her inn to worry about.

"I wish I could help you, Pauline. I really do. But I don't have time to look into this. Summer is my busy season . . ."

"Work during your hours off. You don't have a family."

"Right," Antonia said, feeling slightly affronted, even though it was true. Antonia was quite content being on her own, but when it was pointed out to her, it stung. She would like to have children one day.

"Regardless, I need to work constantly during the summer. This is our busiest time of year."

"I'll pay you well."

"I'm sure you would, but how could I accept payment? What would it be for? I don't even have a P.I. license. My accountants would be all over me."

"What's the slowest month at your inn?"

"Excuse me?"

"What is the slowest month?"

"Um, I suppose February."

"Then I'll rent every room for the month of February, and that will be your payment."

"Pauline, that's very nice . . ."

"Don't say 'but.' I don't like that word. Besides, it would be silly for you to say no. You could use the income."

She spoke the truth. Running an inn and a restaurant in a resort town that had only a three-month high season was expensive. Antonia loved it, but her savings had been whittled down to close to nothing.

A discreet glance at the grandfather clock against the wall revealed that it was almost five o'clock, and Antonia knew she was needed in the kitchen to prep the staff for dinner service. It was time to tactfully extricate herself.

"Let me think about it," she told Pauline.

"Don't fool yourself. You'll do it."

Antonia bristled. She did not enjoy being bossed around. But before she could interject, Pauline continued.

"Come by my house tomorrow and I'll give you all the background information and contact numbers. I won't take no for an answer, at least until you look through what I have. I think you'll be very interested in one of my main suspects."

"Who's that?"

Pauline stood up abruptly. "There was another reason I came to you. The fact is, I believe Susie's killer is a friend of yours."

"What? A friend of mine? Which friend?"

"I'll tell you tomorrow. Seventeen West End Road. Be there at ten."

2

Antonia did a walk-through of the inn's marine blue parlor on her way to the kitchen. Tea service was winding down, and various seating sections were filled with guests of the hotel and locals who had popped in for a quick respite and were currently cocooned deep in the cushioned sofas. Formal tea caddies holding petite trays of miniature sandwiches, scones, and tarts were arranged on tables next to delicate china teapots and cups. The weekly service, held on Thursdays, was very popular, even in the summer months (where iced tea was also an option). It was one of the many warm touches that Antonia provided for her customers.

The Windmill Inn, a sprawling three-story Georgian structure built in 1840, was among the most recognizable buildings in the quaint village of East Hampton. Situated on Main Street (Route 27) it faced both the village pond and the village green and was within walking distance of the town's shops, churches, and well-regarded public library. The inn was now, as it always had been, white-shingled with green shutters, and boasted eight guest rooms, one suite, two small apartments, as well as a restaurant that seated sixty-five, and several public common rooms. Antonia lived in the snug ground-floor apartment, located in the back of the inn with a pleasant view of the garden. The house contained one additional apartment that was situated on the third floor and faced east. Antonia's friend Joseph Fowler, a writer of historical fiction whose wife had recently passed away, had taken up full-time residence there in the fall.

As with most old buildings, the Windmill Inn possessed charm and the enchanting coziness that is inherent in places full of history. The uneven stairs, squeaky floorboards, rickety antique elevator, and countless nooks and crannies in which to curl up and read a book were what people found most captivating. But the finickiness and constant maintenance issues certainly presented a challenge to Antonia and her team, as they were often called upon to fix one thing or another. She frequently felt as if she were hemorrhaging money just to keep the place afloat, especially in the winter months when there were fewer visitors. It was definitely a labor of love, especially the restaurant. Becoming a chef at her own restaurant had always seemed like a far-off dream, and now, even though the reality held financial pressure, she felt more at home here than she ever had in her previous life in California.

Antonia greeted a couple from Pennsylvania before being waved over by Penny Halsey and Ruth Thompson. The ladies were in their seventies and an integral part of the local fabric, with roots going back in the community for generations. Keenly inquisitive and witty, they never failed to cheer Antonia. Ruth was very tall and slim, and wore her white hair short in the style of a 1940s film star. Her features were elegant, from her long neck to her patrician nose and blue eyes. Penny was a bit plumper than her friend, with rosy dimples and eyes that curled up at the edges when she smiled, and today her gray bob was pulled back by a Liberty print headband. Both women were intensely knowledgeable about what was happening in the village.

"We saw Pauline Framingham in here a moment ago," said Penny, who was vigorously buttering a scone. "What's that all about?"

Antonia smiled. These gals didn't miss a trick. "She had some business to talk to me about."

"Did she want to buy you out?" asked Penny.

"No, I'm not for sale."

"You know the Framinghams own most of East Hampton, don't you?" asked Ruth.

"I didn't realize that. But there's definitely an air of entitlement."

"Yes, they bought up all the local real estate in the seventies. Which is why their beloved daughter got away with murder. Everyone was scared to death of them. Didn't want to ruffle any feathers," Penny said between bites of cucumber sandwich.

"That's interesting," Antonia said. *That would explain why Susie's murder was never solved*, she wanted to add, but she refrained.

"I, for one, thought she was innocent," said Ruth. "There was a tennis pro I remember. Lived in the guesthouse. I always thought it was him."

"No, it was Pauline. The father covered it all up," Penny insisted.

"If it was Pauline, the police would have got her. Our police are the best, and they would never have been bought off," Ruth said.

Penny snorted. "I don't know, Ruthie. Money can buy many things."

"I'm not sure about that, Pen."

"Why did you think it was the tennis pro?" Antonia asked.

"I don't know, he just seemed rather, well, sketchy is the word, I suppose," said Ruth. "I recall that he was the tennis pro at the Dune Club for years and lived with the Framinghams. They used to do that at the club, you know—have all the pros live in the guesthouses of the grand estates. And then all of the kids grew up and couldn't afford their own houses so they moved into the guest estates and out went the pros to share houses in Springs. Now these old estates are bursting at the seams . . ."

"Interesting," Antonia interjected, keen for more information. "And then, so, about this pro? What was his name?"

"Hmmm . . . one of those seventies names . . ."

"I think it was Scott," said Penny. She was known for her sharp memory.

"Yes, you're right. Scott. He was at the club for years. I remember back then he drove one of those light blue convertible

Cabriolets. Always had surfboards in the back . . . well, something happened and maybe he was fired from the Dune Club? Or quit? I believe there was some scandal. But he continued to live in the Framinghams' guesthouse. I don't know what he did for a living after that. He was all washed up. I heard he was frequenting Cavagnaro's and McKendry's at all hours, downing vodka tonics."

"He was so handsome, but then alcohol really took its toll," Penny confirmed.

"And it was such a switch. There he was, this good-looking young man, blond hair, always tanned and energized, a smile on his face . . ."

"Called everyone 'dude,'" interjected Penny.

"Yes, he did. He was a Valley Person. Isn't that what they called everyone at that time? Valley People?"

"I believe it was Valley Girls," Antonia said.

"Oh, yes, that's correct. But he was casual and sweet. Just a relaxed fellow. But after that summer he was quite dissipated."

"You think he was hiding a secret?" prompted Antonia.

"I think something sent him over the edge," Ruth confirmed.

"Maybe he was just upset that Susie was murdered?" Antonia suggested.

"Perhaps," Ruth conceded. "Or perhaps he murdered her."

"Nonsense!" Penny said. "Ruthie, I guarantee it was Pauline. Always a cold little fish. Everyone at the club apparently detested her. Zero sportsmanship. And she was known for her questionable line calls in tennis."

"That doesn't mean she was a murderer," Ruth protested.

"I don't know. I think it says a lot about a person's character if they cheat at recreational sports."

As the ladies continued their banter, Antonia's mind wandered to Pauline Framingham. She was an intriguing woman, clearly smart and sophisticated. And yet definitely bossy and used to getting her own way, although Antonia felt that could describe *her* as well. Was Pauline a murderer? Surely she couldn't be if she had asked Antonia to reopen the case and find the true killer. Unless it was a ruse and she wanted to exonerate herself after living under the cloud of suspicion for decades. Whatever happened was so long ago and much of the world had changed. Antonia tried to conjure up an image of East Hampton in 1990. She'd seen pictures, of course, but she had been living in California at the time. A lot had changed since then.

But the truth hadn't. And the fact was, a young girl had been murdered, and her killer had never been brought to justice. And now her mother was dying and needed closure. Suddenly Antonia felt a chill, as if the ghosts of the past were upon her. She glanced around and saw the gauzy white curtains of an open window blowing in the wind. It was as if someone had just passed through, and the thought made Antonia feel restless. Pauline Framingham was right about one thing: Antonia was going to solve this crime.

3

Dinner service, which normally went off as seamlessly as a well-choreographed ballet, was a beat behind that evening. The reason was Kendra, Antonia's sous chef. Kendra was always a bit slower and more intellectual in her manner of cooking than Antonia or her executive chef Marty, though her colleagues were usually able to accommodate that when service started. The more recent delay was due to the fact that Kendra had entered some sort of Instagram cooking competition and was determined to photograph every one of her dishes before they left the kitchen. This made Antonia somewhat stressed and Marty, never one for holding back, downright irate.

"Listen you fat ginger, take your goddamn pictures on your own time," he snapped at her in his flat, gravelly voice as he shook the shallots in the hot oiled pan.

"I love you too, Marty," Kendra replied in a singsong tone.

She snapped one more photo of her tomato basil chèvre tart before passing it on to an impatient waiter.

"I don't need your love, baby," said Marty. "I need you to stop playing with the phone and start making love to your soigné dish and making me some more sea bass crudos because I have three on deck."

"We need to eighty-six the crudos. All out of sea bass," replied Kendra calmly. To "eighty-six" a dish meant to take it off the menu because the kitchen had run out. It was not an ideal situation.

Marty turned and gave Kendra a hostile look. "Now you tell me? Jesus, we are in the goddamn weeds here because of you! Then fire up shrimp scampi à la minute. No one wants to see your stupid pictures anyway. Who even looks at these things?"

Marty was in his late fifties and a restaurant lifer. Since the age of sixteen he had moved from one kitchen to another, climbing up the ladder from dishwasher to line cook to prep cook to sous chef and now executive chef. He was such a pro that Antonia often felt her presence in the kitchen was re-dundant. Marty lived and breathed the kitchen and had little knowledge of or interest in anything outside of the culinary world or Major League Baseball. He was tough as nails—a wiry little whippet with a thin gray ponytail—but he actually had a heart of gold.

That said, Marty was often extremely politically incorrect, and if Kendra were not so thick-skinned, Antonia would be worried that the inn would have some sort of harassment lawsuit coming at it. Fortunately, Kendra was tough, similar to most women who worked in restaurant kitchens. You had to give as good as you got, and Kendra, despite her soft features, could dish it out.

"Let's take it down a notch," Antonia advised. She often had to play the role of mother hen, chiding her chickens to keep in line.

Glen, the maître d' and manager of the restaurant, swept briskly into the kitchen. He was in his mid-thirties, tall and handsome, albeit borderline cheesy with gelled dark hair and a propensity for shiny fabrics and tight-fitting shirts. (Marty called him "metrosexual.") He took his role as gatekeeper to Antonia very seriously. With his mood swings and need for constant recognition, he could be demanding, but he was adept at his job and charmed ladies (and sometimes gentlemen) of all ages.

"Antonia, your friend Larry Lipper has finished his dinner. He said that you agreed to comp him for it and to tell you that you, and I quote, 'better haul your butt in here if you want to ask him your questions because he has a life to lead,'" said Glen in his strong Long Island accent, before adding, "Don't shoot the messenger, I'm just relaying his message."

"Well, that certainly *sounds* like Larry," Antonia said, wiping her hands on her dish towel. "Thanks, Glen."

"I assume he's doing his usual routine and you had no idea he was coming or that you had to buy him dinner," Glen said with certainty.

"Actually, this time he's not lying," Antonia corrected. "I texted him earlier. I do need to ask him something, and the only way I could coerce him here on short notice was through his stomach."

Glen snorted his disapproval and left out the swinging door.

"Gonna go see your boyfriend?" teased Marty.

Antonia bristled. "Good grief, you of all people should know that I find Larry Lipper to be one of the least attractive men on the planet."

"Ya know I'm kidding. No one would be hot for that troll," Marty said as he flipped a pair of pork chops onto the flame. "But he sure is hot for you."

"The man is hot for any woman with a pulse!"

"He never hit on me," Kendra said, taking a picture of lobster tarragon risotto.

"Because look at all those tattoos—yuck!" shrieked Marty.

"Pot calling the kettle black!" retorted Kendra.

"I served my country. That's what servicemen do, get tattoos when we're not dodging bullets and defending our borders."

"You were a cook in the army for about five minutes."

"It's more than you did."

Antonia was happy to leave them to it in the kitchen as she wandered out to the dining room to see Larry. Sometimes she thought Marty and Kendra should take their routine to a sitcom. They had that ongoing bickering repartee like Sam and Diane from *Cheers*, minus the good looks and inevitable romance.

The eggshell and navy dining room had been designed with a mixture of contemporary and traditional elements. While Antonia had gone for a formal look for the rest of the inn, painstakingly scouring the Hamptons and the Internet for antiques, she had decided to make the dining room sleeker and more modern. Abstract art by local artist Dave Demers decorated the walls, and the walnut floor was stained dark, unadorned by the Oriental carpets that ran throughout the rest of the inn. The restaurant, with a cluster of freestanding tables and booths, sat sixty-five people in the most comfortable upholstered chairs Antonia could find. (She discovered that if you had comfortable chairs, men were willing to stay longer and then they ordered more booze.) In the front of the room, there was a lacquered bar with eight button-tufted high-backed bar stools studded with pewter nail head trim.

Most of the dining crowd had thinned out for the evening, leaving just a few stragglers here and there and a cluster of folks at the bar. Antonia waved to a few familiar faces before she spied her friend ensconced in a booth.

Larry Lipper was the crime reporter for the *East Hampton Star*. He and Antonia had a love-hate relationship. Well, actually, she had a love-hate relationship with him; he, on the other hand, was totally oblivious to her occasional hatred and mostly loved her. Despite his short stature, he had an incredibly inflated sense of self. Antonia could concede that he was good-looking—full head of dark hair with streaks of gray, nice blue eyes, chiseled jaw—but he was no Adonis, and she could not for the life of her understand why his ego took up the whole of most rooms. Not to mention that he had incredibly bad manners—he was brusque, demanding, totally unfiltered, and narcissistic. But despite how irritating he was, Antonia did know that a good person lurked inside his tiny body (although it pained her to admit it, even to herself). He was also very smart, something that he unfortunately knew all too well.

She found him reading a smeared copy of the *New Yorker* and eating a bowl of vanilla ice cream with rainbow sprinkles and whipped cream. She sighed; he had very childish taste in food, much to her dismay as a chef.

"Hey, Larry."

He glanced up. "My God, what the hell, Bingham? Don't you ever get out in the sun? I feel like I'm looking at Caspar the Friendly Ghost. You are translucent."

Antonia took a seat across from him. "Nice to see you too, Larry."

He put his spoon down in his bowl. "I'm serious. It's summer. You need to pull your butt out of the kitchen and put a tan on that face. People will think you're dead."

"First off, you know I have no time to go to the beach. Not to mention that until recently I was convalescing after being attacked by a serial killer. And secondly, I have my father's fair skin. No good comes from me in the sun. I either burn or develop red blotchy marks."

"Don't gross me out."

Antonia rolled her eyes. "Blotchy, blotchy, blotchy."

"Seriously, Bingham. Try to maintain some of the mystery. I need the aura, I don't need to know all the down and dirty when you're trying to seduce me."

"Okay, enough. So, what have you got for me?"

Larry took a large bite of his ice cream. His eyes lit up gleefully as he swallowed. "You know it's not going to be that easy."

"I know, it never is. But were you able to secure a meeting for me with your former colleague?"

Larry licked the whipped cream off his spoon. "You only texted me this afternoon, you think I can work my magic that fast?"

Antonia sighed again. "Larry."

"All right, all right. Yes. Chester said he would meet with you."

"Fantastic! When?"

"Well, that's the problem. He's in Maryland."

"He's in Maryland? For how long?"

"Dunno. He said he wasn't sure. A couple of weeks."

The disappointment stung. Chester Saunders had held the crime beat at the *Star* before Larry, and Antonia was certain he would be able to tell her what he knew about Susie's murder. After all, he was there; he covered it.

"Maybe I can talk to him by phone?" she asked hopefully.

Larry plucked the maraschino cherry off his sundae and popped it in his mouth. "Yeah, but he's going on a boat trip. He said it wasn't a great time."

"Did you tell him it was urgent?"

Larry gave her a wide-eyed look. "Urgent? This chick has been dead for more than twenty-five years. How is it urgent?"

Antonia didn't want to concede that he had a point. "Well, I mean, I want to start . . ."

"Ah, now that you're hot on the trail of this cold case, everyone needs to cut short their vacations and stand at attention? Doesn't work that way, sweetie."

"Her mother is dying, Larry. There is a ticking clock here."

"How long does she have?"

"Less than a month."

"She's going to the grave without an answer."

"Larry!"

"What? Don't 'Larry' me, Bingham. You really think you can solve this murder in a couple of weeks?"

"I have no choice. So when is Chester going on the boat trip? Maybe I can talk to him tonight."

"Tomorrow morning."

"Why didn't you tell me right away? I could have called him."

Larry leaned back against the vinyl banquette. "Bingham, relax. I asked him a few questions myself. Figured we could work this case together."

"I would like nothing less."

"You flirt!" Larry laughed. "But you know you need me. I mean, it's pathetic that you just can't admit it. This woman walks into your inn and asks you to figure out who killed her friend, and the first person you call is me? You need my help, Bingham. And I'm willing to help you. We both know you can't do it yourself. Plus, you enjoy having me around."

He was right; she did need him. If she was going to attempt

to run an inn and a restaurant *and* solve a crime simultaneously, she would require assistance. Due to his profession Larry had a network of contacts with law enforcement and local crime buffs. One spin of his Rolodex could give her access to a number of witnesses. Plus he was pushy, and although Antonia was no shrinking violet she would rather Larry be the pest.

Antonia sighed heavily.

"Don't deny it anymore, just accept it," Larry said, dabbing his face with his cloth napkin.

"Just tell me what Chester said."

"It's actually an intriguing case."

"Go on," Antonia prompted. "Tell me what happened."

"I can do better than that."

"What do you mean?"

"I recorded my call with Chester. I had him tell me the story. You can listen to it in his own words."

"Larry, you know what? Sometimes I do love you."

He smiled smugly. "Sometimes, Bingham? *Please.*"

4

The restaurant had emptied out and only Glen remained at the bar, tallying the night's receipts. The busboys had cleared the discarded dishes and blown out the candles that illuminated the tables. Darkness swept through the room, and Antonia stared intently at Larry's iPhone, which he had placed between them. They were riveted to Chester Saunders's husky recorded voice as it came through the phone, describing the crime that had captivated the town a quarter century prior.

"Do I remember it?" Chester asked after Larry had explained the reason for the call. Chester had the strong Bonacker accent unique to the East End of Long Island; some say it is a derivative of the one found in Cornwall, England, from whence some early East Hampton settlers came. "Of course I remember it. I remember it as if it was yesterday. That was big news back then. We didn't catch many murders out there—still don't."

"I know, I wish . . ." Larry's voice interjected, prompting Chester to burst out laughing in a deep bass.

Antonia rolled her eyes at him.

"What?" he spat out at her. "I cover the crime beat, for God's sake. Of course I want crime!"

She put her fingers to her lips and leaned toward the phone.

"Murder makes good copy, but it also makes people crazy," Chester continued.

"That's fine by me, I only care about copy," Larry's recorded voice said, again inciting laughter from Chester. "But tell me all about it. I won't interrupt anymore."

"Fair enough. Let's see now . . . it was summer. End of August, I think. Yes, around the twenty-third—my wife's birthday was that week. Anyhow, of course I had the police scanner, and that's how I got tipped off to everything that was going on around town. I'm at my desk, it's around five p.m., give or take, and I pick up the nine-one-one call to seventeen West End Road. I'm thinking, West End Road? Why, that's right by Steven Spielberg's house, and, this sounds crazy, but I'm thinking, maybe they're filming a movie and the caller thought it was real. But of course, that wasn't the case. So the nine-one-one call says that a girl's head is cut and she's bleeding and they need an ambulance right away."

"Who made the call?" Larry asked.

"It was Pauline Framingham. And you know she was real calm, cool as a cucumber. You'd think, you know, your friend is bleeding to death, maybe you're a little bit hysterical? But no.

Not this gal. And that's how she was the entire investigation. Just cool as a cucumber . . ."

"You think that's why they thought she was guilty?"

"Could be. They zeroed right in on her, that's for sure. Old Tubby Walters was the chief of police back then. You didn't know him; he retired a year later and moved down to Florida. A lot of folks thought he was paid off by the family, actually. Never solved the case and moved away. I don't think so; he was an honest guy. I just think he was out of his depth. He was a local cop and this was Big City business. The Framinghams and their friends were Big City. Anyhow, I wait awhile, thinking maybe it's just an accident, because, you know, the caller was so calm, and who would have thought murder? I wait, but then I hear the call for backup and detectives and a wagon and I know I need to head over there.

"You know, I didn't spend that much time in that part of town, down by Georgica Beach. It's pretty swank over there. And I pull on the road, and they're all up at that house on the dunes, the Framingham house. I ask my buddies what happened and they say a seventeen-year-old girl is dead. Pummeled to death with a tennis racket. One guy said he'd never seen anything so gruesome, but I suppose that's not saying a lot, he'd probably never caught a murder before. They said they were talking to the Framingham girl, but before they even got to her, the lawyer Tom Schultz arrived. He's a powerhouse, to boot. To this day, I don't know how they got him there that fast, but he was there by the time I was. She lawyered up and then that was that."

"Was Pauline the only suspect?" asked Larry.

"She was the only one who was there at the time. Well, there was a tennis pro living on the property, Scott Stewart, but he was teaching at the club at the time, and people vouched for him. They looked at the housekeeper and the maid, but one was sixty-five years old and wouldn't have had the strength to do anything like that, and the other was at the grocery store. Pauline had a brother, Russell, but he was on his boat at the yacht club, someone vouched for that. The only other people investigated were Pauline's boyfriend, Dougie Marshall, and the landscaper, Kevin Powers."

A lightbulb went off in Antonia's head. She knew Kevin Powers, not well, but she was good friends with his brother, Len, and Len's wife, Sylvia. Pauline had said that the person she suspected of killing Susie was a friend of Antonia's. This must be to whom she was referring.

"Did you think either of them were good for it?" asked Larry.

There was a pause on Chester's end. "I actually liked the brother for it. I thought there was something off about him . . . I'm not sure what."

"But you said he had an alibi?" asked Larry.

"Yes, yes. But I don't know . . . there was something not right about him. It felt as if he was hiding something."

"Why didn't they look at him harder?" pressed Larry.

"I think they were overwhelmed. The family lawyered up; they weren't cooperating at all. Dougie Marshall was a degenerate, one of those snot-nosed spoiled brats. They would have loved it to be him. And Kevin, well, I never thought he could have done it. He was a lightweight. Surfed a lot, smoked a little weed, I hear he's legit now, but, well . . . I think we got into a little bit of a class warfare on that one."

"How do you mean?" asked Larry.

"Well, God forbid it's a rich person who did it! It had to be a Bonacker: a local. At least that was the rumor the family was spreading."

"Why would the brother—Russell—why would he have killed Susie?"

"I don't know . . . maybe he fancied her. I'm not saying he did, but there was something there. Something I can't pinpoint."

"Got it."

"But you know, I could be all wrong. Could have been Pauline Framingham, like everyone else thought. She was one cold gal."

"You think a girl like that kills her best friend?"

"Yeah, that's where it all fell apart. No real motive, not for any of them."

"Anything wonky about the vic?"

"Naw. Everyone loved her. A pretty girl. I remember when her parents came down to I.D. the body. I was hanging around. They were shell-shocked. I'm haunted to this day by the looks on their faces."

Larry turned off the recording.

"So what do you think? You got your work cut out for you, Bingham."

"It's very sad. Gosh, now all I can think about is her parents. And to know that her mom is so sick . . ."

"There are a lot of casualties around a murder, and not only the victim."

"You're right."

"Are you ready to exonerate a possible murderer? Who is 'cool as a cucumber' when their friend gets whacked?"

Antonia cocked her head and stared at him. "I was interested in what Chester said about the nine-one-one call."

"What, that she was calm?"

"No. Nobody knows how they'll react when confronted with that situation."

"What then?"

"Pauline Framingham said her friend had been cut. She didn't say beaten to death or pummeled, she just said cut. That's different."

"What does it matter? It's just semantics."

"I don't know . . . if she had killed her and intended to kill her, she would have said she was dead. I think it matters."

5

Friday mornings in the summer were a whirling bustle of zest and activity at the Windmill Inn. There were new guests arriving—usually earlier than their appointed check-in time—who were eager to unpack and hit the beach as soon as possible. Then there were the reluctant departees, whose languid efforts at checkout always caused tremendous consternation to the housekeepers and front desk. Even when gently reminded that departure time had come and gone they would situate themselves in the public salons before reluctantly retrieving their belongings from their now overdue rooms.

These were the moments when Antonia channeled her inner Camp Director, and she was in her element. She would stand at her post, next to Connie, who worked at reception, and Jonathan, the manager of the inn, and dictate, designate, and troubleshoot. After assigning early visitors the shiny blue bikes that the inn offered and providing them with maps and restaurant and beach information, she wished she had a giant whistle around her neck that she could blow to send them on their merry way until their accommodations were ready. And although she would have preferred to rebuke the guests who had worn out their welcome, she knew that she had to take it as a compliment that they were so entranced by her inn that they didn't want to return home.

"How are you doing this morning, my dear?" asked Joseph Fowler, as he scootered past the desk en route to the front door.

Joseph, Antonia's friend and lodger, had suffered from polio as a child and now walked with the assistance of crutches or zipped around on his shiny red scooter. A distinguished and handsome man in his early sixties, his appearance was always meticulous (he had a penchant for bow ties and dressing formally, regardless of the season—today it was a seersucker blazer over a pale yellow polo shirt with khakis) and his demeanor unflappable. He and Antonia shared a special bond; he reminded her so much of her late father and was always a supportive friend and adviser.

"Frazzled," replied Antonia. "But managing."

"Make sure you give yourself a break! Just because you feel better physically doesn't mean the wounds have completely healed."

He worried about Antonia's health after her hospital stay. It was sweet. "I'm fine."

"Pamper yourself a little! Head to the beach one day."

"You sound like Larry Lipper," said Antonia.

"Oh, then forget I said anything," Joseph replied. He was

not a big fan of Larry—he found him churlish and inappropriate—and he particularly despised the brusque and sometimes "disrespectful" tone Larry used when he talked to Antonia.

"No, I just mean he said I look too pale."

"You look wonderful."

Antonia smiled. They didn't make men like him anymore, Antonia mused. Always chivalrous and courteous, Joseph had all of the older ladies who came for tea contending for his attention.

"Are you headed to the library today?"

"Indeed I am. I ordered some recondite biographies on lesser-known Russian royals from a library upstate."

"Sounds interesting. How's the book going?"

Joseph's historical fiction was critically acclaimed, and one of his books had been nominated for a Pulitzer Prize. All his books were set in the World War I era, with his latest taking place in Russia. "Slowly, as usual."

"I'm sure it's great," Antonia said with certainty. "Hey listen, if you have time while you're there, would you mind searching through some old copies of the *East Hampton Star* for me? Pauline Framingham asked me to look into the murder of her friend Susie Whitaker."

Joseph raised his eyebrows. "Aha, just can't stay away from murder, can you?"

"I want to . . . but now my brain is full with Susie Whitaker and I feel compelled to help find her killer."

She filled him in on everything that had transpired between her visit with Pauline and Chester's commentary.

Joseph left with the promise that he would look into the back issues at the library. He was an incredible researcher so she knew he would have plenty of information assembled by dinnertime.

Antonia poked around the parlor and made sure that all of the breakfast fare had been cleared and the discarded newspapers returned to the racks against the wall or neatly aligned on the coffee tables. The staff had fluffed the pillows, and the furniture had been restored to its immaculate condition, no longer bearing the posterior indentations of the breakfast diners. One more survey of the room rendered Antonia satisfied. She was particularly enamored of the clusters of peonies on various tabletops, housed in delicate silver julep cups. At the end of the day, despite the financial burden and the hard work it entailed, she loved her inn and it made her truly happy. Life was about appreciating the small things, Antonia's mother often said, and she was so grateful that she was now surrounded by love and beauty in a place she cherished.

Antonia headed into the kitchen and helped herself to a plate of plump blueberries and a banana nut muffin that was hot out of the oven. The moist treat practically melted in her mouth, and after adding one more to her plate, she made her way to her office. She was looking forward to a moment of quiet where she could enjoy a cup of milky English Breakfast tea with her meal. She couldn't shake Susie Whitaker from her mind and she wanted to think more about how she would proceed in her investigation.

In the front hall, a man descending the stairs stopped her.

He was in his mid-fifties, balding, with a thin black mustache impeccably groomed. He wore a neatly pressed pale blue shirt and a white linen sports coat over it and clutched a fedora in his long-fingered hand. Antonia noted that it was not the type of fedora currently favored by hipsters in Montauk but rather had the air of authenticity about it. He spoke with an Italian accent—her father would have remarked that he was "straight out of Central Casting"—and had an amiable face and pleasant demeanor that Antonia immediately responded to.

"Excuse me," he began. Antonia noted that he said it more like *Excusa me!*

"Yes, can I help you?"

"Thank you. You are the owner of the inn, *si?*"

"Yes, I'm Antonia Bingham. Welcome."

"Thank you." (Again, more *Thank-a you.*) "I wanted to know your advice. Are you familiar with a woman who calls herself Elizabeth?"

"Elizabeth? Elizabeth who?"

"I don't know her last name. Elizabeth."

"Hmm . . . what does she look like?"

"She is about this high," he said, indicating his height, "and she has dark hair and beautiful brown eyes. *Bellissimo.* Like a baby deer."

"Ooh, don't say that around these parts. People are not too fond of deer," said Antonia.

The man gave her a quizzical look.

Antonia continued. "Because they're overpopulated. They eat all of the vegetation. They used to eat just certain plants, but now they're eating everything from the yew trees to the hydrangeas. They're destroying the ecosystem . . ."

She trailed off when she noticed confusion in his expression.

"But they are so cute, no?"

"Well, I suppose . . . but people are throwing up fences everywhere to keep them out. There's just too many. It's sad. They're starving, and plants are dying. It's lose-lose."

She could tell that the man wasn't exactly following, so she stopped herself. Sometimes her logorrhea got to be too much. "So, this Elizabeth? She has pretty eyes?"

The man's face became awash with joy. "The prettiest eyes in the world. You see straight into her heart. The eyes that you cannot forget. At least, I cannot, and I am certain no one else could."

"Wow! Sounds very special."

"I met her here in East Hampton. It was in October. I was here for the Hamptons Film Festival. I am an investor in small films. I live in Milano."

"How interesting."

"It is. I met her at Cittanuova, the Italian restaurant in town. She was at the bar; I was at the bar. We discussed. She says this was her first time at the festival. She always comes to East Hampton in July and August. We talked and talked. And then she said it was time for her to go to her film, and she did not reveal her last name. I know only, Elizabeth. Now I have been thinking about her for all these months, and I decided I need to come back and see her again."

Antonia was truly touched. She put her hand to her heart. "That is the sweetest story I've ever heard!"

"I hope it is not the ending of the story, but the beginning. I am going now to the offices of the Hamptons Film Festival to ask their information on people named Elizabeth. But I ask of you to think or ask your friends . . . maybe they know her."

"I definitely will. Hmmm . . . I'm running through everyone I know now and drawing a blank. But I definitely want to help. What's your name?"

"I am Giorgio Leguzzi. Here is my card."

He produced a manila card from his black leather wallet.

"Nice to meet you. I'm going to spread the word and see if we can track down Elizabeth. I must know someone who knows her."

"*Grazie*," he said with a slight bow before leaving the inn.

Wow, Antonia thought. She wondered how it would feel to have someone cross an ocean to find you after meeting you just once. To be that lucky in love. That wasn't even in her wheelhouse. She had sabotaged her last romantic dalliance by accusing the guy of being a murderer. That was probably a giant no-no in the rule book on how to land a man. She was no good at love or romance. Her ex-husband was a monster who had been physically abusive and had inadvertently caused the death of her father. These days, she spent her time pining over a married movie star who was her morning beach walk partner. Yup, she was definitely self-destructive in the relationship department. However, just because she was bad at romance in her own life, it didn't mean that she couldn't help others.

Antonia spent the afternoon sending out emails to local friends inquiring if they knew any charming brunettes named Elizabeth. It was these sorts of distractions that often derailed Antonia's day, but brought her so much joy. One of the perks of owning an inn was connecting with the guests. And Mr. Leguzzi was so lovely, it was fun to help him. Of course, not all of the guests were receptive to help. She remembered that last month there had been an odd young woman named Bridget Curtis who had stayed at the inn. A skittish girl who had behaved strangely. Antonia had tried to help her but had been rebuffed. *Oh well*, Antonia told herself. *You can only help those that want help.* And maybe she would find Mr. Leguzzi's love.

6

The air in East Hampton was redolent with the salty scent of the ocean and the lush perfume of soil and flowering trees. The aroma of blooming privet and honeysuckle bushes was especially strong this summer. Not a day went by without Antonia feeling an overwhelming sense of gratitude that she had ended up in this scenic, soulful, aromatic town. She had her best friend Genevieve to thank for that. If Gen hadn't encouraged her to quit her life in California and join her on the East Coast, Antonia might never have discovered the beauty that awaited her. There was a reason artists had flocked to this town to paint—the colors were luminescent and poetic and the light was spectacular. What Antonia felt most of all was inspiration.

East Hampton is the easternmost town in the state of New York, and in Antonia's opinion, the most beautiful. Sited on a peninsula, it is bounded by the Atlantic Ocean, Block Island, and three bays—Gardiners, Napeague, and Fort Pond. The town includes the village of East Hampton as well as the hamlets of Montauk, Amagansett, Wainscott, Springs, and part of the village of Sag Harbor. It was the first English settlement in New York State, though it had been populated by Native Americans for centuries.

An agrarian community for its first 250 years, East Hampton village's design remains exactly the same as when the settlement was laid out in 1648. Which meant that the view from Antonia's Windmill Inn, of church tops, windmills, historic houses, and the South End Cemetery—where Lion Gardiner, one of the first settlers, is entombed—was more or less the same view that prior generations saw for centuries. Antonia felt a sense of history and place whenever she stood on the grassy lawn in front of her inn.

Now, as she drove down Apaquogue Road toward Pauline's estate on West End Road—dodging the clutter of joggers, bikers, and amblers—Antonia was filled with a mixture of anticipation and anxiety. There were no two ways about it: Pauline Framingham intimidated her. Antonia respected the fact that Pauline was forthcoming; it was refreshing. But the more time she had to think about Pauline, the more unnerved Antonia became. She tried to break it down in her mind. If she could decipher the root of it, she might feel better.

Could it be because Pauline was so rich? Until Antonia had moved to East Hampton (she hated to say "the Hamptons"—so tacky) she had never met super wealthy people. Well, that wasn't completely true; during her catering days she had done events for affluent vintners and some of the wine-country crowd. But this was on an entirely different level. A lot of people who summered in East Hampton had more money than small Latin American countries. Or even big Latin American countries. But in the three years since she had moved here, she had consorted with rich, even very rich people at benefits for Guild Hall or the Group for the East End. They had even dined at her restaurant. And now, for the most part, she was used to people with money, which was almost absurd. Her father would have had a good laugh at that.

Could she be intimidated because Pauline was "old money" as opposed to "new money," more *to the manner born*? That couldn't be it either. Antonia had a side job as a caretaker where she looked after the Lily Pond Lane home of the Masterson family. Her duties included checking on the house when they weren't there and being present for any deliveries or maintenance. Robert and Joan Masterson were very old money. Someone had told Antonia that Robert's family had come over on the *Mayflower* and Joan was a Daughter of the American Revolution, which was apparently a big deal in society. Or at least it used to be. But the Mastersons were very nice, and Antonia never felt intimidated by them.

It was Pauline herself who was daunting. That could be because Antonia had suspected her of a different crime, or maybe it was because she had been suspected of killing her best friend, but Antonia didn't think that was the reason either. Pauline had this aura around her—this confidence and entitlement coupled with—the word popped into Antonia's head as she passed Steven Spielberg's house—ruthlessness.

* * * * *

"Wow, what a beautiful house," mused Antonia as she was led through the spacious pale green living room with windows facing the Atlantic Ocean. There were several clusters of furniture upholstered in pastel colors with floral throw pillows, a skirted corner table with an abundance of framed photographs, and an impressive oil portrait above the marble fireplace mantel of an elegant woman sporting a large diamond and sapphire necklace.

"It's a teardown," said Pauline without a lick of emotion in her voice.

"A teardown? No way," Antonia disputed as she glanced around.

The enormous weather-beaten, gray-shingled house loomed on the dunes with a large expanse of newly mowed lawn in front of it. It was one of those iconic beach houses, probably a hundred years old, that no doubt had been referred to as a "cottage" back in the day. There were no frills—well, that is if you didn't count amenities such as a tennis court, a saltwater pool, an outdoor shower, a guesthouse, a spectacular view of the ocean, as well as probably multiple bedrooms and as many baths. In the era of shiny new McMansions all attempting to emulate such original beauty, it was stunning to see inside the real thing.

"Of course it is," said Pauline. She diverted her attention from Antonia momentarily to ask her uniformed maid to bring the iced tea to the sunroom. She then returned her focus to Antonia.

"Why do you say that?" Antonia asked peevishly.

Pauline gave her a slight condescending smile that made Antonia feel self-conscious. She worried that she would start perspiring and wished she had not worn her gauzy shirt, which would immediately show any sweat marks. Pauline, on the other hand, looked fresh in her neatly pressed tennis whites with her dark hair slicked back in a swinging ponytail. Although she was in her mid-forties, she was as fit as a teenager with toned and tanned hairless legs and arms and a flat stomach.

"In this day and age, everything out here over twelve years old is a teardown," Pauline said with strained patience. "The people with money have no loyalty to history, they just want convenience. You can't blame them, really. It's no longer fashionable to have Jack and Jill bathrooms, everyone wants 'en suite.' They want to feel like they're in a hotel. And this house has low ceilings—there's no charm in that, they all want cathedral. Not to mention we don't have a basement, so they would have to lift up the house and dig under it, and at that point why bother . . ."

"Do they really need a basement?" asked Antonia naively. "Seems as if you have enough storage space."

Pauline looked at her as if she were insane. "You have to have a basement in this day and age for your media rooms or kids' playrooms or especially if you want central air—a perk we don't have. For us, it was always fine to use the ocean breeze to keep us from overheating. But apparently that is not de rigueur these days."

"But there's so much charm in these old houses . . ." Antonia protested.

"Who cares about charm when you pay sixty-five million for a house?"

Antonia's eyes widened and Pauline continued.

"I'm not trying to be gauche, we both know how much this type of house would fetch. And I am most likely low-balling. The one on Further Lane went for one hundred and twenty-seven million and that was also a teardown."

"I don't know . . . this house has style."

"Style is ephemeral. This house has quirks, and people don't have patience for that anymore. We have a dozen bedrooms of varying sizes, but buyers want a uniform size. They don't want the staff on the same floor, so they either stuff them in newly built rooms in the basement or outsource them. My neighbors, who bought their house for twenty million ten years ago before promptly tearing it down, rent a house for their chef and housekeeper in the Springs."

"The world is really changing. I happen to love quirkiness . . ."

"Clearly," said Pauline. "But quirky means forcing yourself to adapt to something uncomfortable and inconvenient and spinning it to make it sound charming."

Antonia opened her mouth to protest but Pauline continued. "Quirkiness works for me here because it's a habit. I'm used to this house. It's the repository for my childhood memories, my mental garbage can. When the third step on the back stairs creaks, it reminds me of sneaking out when I was fifteen. I like the fact we haven't dug our power lines underground because I quite enjoy losing power during a hurricane. It reminds me of Hurricane Gloria when I made out with Henry Johnson for the first time. But someone new who doesn't have these memories will care less about them. They want their own."

"I suppose . . ."

"At the end of the day, it's irrelevant, because I'm not planning on selling, now or ever."

"That's great."

Somehow, Antonia felt as if she had been dressed down by a teacher. She followed Pauline in silence until they arrived at the sunroom. Antonia realized she had seen this house from the beach many times on her early-morning walks. It was surreal to be on the opposite side, staring out rather than in.

The sunroom was not fancy or in any way impressive except for the wall of windows and screen doors that afforded a spectacular 180-degree view of the beach. There was a beadboard ceiling and shingled interior walls awash in white paint. The décor consisted of white chipped cane furniture with sagging cushions in faded green, white, and pink chintz—a somewhat sad pattern of fat peonies and roses. The floors were a milky cream tile overlaid with a small natural-colored sisal rug and a glass-topped coffee table atop that. There were some bleached wood-framed prints of plants and flowers adorning the walls and an endless collection of jars of varying sizes housing sea glass—no doubt collected from the beach below—on every surface. It was a WASPy paradise and smelled faintly of mildew.

Pauline motioned to a rickety armchair that appeared to be the least comfortable seating option in the room for Antonia to place herself on, while opting for the sofa herself.

Antonia wedged her frame into the seat as gracefully as possible but couldn't help but feeling that the chair was meant for a child, not a grown woman.

"I talked to Mrs. Whitaker last night and she was so heartened that you have decided to help us find Susie's killer," Pauline said.

"I'll do my best."

"It really means a lot to her. It's very sad because she's so sick, but she's still totally lucid. And she still talks about Susie as if she just left the room."

"That's heartbreaking."

"I know. The nurses say she is holding on in order to get an answer . . ."

They both sat in silence for a minute. Antonia studied Pauline, who looked distraught. Surely she couldn't have murdered her friend if she's this despondent, Antonia mused.

Suddenly, Pauline's manner changed and she was at once all business. "I need you now to sign all these documents and then we can commence."

She motioned to a pile of legal contracts that Antonia had not noticed upon entering.

"What are these?"

"Nondisclosures, payment agreements, liability waivers."

Antonia gulped. "Um, I guess I'm not really prepared for this. Maybe I should have my lawyer look at it?"

She did some mental math on how much her lawyer charged per hour and how much this endeavor would cost her. She had never thought about liability. Maybe she was putting herself in a precarious position. This was definitely above her pay grade, literally and figuratively.

"Nonsense. I'm all for lawyers, believe me, I have a lawyer for every possible need, but I'm also a reputable person from a very wellconnected family. Let's be honest here, my lawyers could crush your local lawyer. So just sign and let's be done with it."

Antonia didn't know how to respond.

"You have to trust me for this to work," Pauline prompted.

"Well . . ."

Before Antonia could finish her sentence, the maid entered with a pitcher perched atop a tray.

"Ah, here's Elsa with the snacks," said Pauline with light cheer in her voice. She began pouring the iced tea into tall melamine glasses. The maid, who had a broad Slavic face and thin blond hair, looked to be in her late twenties. She asked Pauline if there was anything else and, when told no, left quietly.

Antonia glanced down and saw that, in addition to drinks, there was a plate of Pepperidge Farm Milano cookies.

Pauline caught her ogling them. "I had her bring treats for you as well. I know you have a sweet tooth, but I don't do sugar. I'll set us up while you sign."

7

With the official business finished and Antonia still in doubt as to whether she had just signed away her inn or her firstborn child or both, Pauline was finally ready to begin discussing the past. Antonia pulled out a notebook from her handbag and began to take sporadic notes. She wasn't sure if that's what she was supposed to do. Should she be recording Pauline? She needed to go to private eye school; even an online seminar might help. Ask her anything about cooking or antiquing and Antonia was a pro, but this was out of her comfort zone.

"Let's see . . . where shall I start?" Pauline asked, smoothing her tennis skirt. There was a tiny blue whale folded between the pleats on the left side, and every time Pauline moved Antonia got the impression he was bobbing in a milk bath.

"Well, why don't you tell me how you knew Susie?"

"Right. Contextualize, good idea. Susie and I met at Brearley. That's an all-girls school in New York. She had been there since kindergarten, and I came as a new student in fifth grade. Prior to that, my family had been living in Europe, mostly London, but a few years in Belgium. My father was the ambassador."

"Really?" Antonia looked up. "I thought he was in the pharmaceutical business?"

"He was, but this was a political appointment. He was a huge supporter of Ronald Reagan."

"Got it."

"Susie was very popular, always. She was a really supportive friend, very loyal, your victories were her victories, she was not competitive at all. She liked most people and wanted to be liked. I guess what some might call a people-pleaser. I suppose what others call a kiss ass."

Antonia raised her eyebrow as she glanced down and pretended to scribble something. Had Pauline said that with disdain or neutrality?

"Don't worry, this is nothing I wouldn't have teased Susie about! We all did. Well, our posse. That's what we called ourselves in later years, 'The Posse.' It was me, Susie, and our other best friend, Alida Jenkins."

"Alida Jenkins . . . isn't she a model?"

"Yes. The top-earning African-American model of all time. She was always stunning."

"I know. I remember her ads for Calvin Klein. It's funny, but I thought I saw her out here once . . ."

"You probably did. She has a house in Sag Harbor."

"Really? I had no idea . . . that's interesting."

"You'll want to meet with her as well. To hear her thoughts on this whole sad affair."

The way she said "sad affair" sounded hollow to Antonia. Was it just her pat answer because she had been asked so much about Susie's death? Or did she find it a nuisance?

"Yes, I will definitely want to talk to her . . . to contextualize."

"Good."

Pauline took a sip of her iced tea. The sunflower that had once been etched into the side of the glass was vanishing from years of dishwasher use.

"Where was I?" Pauline asked, her eyes sparkling. Antonia noticed that they had changed color; they were more green today than hazel. Perhaps it was the blue sky and ocean being reflected in them.

"You were telling me about your . . . posse."

"Ah yes, yes. The posse. Alida, Susie, and I were all best friends. In the summers, Alida would be at her family house in Sag Harbor, and Susie would come stay with me out here. Starting from when we were about thirteen. We would bike to town, hang out at the movie theater, buy ice cream at Sedutto, go riding at Swan Creek, spend our days at the club. There wasn't a whole lot to do here back then, but it wasn't crowded, which was nice. I used to have this little toy car, motorized; my parents got it for me from England. It went up to forty miles an hour and looked just like a VW bug. We used to drive up and down these streets. Once a reporter from the *East Hampton*

Star snapped a picture and we were in the next issue under the headline 'What is it?' It was funny . . ."

Her voice trailed off as if she was awash in memories. She glanced down at her hands before continuing. "I adored the town back then. And just before Susie died, we were at the age where we started going to the Talkhouse and Bay Street to hear bands. And of course dinners at Little Rock Rodeo followed by Snowflake. There were bonfires on the beach. Yes, the posse sure did have fun."

"Sounds like it," admitted Antonia. "Didn't Susie have her own country house?"

"Not everyone has a country house," Pauline rebuked.

Antonia reddened with embarrassment. "I know . . . of course I know that, I'm sorry," she sputtered.

Pauline smirked. "But, yes, Susie's family did have a second home. It was in Litchfield, Connecticut, which was terribly boring. She lived on a thousand acres with no neighbors in sight, and she was an only child with older parents so she went out of her mind. If she'd had horses, that would have been one thing. I would have been up there every weekend to ride—with or without her. But they didn't have anything of the sort. Just a murky pond coated in algae and lily pads."

"Sounds terrible."

"For a teenager, yes. And I enjoyed having her here. I didn't have a sister, only Russell, my older brother . . ."

"Right, how much older is he?"

"Three years older."

"Does he still come out here?"

Pauline rolled her eyes. "Unfortunately . . ."

"Oh . . . sorry for asking."

"It's fine. It's just difficult now that my parents are dead . . . sharing a house. It's similar to a ship without a captain so there's always mutiny."

"I see . . . is he married?"

"Divorced. He has a daughter and a son who live with their mother in Florida. And there is always a revolving door of girlfriends. Younger and younger, with bigger and faker tits every time."

Pauline took a hurried swig of her iced tea, as if to wash the distaste for her brother out of her mouth.

"And was he . . . did he hang out with you and your friends?"

Pauline cocked her head to the side. "Not really . . . he was a bit of a nerd. He did have a girlfriend for a long time back then . . . Holly Wender . . . then they broke up. Funny, we were all glad when they broke up, didn't care for her at all, but now she would be a godsend compared to the trash he brings home."

She looked as if she was going to continue but stopped abruptly. Antonia waited before finally speaking when it was clear Pauline wasn't going to proceed. "Was he dating Holly when Susie died?"

"Yes."

"But they weren't at the house that day?"

"Not at that time."

"You know, why don't you just tell me about that day."

Pauline nodded. "That day. That day. It's funny how one

day in your life can be the one day of your life that defines you. On my tombstone it will say December 16, 1973—the day I was born—and then whatever day I die, and it might as well include August 23, 1990, as well, because that is the most notorious date in my life. The date that Susie died. And actually, I'm sure no one cares about the other two dates—my birth and my death. Because when it comes to me, it's all about what happened to Susie and whether or not I killed her."

"I'm sure that's not true . . ."

"Isn't it?" asked Pauline, staring carefully at Antonia. They stared at each other for what seemed to Antonia like a full minute. Antonia looked away first. "But I don't care anyway," Pauline continued. "My conscience is clear."

"Can you tell me what happened?"

"Certainly, but don't you want to record this? Or are you very skilled at shorthand?"

Antonia pulled out her smartphone. "Yes, of course. I wasn't sure if you wanted me to."

Pauline shrugged. "I want to make sure you have the facts."

8

At the end of the driveway, Antonia stopped abruptly as a gardener passed in front of her. A tiny, weathered old man, he nodded at her before crossing toward the large maple tree. He bent down and began weeding the pachysandra that surrounded it. Antonia watched him as he diligently worked, yanking the weeds and flicking them into his bucket. She had a superb gardener at the inn, Hector, which was fortunate as she was totally useless with plants.

Instead of making a right toward home, Antonia made a left and slowly drove by the entire Framingham property. She wanted to absorb the neighborhood and gage the surroundings. Through the scattered bushes the house came into view as she moved along the road. On the westernmost end, as far as possible from the main house, was the guesthouse, which practically abutted the split rail fence. It was separated by only a few overgrown boxwoods, which shadowed its entrance. It

was there that Scott Stewart, the tennis pro, had spent his summers. Next to it was a chain-link fence enveloped by vines; the
tennis court. Antonia craned her neck to get a better look, but
the foliage created an impenetrable screen.

West End Road was not only a very narrow paved road
but also a dead end. Clearly the inhabitants had gotten tired
of people turning around on their lawns because there were
pointy stakes thrust into the earth and rows of large white-
painted rocks lining the lush grass outside their fences, making
it difficult for a car to make a U-turn. The road was unique
in that both sides of the street were on the waterfront (one
side the Atlantic, the other side the fabled Georgica Pond). It
boasted a variety of enormous houses in various architectural
styles teetering on the ocean dunes, with equally impressive
abodes across the street on the pond side. One house resembled
a castle, another bore a resemblance to a dollhouse, several were
newer imitations of the Framingham mansion, and there was
one very bizarre one-story dwelling that looked not unlike a
fast-food restaurant. *Now* that's *a teardown*, Antonia thought
to herself.

This time of year the vegetation was dense and the hedges
thick, which somewhat obscured Antonia's view of many of the
houses. East Hampton was a natural paradise in the summer,
bursting with color, fragrant with flowers, with the ocean a
lively cobalt color and the pond a deep sapphire. Everything
grew with full force, from the hydrangeas to the sea grass to
the ferns. Antonia thought of it as a jungle, full of lushness and
sensuality, albeit a curated one. Teams of landscapers buzzed

around the neighborhood, maintaining the wildlife. Lawns were mowed, hedges clipped, bushes pruned, and flowers coddled, and just when one round was finished, the gardeners came back and started all over again. The landscaping noise on weekdays was almost unbearable.

The road narrowed and then Antonia reached a "Private: No Trespassing" sign that forced her to make a U-turn in a gravel driveway. Luckily her old Saab was compact enough not to require a three-point turn. Someone had told her that there was a public beach access at the end of the road, but the owners had put up "Private Property" signs to deter visitors, and the town had not taken them to task for it. Antonia continued back toward the inn, passing the Framingham house again and waving at the gardener before pausing at the stop sign in front of Grey Gardens.

Antonia wondered if there was some irony in the fact that the Framingham house and Grey Gardens were so close to one another. They were both notorious in their own way. The Framinghams' for murder and Grey Gardens for once being the decrepit residence of the impoverished Beales—Jackie Onassis's aunt and cousin. There had been documentaries, plays, and movies made about Grey Gardens. Perhaps one day there would be one about Pauline Framingham's home. It was ripe for a TV movie, at least. Or maybe an episode of *Law and Order*, if it was still on the air.

Antonia was still processing her interview with Pauline and wanted to mull it over before she came to any conclusions. Her plan was to throw herself into dinner service and then discuss it with Joseph afterward. She was glad she had recorded it so she could play him everything in Pauline's voice. It would be good to have an outside opinion.

* * * * *

Growing up, Antonia had always preferred her family's feast on the night before Thanksgiving to the actual holiday banquet of turkey, mashed potatoes, and stuffing. On that Wednesday night, Antonia and her parents would host her aunt and uncle for a steak dinner. It was smaller and more intimate than their Thursday affair, when extended relations, family friends, and the usual stragglers would descend for the traditional fare. But what Antonia really loved was that, in addition to steak, her mother would make double-stuffed potatoes and Antonia's all time favorite dish: creamed corn.

This, however, was no ordinary creamed corn. First her mother would fry bacon, then, after removing the crisp strips from the pan for Antonia to chop into bits, Mrs. Bingham would sauté chopped red onion in some of the reserved bacon fat. Then she would add the corn kernels (frozen) and sauté them in the bacon grease as well. After they were cooked through, she turned off the flame and added sour cream and the bacon bits. It was definitely not a recipe for those suffering from high cholesterol, but Antonia adored it.

Since it was late July and there was an abundance of corn, Antonia had decided to add it to her menu that evening. Rave reviews from diners had been pouring in all night. Antonia knew that customers loved delicious comfort foods. She enjoyed reading about all of the latest food trends, like sous vide and foams and liquid nitrogen, but none of those fancier culinary tricks would ever be her forte, and the menu at the Windmill Inn reflected that. Good thing a lot of other people felt the same way and the restaurant was doing well.

"We've got two more sides of that goddamned corn," Marty snapped as he whipped the chits with the incoming orders off the board. "Soyla, you better work faster."

"Yes, Marty," Soyla said complacently. Whereas Marty and Kendra were larger-than-life personalities in the kitchen, Soyla, the petite hardworking wife of Antonia's gardener, Hector, was the quiet and unassuming worker bee. She had started with no real experience but was now running breakfast service and prepping dinner service. Currently, she was at her station, furiously shucking corn and slicing the kernels off the cobs, and she had been at it nonstop all night. They normally did prep work in advance but they'd had no idea that the corn would be so popular. Anyway, corn was best served freshly shucked.

"Thanks, Soyla," Antonia said.

Friday nights were busy, and the heat was on in the kitchen. The hours had spun by for Antonia in a whirl of plating butter-and-thyme-roasted French radishes with rock shrimp tempura over beds of dressed mâche as well as cutting the fish for the ceviche. In addition, she also had to gently remind Kendra to stop Instagramming long enough to fulfill her orders.

"Kendra, move it on the pasta," shrieked Marty. "I've got two lambs dying on the pass waiting for you to be done."

"I'm almost finished," she said, while snapping one more shot with her smartphone.

"Kendra, when does this contest end?" Antonia asked gently. She wanted to give her employees wings and let them fly . . . but not if it made the customers fly away because service was so slow.

"One more week. I promise," Kendra said, wiping her face on a dishrag.

Antonia could not help but note that Kendra did not look particularly healthy. Puffier than usual, she had a glossy pale sheen and was sweating from the steam coming off the burners. Her red hair was pulled back in a blue bandanna, and her doughy white features had not seen the sun this season. If Larry Lipper thought Antonia's complexion was bad . . .

"Okay. I hope you win. But I hope you win soon," Antonia said.

Glen opened the swinging door to the kitchen and popped his head in. "Antonia, Genevieve is here."

He gave her a strange look.

"Uh-oh, what is it?"

"She's doing shots at the bar . . ."

"Is she out of control?"

"No . . ." he answered without conviction.

Despite being only two years younger than Antonia, Genevieve behaved as if she were a teenager. If there was a female equivalent of the Peter Pan syndrome, Genevieve suffered from it. After a few peripatetic years where she jumped back and forth between Northern and Southern California—attempting to be an actress, then a vintner, but ultimately working as a caterer and following any guy that caught her fancy—she was now a manager at one of the local Ralph Lauren stores (there were, rather impressively, four in town) and was quite successful at her job. That didn't change the fact that she was, at times, immature and infantile and could still be found engaging in the same activities as people twenty years her junior. Examples included: attending Justin Bieber concerts, putting toilet paper around neighbors' bushes at Halloween, and prank calling "enemies" from burner phones. She had terrible taste in men—not only attracting losers and cheaters—but was completely oblivious to any warning signs and resolutely refused guidance. If she found a man handsome, it wouldn't make a difference if he was wearing an orange prison jumpsuit, his hands were in cuffs, and two federal agents held him by the arms; she would go for it. But she was fun and loyal as heck and those were only two of the many good reasons why she and Antonia were best friends.

As soon as the orders died down, Antonia took off her apron and made her way through the restaurant to find Genevieve. It was not hard, as her voice preceded her.

"Come on! You can do better than that!" Genevieve coaxed loudly. "Woo! Woo! Woo!"

Antonia found her at the bar with two older men in suits, one with short dark hair and the other with a mop of steel wool–colored hair and the type of wire-rimmed glasses that had been popular in the seventies. Genevieve—her long, lanky figure clad in a floor-length floral spaghetti strap dress with tasseled leather earrings dangling from her lobes—towered over the two men. She was egging them on to drink some sort of flaming red liquid shot, and they were up to the challenge. Fortunately, rather than offend or disrupt the remaining clients, this seemed to have energized them. The remaining diners were clapping along, and the other guests at the bar were smiling with encouragement.

"Antonia!" Genevieve boomed with excitement as soon as she saw her friend.

"Hey, Genevieve, what's going on?"

"This is Heinrich and Chang."

"Ching," asserted the dark-haired man.

"Ching! Right. And we are celebrating!"

The two men downed their shots to the applause of the room. They were both perspiring as if they had been running and their eyes were slightly bleary and bloodshot.

"What are you celebrating?" Antonia asked. "And *how long* have you been celebrating for?"

"We are celebrating our new friendship," Genevieve said loudly before leaning in and whispering to her friend, "They just spent forty thousand dollars in the store. I earned the fattest commission of my life. Apparently they live in Singapore, they're here for some business associate's daughter's wedding or something random and they wanted to buy souvenirs for their family! Can you even?"

"That's great," Antonia said.

She didn't want to quash her friend's ebullient mood, but Antonia wasn't sure she was excited to have such a festive atmosphere in her restaurant. It irritated her a bit. Or was she overthinking it? Was it a good thing that people came to her bar to 'party'?

"Turns out they're staying *here* this weekend! I insisted we have the best champagne and drinks so they can drop some more coin in your inn as well. I have them ordering only the most expensive stuff. But don't worry, I'm dumping whatever I can when they're not looking. Then they're only too happy to buy me more!"

Immediately Antonia felt bad. No matter how scattered and lacking in common sense Genevieve could be, at her core she had Antonia's best interests in mind and, in her own clumsy and often inappropriate style, she always meant well. Antonia should have known by now not to doubt her.

"Thanks, Genevieve."

"You betcha," she said, crinkling up her nose. Unlike Antonia's pale complexion, Genevieve's naturally olive skin was bronzed and tanned. She was a stunning woman with beautiful big green eyes and a tawny, even complexion. Her features were a little asymmetrical, but in Antonia's mind, these quirks only enhanced her beauty. Genevieve had never failed to attract male attention, but it was always the quality of her admirers that was the issue.

"Listen, when you're not busy—and when you're totally sober—I want to ask you about something," Antonia told her.

"Uh-oh, am I in trouble?"

"No, I need some information on everything you know about East Hampton in the summer of 1990. I know you were here then."

"Nineteen-ninety?"

"Yes."

"Okay. I mean, I was here, but I was pre-pubescent. Although I might have had breasts, I did develop early . . . unfortunately, I also stopped developing early . . . why do you want to know about that?"

Before Antonia could answer, Genevieve's drinking buddies coaxed her away and she did another shot with them, to the backdrop of the chanting crowd. Antonia motioned to the bartender to keep an eye on the drunken triumvirate. The German downed a shot and swaggered over to Antonia.

"You are a beautiful woman," he said, his breath fragrant with alcohol.

"Thank you."

"I mean it. A beautiful woman."

"That's very nice of you."

"Genevieve says you are single. I am also single."

"Yes, I'm single."

Heinrich swayed slightly, woozy from alcohol, but kept his eyes locked on Antonia. "A beautiful woman like you shouldn't be single. Come, have a drink with me. Let's go sit over there, away from the noise."

"I'm flattered, but I need to return to the kitchen. Time to wind down dinner service."

He sighed deeply. "I see. Genevieve said you were single, but it appears you have your heart set on another man."

Antonia didn't want to protest, it wasn't worth it. "You're right. I'm in love with someone. But thanks for the offer of the drink. I'll head back into the kitchen now."

Heinrich gave her a nod. "I hope this man is worth it. Genevieve speaks very highly of you."

"Yes I do," said Genevieve, swooping in on the tail end of the conversation just as Heinrich walked away. "What was that all about?"

"He was hitting on me."

"As well he should! You need to get out there, Antonia."

"I need to get back to work. I have to meet Joseph in the library at eleven."

"But wait, what were you saying before?" asked Genevieve, returning her attention to Antonia. "What happened in 1990?"

Antonia sighed. "It's a long story, but Pauline Framingham asked me to look into her friend Susie's murder."

"SHUT UP!"

"It's true."

"That is so awesome, another murder!"

"Um, awesome and *tragic*?"

"Yeah, totally. I didn't mean to be callous. I just meant that you are so good at solving crimes, Miss Marple. Okay, yes we have to brainstorm and I will try and remember everything. Of course that was a *major* event that summer. I probably wrote about it in my diary, which I still have . . . Hello Kitty, so cute . . ."

"Okay, well, see what you come up with."

"For sure!"

Antonia started to walk away when Genevieve laid a hand on her arm, stopping her.

"And of course you need to talk to my sister."

"Victoria? Why?"

"Because her best friend Holly was dating Pauline's brother at the time."

"Really? She was friends with Holly Wender?"

"Yeah. Small world."

"It is indeed," mused Antonia. "Okay, I'll call Victoria."

"Or come by. She's staying with me for the week."

As she left the room Heinrich blew her a kiss. Antonia was tickled. It was nice to have a man tell you that you were beautiful. No matter how intoxicated he was. But her mind immediately jumped to Nick Darrow. If only he knew how much she thought about him. If only he were available.

9

That Antonia was meeting Joseph in the library of the inn to listen to Pauline's recording recounting Susie's murder was a little ironic since that's where she had met with Pauline just the day before; hearing Pauline's voice come through the phone was déjà vu. But Antonia always preferred to sit in the library after dinner. Most of the hotel guests who were returning home from their dinners or events flocked to the parlor, where they could still order drinks and snacks until midnight. The library afforded some privacy.

Because the Windmill Inn was open year-round, it was crucial that the décor be appropriate for all seasons. It meant that Antonia had to establish a delicate balance between cozy and charming, more fitting for fall and winter, and bright and airy, for spring and summer. She found that switching out the throw pillows from darker hues to brighter colors in the warmer season added an incredible amount of light. The heavy curtains were removed from the windows of the downstairs public rooms, leaving just the bamboo matchstick shades, and in some places thin white curtains were added as the only protection from the sunlight that flowed into the inn. Antonia also pulled up many of the area carpets and left the polished floors bare for the summer. Streamlining the décor made all the difference.

The library, with its shelves of hardcover books and its blue-painted wicker furniture and green-striped cushions was the perfect blend of comfortable and lively. Antonia was always inspired by an abundance of books, and she had carefully curated the selection that she offered on loan. Of course, some disappeared forever in the hands of guests, but that was to be expected.

She found Joseph ensconced in the corner chair, perusing the latest issue of *The Atlantic,* one of the many periodicals that Antonia stocked on the magazine racks of the inn. She was of the belief that if you were surrounded by reading material it elevated your behavior.

"Dinner was delicious as always, my dear."

"Thanks, Joseph," Antonia replied, handing him one of the glasses of sherry that she had brought in from the bar. Having a nightcap always made Antonia feel retro, as if she were stepping into an episode of *Mad Men.*

She sat down on the couch and placed her phone on the white lacquered coffee table in front of her. She slid the potted geranium over so her view of Joseph was unobstructed.

"I'm intrigued," Joseph confessed. "I imagine this was what

it was like back in the day when there was no TV and people listened to radio shows."

"You mean when you were young?" Antonia teased.

"Very funny. I may be old but not that old," he replied, his blue eyes twinkling.

"I want to show you this first."

Antonia pulled a photograph out of the roomy pocket of her cardigan and handed it to Joseph. It was a close-up picture of Susie on the beach taken the year she died. Pauline had peeled it out of her monogrammed leather-bound photo album and handed it to Antonia. The colors were vibrant. Susie had been a pretty girl—with long blond hair and cornflower blue eyes. She had a round face and a smattering of freckles and was tanned with slightly chubby cheeks. She looked wholesome, youthful, and vivacious. Back in the day one might have called her a Breck girl, although if you were to ask a current teenager what that meant they would draw a blank.

Antonia thought hard about what Susie would have looked like now. No doubt her baby fat would have melted away and her jawline would have been stronger. She would have been even more attractive when she was older as her features became more pronounced.

"Pretty girl."

"Yes," Antonia agreed.

"Very all-American," remarked Joseph. He shook his head with sadness. "Such a tragedy."

"I know. The more I look at her, the more I feel . . . I don't know, a kinship with her. Sort of a familiarity. She looks like so many of the girls that I grew up with in California. She looks so excited in this picture. She had all of her hopes and dreams, everything in front of her . . . and then it was extinguished."

Joseph continued to study her picture. "I wonder if Miss Framingham has any video of her?"

"I should ask. Good idea."

Joseph put the picture down, and Antonia pressed the button on her phone. Seconds later Pauline's clear patrician voice came through the speaker:

Susie was living with me that summer, as she always did. For the month of July and part of August we worked in the stables at Swan Creek, but we had both arranged for our jobs to end August fifteenth so we had the last few weeks of summer to sleep in and go to the beach and hang out. Some mornings we would go riding, but other days we just brought a ton of magazines to the club and stayed as late as possible on the beach with our friends. Alida often joined us, but she was working as a counselor at Boys Harbor during the weekdays, so usually only on weekends. Plus she had started modeling already so she often headed to the city for shoots.

So on that day—August twenty-third—Susie and I had gone to the club and got home at about four. My parents were in Europe so it was just us. We decided that we had been lazy so we would play tennis. We went down to the court—you drove past it on your way up to the house—and we started to hit. Alida said she would come by to hit with us, and I left a message for my boyfriend, Dougie, to join us as well, so we were kind of waiting for them to play doubles. It was boring to play with Susie because I was a much better player than her. I easily beat her 6-0 in the first set without even breaking a sweat. She wasn't competitive at all, which also made her not that fun to play with. She'd just laugh a lot.

I told Susie to work on her serve while I went up to the house to call Alida and Dougie again and find out where the hell they were. Dougie hadn't been at the beach that day, but his mom said he wasn't home, and there was no answer at Alida's. So I had Rosamund—she was our housekeeper at the time—make up a tray of lemonade and snacks, and I brought it down to the court.

At first I didn't see Susie anywhere, and I called her name, but there was no way she would have heard me, even if she weren't already dead, because your friend Kevin Powers was mowing the grass with one of those beyond noisy lawn mowers. He wore headphones, of course, so the sound didn't bother him, but it was a nightmare for the rest of us. Not to mention that he wasn't supposed to mow the grass at that time. The rule was he did that type of work when we were out at the beach or away from home. Not when we were there. My father told him that repeatedly. He didn't listen . . . but more on that later.

So I called for Susie. I put the lemonade down on the table and then I saw that the gate at the far end was open. We never ever used that gate; we always came in from the gate closest to the house, and that was the gate closest to the street. I walked over and noticed a pile of laundry there, half on the court, half on the grass, and I was confused as to what it was. And then I realized it's not laundry but Susie. At first I thought she was faking and I told her to stop being annoying and just get up. But she didn't move and when I leaned in I noticed that her head was bleeding. I couldn't see her face or her eyes. But I felt her pulse and she was still alive, so I rolled her over and saw a gash on her head, as if she'd been cut. So I run up to the house and call nine-one-one. You know the rest.

There was a pause before Antonia's voice broke the silence with a follow-up question. "Who do you think killed her?"

My parents believed Kevin Powers did it. I had complained earlier in the summer to them that he was a creep, always leering at us when we were in bathing suits by the pool. And he was always around. It was so annoying, he bothered the hell out of me. And he knew it too. What bugged me is, whenever I wasn't there, he would corner Susie and talk to her, and she was too nice to blow him off. She also felt awkward because it wasn't her house so she couldn't really say scram. But I could and did.

My father thought that Kevin went up to the house to talk to Susie and she finally blew him off and he freaked out and hit her with her tennis racket. You know he was a big druggie. The guy was a loser, in his twenties and mowing two or three lawns a week for a living. But the police defended him because he was from an old local family and they stick together. They said he had no history of violence, blah, blah, whatever. My father always insisted he did it.

Antonia spoke again. "Where were Alida and Dougie? Did you ever find out?"

Alida stayed late at Boys Harbor because there was some camper play or awards ceremony or something like that. Dougie was AWOL all day because his dad made him play eighteen holes of golf with some business associates, which takes hours. There was no one else here but me, Susie, Rosamund—our housekeeper—and Kevin. My brother, Russell, was at the yacht club with his girlfriend,

Holly. And Scott, the tennis pro who lived in our guesthouse, was teaching. No one had any motive but Kevin—a spurned lover. But that wasn't the story the police or press wanted—too boring. They wanted it to be me. Poor little rich girl who killed her best friend. It was absurd.

Antonia turned off the recording.

"What do you think?" she asked Joseph.

"This is a tough one," he remarked. "It would be ideal if we could see the police files and find out why they didn't pursue Kevin Powers."

"I know. I may have to pay a visit to my pal Officer Flanagan." Antonia had "worked" with him on her last case. What had started as an acrimonious relationship—Antonia was wary of cops—had actually blossomed into a semi-friendship.

"It's interesting that Pauline dodges the question when you ask her who she thinks did it."

"What do you mean? She says Kevin Powers."

"No. She says that her parents and in particular *her father* believed it was Kevin Powers. But she doesn't state that as her own opinion."

"Oh, you're right."

"Are you planning on interviewing others?"

"As many as I can find. Pauline said Rosamund, the housekeeper, is dead. The other woman who worked for them moved back to Colombia years ago. She gave me Alida and Dougie's contact info, but otherwise I'm on my own."

"What about Susie's mother?"

"I asked Pauline if I could interview her and she said

she would check with the nurses. The mother is very sick so it doesn't seem likely. Not sure how much she would know, anyway, as she wasn't here."

"You have your work cut out for you, my dear."

"Yes," Antonia agreed. "It is a bit daunting on so many levels. Pauline Framingham is intimidating and although I fancy myself as strong, there is that vulnerable side of me that she has a talent of tapping into. She's a bully, and I don't do well with bullies, as you know."

Joseph nodded. He knew Antonia's history with her ex-husband Philip and how he was able to tap into that side of her as well. "If that's the case maybe you don't want to do this investigation. Why put yourself in a position of weakness rather than strength?"

"You have a point. But my reason for doing it is for Susie, not for Pauline. Look at this picture . . ." Antonia held up the photograph of Susie. "She deserves justice."

"She does."

"I want to bring it to her. It's the least I can do. But I don't know the first thing about cold cases. I know I am a good snoop, but the technical aspect is a challenge. Even if I gain access to the police files, I have no idea how to analyze evidence such as fingerprinting or DNA. What if there's DNA that needs to be looked at? I don't know anything about that other than what I've seen on TV."

"But you know people. And you understand them. And don't forget, profiling and criminal psychology are just as important to solving a crime as forensics. There may be a 'what, where, and when' in an investigation, but your job is to find the 'who' and the 'why.'"

"That's true."

"Remember the words of advice from that legendary detective Hercule Poirot."

"What was that?"

"He said, 'Until you know exactly what sort of person the victim was, you cannot begin to see the circumstances of the crime clearly.'"

"In other words, start with Susie."

"Exactly. If anyone can do it, it's you, my dear."

10

Antonia liked to take an early-morning walk every day in order to clear her head before the crazy busy workday unfolded. She'd made a promise to herself when she first moved to East Hampton to do it every day, but she had found that the promise was much easier to keep during the off-season when business at the inn was slower. Summer was nonstop for Antonia, and it took a Herculean effort just to leave the inn for an hour to meander along the picturesque coastline just a few blocks away.

That Saturday morning, Antonia was determined to hit the beach. She wanted the soft sand under her feet. She wanted the cool frothy water to lap at her toes. She wanted to search for interesting shells and rocks and watch the sun rise high in the sky. She knew it would help her sift through some of the information that Pauline had given her and help her formulate a plan of attack. She parked her old Saab at Georgica Beach and set off westward in the direction of Wainscott. She needed to take another look at the Framingham house.

When she reached it, she paused and stared. The house looked different from the beach side. It was still large and majestic, but without the giant yard that unfurled in the front, it was less imposing. Antonia's eyes flitted to the screened porch where she had recently sat with Pauline. She couldn't see anyone inside. In fact, the house looked deserted.

"Beautiful house, isn't it?"

Antonia was startled. She hadn't heard anyone approach. She glanced over and saw a woman dressed in tight athletic clothing, gripping two hand weights in her palms. She was attractive and fit, probably in her early sixties, but she'd had a lot of facial work done in order to appear younger.

"It is."

"It's too bad that such a nice house is home to such an evil person."

Antonia cocked her head to the side. "Why do you say that?"

"The woman who lives there is a murderer."

"Pauline Framingham?"

The woman gave her a fake smile. "Also known as a spoiled brat who enjoys wrecking people's lives."

Antonia nodded. She didn't want to engage, what was she supposed to say? It would be impossible to defend Pauline and this woman clearly had experienced some distasteful interaction with her.

"I would discourage anyone from getting mixed up with her."

"What do you mean?"

The woman shrugged. "It doesn't end well. Let's just say I know where the bodies are buried. And I'm not talking about Susie Whitaker's."

"I'm sorry I didn't get your name? I'm Antonia . . ."

"My Fitbit just went off. Have to finish this run before I cramp up. Bye."

The woman took off in a run, leaving Antonia alone in front of the Framingham house. What was that all about? Antonia mused. Was it a coincidence or was that woman threatening her? She decided to shake it off.

The tide was low, so Antonia walked down close to the shoreline. Her bare feet made imprints in the wet sand. Maybe it was a good thing that she had been avoiding the beach. You never knew who you would run into. Although if she had, she never would have met *him.*

She had met Nick Darrow one morning on the beach when he was walking his dogs and they had become friends and confidants. He hadn't led her on; in fact, he most likely assumed she knew he was married, because, well, everyone on the planet knew that. But Antonia wasn't big on celebrity gossip and had serious disdain for tabloid journalism, and so she was quite out of the loop on the personal lives of celebrities. If she *had* been interested, she would have known about Nick's tempestuous on-and-off-again marriage to Melanie Wells, a well-known actress. And despite all the drama surrounding their union, it didn't appear to be dissolving any time soon.

Against every single morsel of her being, Antonia knew that

being in love with a married man, let alone a married movie star, was not only absurd but self-destructive. And yet, she couldn't help herself. "The heart wants what the heart wants," Woody Allen had disgustingly said in defense of marrying Soon-Yi. He was a bad example and yet there was truth there, and the fact that he said it then, while defending a terribly immoral union, proved how accurate that phrase was. The heart wants what it wants. But. You also have to control the heart and not let it go in the wrong direction. And Antonia was making her best effort at this type of control. Of course it helped that Nick Darrow was currently out of town filming a movie in some far-flung exotic destination, with his wife and son.

As Antonia ambled past the staggeringly beautiful mansions hovering in the dunes, she attempted to examine why she made bad choices when it came to relationships. Her parents had been happily married until her mother's death when Antonia was twenty-one. Her father had grieved and remained true to her mother's memory until his passing ten years later. They were a beautiful example of devotion and kindness and love. But despite that model, Antonia had married Philip, an abusive cop who had only become more violent and aggressive as the marriage continued. And why hadn't she left that situation earlier? She was a strong, competent woman. His friends—fellow cops—kept assuring her that he would change, that Antonia was overreacting. It did a number on her. In retrospect, she couldn't relate to the person she was back then. She'd had resources. Her father would have helped her—as soon as he learned what was going on he had sprung into action. She had friends and extended family she could have reached out to for assistance. It was an aberration—as if she had lived that part of her life in a daze, which confounded her now because she had the strength and clarity to do something about it. Sadly, it took the death of her father after a blow from Philip to extricate Antonia from him forever. Even now, Antonia was still reeling from her father's death and felt she hadn't completely processed it.

Since then there had been a few dates and dalliances here and there but nothing heavy in the romance department. Antonia would love to be married and she wanted children too, but she wondered if it would ever happen for her. Certainly not when she was so distracted by Nick Darrow. It wasn't because he was gorgeous (although he was) or because he was famous (that was almost a negative); it was his intensity and brilliance that she admired. He would listen to her talk— really listen—and reference things in later conversations that she hadn't even remembered saying. He never bothered with chitchat or gossip, instead preferring to discuss cerebral and philosophical issues, which Antonia found thrilling. They had once had an intense conversation about God and religion and the meaning of life that Antonia had found deeply moving. Nick was a religious, churchgoing person and persuasive in his belief in a higher power. They had conversed in a way she never had with anyone else.

Thank God he was away. It couldn't go on like this. She hoped that distance would make her heart grow less fond. If she kept harboring this crush she would be single forever.

Antonia wondered why Pauline Framingham was still single. Antonia didn't feel comfortable passing judgment on people's romantic decisions, but Pauline was forty-four—eight years older than Antonia, and she was a beautiful and rich woman. Did Pauline have a boyfriend? What had her romantic life been like since Dougie? Antonia hadn't even thought to ask. There had been whispers that perhaps Susie and Pauline had been lovers, and Antonia had dismissed it, but maybe Pauline was gay. Antonia wasn't sure how important it was, but if she was investigating everyone she would have to find out. Only then would she discover who killed Susie.

* * * * *

Alida Jenkins was the first person Antonia reached out to because she thought Alida would be the hardest to pin down, but the opposite turned out to be true. When Antonia called and introduced herself, Alida had told her that Pauline had said she would be calling and there was no time like the present so why didn't they meet now? As soon as breakfast service came to a conclusion, Antonia did just that. Unfortunately, she had to bring company to Alida's.

Larry Lipper, in exchange for putting her in touch with Chester Saunders, had demanded that he be present for any of Antonia's interviews. She had attempted to rebuff him, but he held firm. An arrangement between Antonia and Larry had been brokered: she had guaranteed him the exclusive story rights, had promised to allow him to participate in some of the interviews (she could decide which ones at her discretion), while he had agreed to use his police contacts to ascertain any pertinent information. Antonia couldn't help feeling as if she were making a deal with the devil.

"Thank God we're interviewing someone hot," Larry remarked from behind the wheel of his jazzy new BMW convertible. Larry had sold the film rights to the series of articles he'd written about the serial killer in East Hampton, which had provided some cash flow. That the movie might never be made was a sore spot for him. That Nick Darrow would play him remained his confident belief.

"Must you be so superficial?" Antonia scolded. Antonia hated being a passenger in Larry's car—he always drove too fast and passed people and spun around corners—but he had insisted. She assumed that his love of being behind the wheel was a deeply Freudian and phallic need, so she didn't bother fighting him.

"Whatever. Seeing Alida Jenkins in the flesh will be very helpful to me. I hope she wears something skimpy. Man, I wore out that *Sports Illustrated* bathing suit issue she was on the cover of."

"You're vile," sniffed Antonia.

Their interactions always devolved into such prurience. He definitely didn't bring out the best in Antonia, and she hated that about him.

"I'm not vile, I'm a hot-blooded man."

Antonia couldn't see his eyes behind the mirrored lenses of his aviator sunglasses, but his chin had about two days' worth of stubble and he was very tan. For a fleeting second Antonia thought he looked semi-attractive but then she remembered who he was.

They were cruising on Route 114 headed into Sag Harbor, the whaling hamlet where Alida had a house. Antonia thought it was somewhat ironic that Sag Harbor—long described as "Least Hampton"—is actually the only East End village situated in two Hamptons. About three-fifths of the village, including Main Street, the Old Whalers' Church, the Whaling Museum, and other noted landmarks, are in Southampton, while the remaining two-fifths, including the bay front and the high school, are in East Hampton. Despite the geographic tug-of-war, Sag Harbor has maintained its unique character for most of its three-hundred-plus-year life span. But in the past few years it did seem to Antonia as if the outside world had suddenly discovered Sag Harbor and the secret was blown. As Larry edged closer to town, the traffic thickened.

It made sense to Antonia why it was so popular these days. Sag Harbor's history is a full one. Among other things, it has been a whaling port, a writer's colony, a historic African-American community, a stop on the Underground Railroad, a summer residence for a United States president, and a reference in such iconic novels as *Moby-Dick* and *Jaws*. The village is picturesque, with houses situated on small leafy lots reminiscent of New England and a business center devoid of the chain stores that can be found in every other town and strip mall in America. The town leaders were struggling to contain the tsunami of development that was accosting the town. Antonia hoped they would be successful. Overdevelopment was the scourge of the East End and would be its ultimate demise.

"I talked to some people at the paper who remember the case. They said all roads lead back to Pauline Framingham. She was always suspect Numero Uno. But they had no evidence."

"Maybe they had no evidence because she didn't do it and that's why they never solved the case," Antonia said with confidence. "I won't make the same mistake."

"Look at you, Bingham. All bulled up on yourself. I like it."

11

Alida Jenkins's house was located on one of the most
sought-after streets in the Sag Harbor historic district.
Sitting prominently on a hill, the late-1800s shingled home
had white trim and a large front porch with several seating
arrangements. The lots in Sag Harbor Village were small—
whereas you might live on a two-acre plot in the village of East
Hampton, in Sag Harbor that was extremely rare. Antonia es-
timated that although Alida's was one of the bigger properties,
it was probably situated on only three quarters of an acre, give
or take a few feet.

"Nice pad," Larry said after they had parked on the street
in front and commenced climbing up the series of stone steps
situated in the lawn. "I'll be very happy here."

"I'm sure you will," replied Antonia. "In your dreams." She
glanced around the yard. "Beautifully maintained property. I

like how they kept a lot of the big evergreens and ferns. Nowa-days all you see is boxwoods, no one has anything else."

"Because of the deer. They eat everything," Larry said. They had finally reached the front door, and he pressed the bell.

The front door swung open and Alida Jenkins stood on the threshold. It took an embarrassing beat for Antonia and Larry to respond. Antonia had been in the presence of beauty, but she quickly realized that it was nothing compared to Alida Jen-kins—she was a whole other level of gorgeous. Alida had a per-fect angel's face in the shape of an oval. From her flawless dark skin to her beautiful eyes with thick black lashes (the kind that most woman have to glue on), she was stunning and possessed the sort of haunting beauty you can't look away from. It wasn't only her face that was enviable; she was tall and thin with end-less legs, perfect breasts, and an amazing butt. Even now, clad in a gossamer emerald green tunic over a damp bikini, with her hair slicked back in a bun, she was the epitome of regal magnificence. It was no wonder that she had been one of the top-earning models of all time.

"Hi! You must be Antonia and . . ."

"Larry Lipper," he said, thrusting out his hand so abruptly that their hostess took a step back before recovering and offer-ing him her palm. Alida Jenkins was about a foot taller than Larry, and Antonia was amused to spy Larry standing on his tiptoes in an effort to look distinguished. *Nice try*, she wanted to mutter under her breath.

"It's a pleasure to meet you," Alida said. "Please come in."

They both followed her through the front door quietly, which was uncharacteristic for Larry. That's when Antonia confirmed to herself just how smitten he was with Miss Jenkins.

"I was swimming with my children . . . it's so hot today, don't you think? They're still out by the pool, so let's go in here."

Although the exterior of the house was antiquated and old, the inside had been completely renovated and gutted, achieving a somewhat startling modern loft-like look behind the traditional frame. Walls had been removed, and the downstairs was open plan with a family room that melted into a living room that melted into a dining room—the only separation between designated sections was the two-sided slate fireplace. The remaining walls were a light creamy gray, the large-planked caramel wood floors were mostly barren except for some sisal area rugs, and the furniture was definitely modern—probably Scandinavian, Antonia conjectured. The art was scarce, but lining the staircase were some colorful collages and prints that, from Antonia's untrained eye, appeared to be African, as well as portraits of Alida from her modeling days.

Alida led them to the farthest part of the house, which was a sitting area, and invited Antonia to sit down on the white sofa, while she curled herself up into a sheepskin chair with her manicured toes tucked under her. Atop the coffee table was a tortoiseshell tray hosting a variety of water bottles—Poland Spring, Evian, Vittel, Arrowhead, and Volvic.

"Please help yourselves to water. I wasn't sure what kind you drank."

Antonia could see Larry use all of his self-control to refrain from making the kind of snarky comment he would normally dispense if he wasn't so bowled over by Alida's looks. In an effort to keep his tongue in check he grabbed a bottle of Arrowhead, cracked the top, and gulped it down.

"Thank you so much for taking the time to meet with us," Antonia said.

"No problem," Alida replied, staring at them penetratingly. Her eyes were disarming, endless pools of depth, revealing little about what she was feeling. Not unlike her friend Pauline, Alida appeared totally self-possessed and completely in command of her environment.

Antonia shifted in her seat. She couldn't help feeling completely unglamorous in Alida's presence. "As Pauline explained, she has asked me to look into Susie's murder."

"Yes, and she told me to be as forthcoming as possible," Alida said.

"Great."

"You're very brave to do this."

"Why do you say that?" Antonia asked.

It was only a flicker, but Antonia saw something dark pass behind Alida's eyes. She wasn't sure what it meant. She was about to press Alida on it when Larry interrupted.

"I realize how difficult this must be for you to discuss. You can cry if you want to," he blurted before adding lamely, "we won't judge."

A hint of amusement flashed across Alida's face before instantly vanishing. "Thank you," she murmured softly.

"Do you mind telling us anything pertinent or any of your reflections or thoughts . . ."

Alida sighed deeply. "It's been so long, and I feel as if I have talked about this so many times that I'm not sure what I really remember or what I think I remember, do you know what I mean?"

"Totally," Larry said supportively.

Alida gave him a small smile, flashing perfect white teeth. "We were all very close—me, Susie, and Pauline. You know, when you attend an all-girls school for thirteen years as I did, you experience a fluidity with friendships, an ebb and flow if you will, where you attach yourself to one group of girls and then, a few years later, you discover another group. I wasn't really friends with Susie and Pauline until about seventh grade. That was after I quit the gymnastics team and . . ."

"Wait one second," Larry interrupted.

Both Alida and Antonia turned toward him.

"You were on the gymnastics team?" Larry asked.

"Yes, why?"

Larry shook his head with wonder. "You must be so flexible."

Antonia glowered at him. "Larry, please, let's not interrupt."

"I'm sorry," Larry said. "But it's just amazing. Is there nothing you *can't* do?"

Alida endowed upon him a smile that one would give an insane person. "There's a lot I can't do . . ."

"I doubt that," Larry said with his usual confidence.

"Larry, let's return to Alida's story without interruption," Antonia reprimanded. She turned to Alida. "Sorry about that."

"No worries," Alida said. "Where was I?"

"Gymnastics," replied Larry at the same time as Antonia said, "Seventh grade."

"Right," Alida concurred.

Antonia was mortified. It was now clear to the supermodel that she was dealing with amateurs.

"We'll let you continue without interruption," Antonia promised, glaring at Larry.

"Okay. Well, we became friends in seventh grade and were pretty much inseparable until . . . Susie died."

She paused, and Antonia could see Larry was about to interrupt but she gave him her meanest look and he stopped himself. Instead, Antonia spoke.

"What sort of person was Susie?" she inquired, taking Hercule Poirot's procedures into account.

"Susie? She was a great friend: supportive, kind, generous. One of the most surreal aspects of Susie's death was that she was one of those people who you could totally visualize in the future. You could just see her married to some preppy guy and living in Greenwich with four or five kids and a golden retriever. She'd be running the PTA or the school auction or some committees, focused on family. She was never really a city person, and she never really had big aspirations, professionally that is. She wanted to be in love and get married and have a bunch of kids. She was lonely being an only child, that's why she spent so much time with the Framinghams."

"Was Susie . . . temperamental? Quick to anger? Volatile?" Antonia asked, still trying to get a feel for Susie's character.

Alida shook her head. "No. She was very easygoing. A joiner, definitely not a leader. Although . . . perhaps her detractors would say she was a little cliquey. She enjoyed being part of our posse and was possessive of her friendships with me and Pauline. She wanted as much of our time and attention as possible."

Antonia took a second to process that. Larry jumped at the pause to insert himself.

"Did Susie have a boyfriend when she died?" he asked.

Alida shook her head. "She wasn't really that lucky with guys . . . they all sort of thought of her as their 'pal' or their little sister. Susie was cute but she wasn't really . . . sexy or mysterious. And she always had crushes on the wrong guys."

"Like who?" Antonia asked.

Alida cocked her head to the side as if thinking. "Well, she was madly in love with Scott, the tennis pro who lived in the Framinghams' guesthouse, but he was older . . ."

"Did he know she was hot for him?" Larry asked.

"Yes, she was like a puppy around him," Alida said, bending down and taking a bottle of Vittel. She cracked it open and took a sip. "But he didn't take her seriously. She was young, and he had it pretty good, living free at the Framinghams'. He would never have jeopardized that."

"Who else did she have a crush on?" Antonia asked.

"Oh, you name it," Alida said. "It wasn't ever for very long. She would be into some unattainable guy and then on to the next."

"What about Russell?"

Alida looked surprised. "You mean Pauline's brother?"

"Yes," Antonia replied. "Did she have a crush on him?"

"Um, have you met him yet?" Alida asked carefully.

"No . . ."

Alida took a deep breath. "He's a little odd."

"How so?"

"I don't want to be unkind . . ."

"Please be unkind," Larry retorted.

"It's very important to our investigation that you be candid," Antonia explained. "And please be reassured that we will be very discreet with all of the information we learn from you."

"I would appreciate it," Alida said. "I don't want to be quoted anywhere."

"We understand," Antonia replied.

Alida took a sip of her water before responding. "Russell completely lacks social skills. It's almost like he has Asperger's or something of the sort. There is something a bit off. And he has this inflated ego and very grandiose sense of self. We didn't hang out with him at all. Pauline loathed him."

"What did he think of you and Susie? The posse, if you will?"

"He didn't really pay attention to us. He had a girlfriend, which is actually surprising because he was so odd, but she was also a bit odd herself."

"In what way?" Larry asked.

"She was a . . . the word that pops into my head is 'wannabe.' She was always reinventing herself and her style. Pauline even nicknamed her Madonna—after the singer, not the Blessed Virgin. One minute she was dressing very provocatively, and the next she was demure. I think there was an absence of self and she was very insecure. She made initial overtures to be friendly, but when Pauline rebuffed her she became very sarcastic and bitchy toward all of us. There was a lot of tension in the house. Pauline and Russell's parents were absentee and formal. They were of that 'children are to be seen and not heard but also preferably not seen' generation. They traveled constantly, and when they were in town they were on the golf course all day. They didn't appear to be particularly interested in their children."

"Do you think it's possible that Russell, or even his girlfriend, killed Susie? Perhaps to set Pauline up?"

Alida shook her head. "Of course, that was one of the theories. Every person attached to the case has been a suspect at one time or another, but I don't think so. Russell seemed blithely ignorant of Susie's existence. Even though she was a constant presence, she was one that he ignored. I told you there's something off about him—antisocial. He paid no attention to us. And I don't think he needed to kill Susie to leverage anything in the family . . ."

"Maybe he had a crush on her?" asked Larry.

Alida squinted as if she was considering the notion before dismissing it. "I doubt it. I didn't see anything that would suggest that."

"But the police had their doubts about him," Antonia insisted.

"I know, and I can totally see that. But I believe it's because he's so strange. He always acted suspicious, and I assume he acted that way when they interrogated him about Susie. I'm sure he had no interest, no inclination, and no reason to kill her. She was a nonfactor."

"And what about Holly?" Antonia asked.

"Holly doesn't strike me as someone smart or skillful enough to murder someone in broad daylight and get away with it. Plus, she was with Russell. They gave each other alibis."

"What about Pauline's boyfriend, Dougie?" asked Larry. "He sounds like a real jerk, if you ask me."

Alida laughed. "Mr. Lipper, you don't mince words."

"Larry."

"Larry," she responded in her velvety voice. She gave him one of her multimillion-dollar smiles before continuing. "Dougie was a bit of a buffoon. I only realized that in retrospect. At the time we thought he was fun and so cool and popular. But he was basically just a rich kid who had nothing going on. He smoked pot, he sailed, he golfed, and he partied. If you asked him what he was doing with his life, he would say 'waiting until I'm thirty-five.'"

"What does that mean?" Antonia asked.

Alida turned toward her, a disapproving look on her face. "He received his trust fund at thirty-five. All he had to do was hang in there until then and he would have enough money to live very well for the rest of his life."

"Whatever happened to him?" Larry asked.

"Oh, he's around. But not much has happened to him. After Susie's murder he was expelled from St. George's for getting drunk. Then he somehow made it to Rollins College in Florida, until he was expelled for bad grades. He stayed down there, hanging out at his former fraternity. And he had a delightful scam going where he would ask his friends when they were arriving and what their suitcases looked like, and when their plane landed he would take their suitcases and they would then approach the airline and say that their luggage was stolen and, at the time, Orlando Airport would shell out $150 per bag, no questions asked. Then Dougie and the so-called victim would split the cash. That's how he survived for years."

"Pathetic," said Larry.

"Yes. After Pauline he dated a series of rich girls who subsidized him. Then I suppose he ultimately turned thirty-five and received his inheritance. I did hear that he married a stripper at one point. But maybe that was a rumor. I believe he still hangs out at the Dune Club in the summer, chugging Southsides."

"This guy sounds like a world-class loser," Larry said.

"Pretty much. But you see, that's why I don't think he would have killed Susie. She wasn't rich enough or pretty enough to capture his attention at all. Susie wasn't threatening and was perfectly happy to disappear when Pauline and Dougie wanted to be alone. And I don't think he would have harbored a secret crush on her. Dougie had two types of women he desired: the very rich girls who helped him out and the promiscuous type. Susie was neither."

Antonia pressed on. "But then if it wasn't Russell or Dougie, who did you suspect, Alida? Was there ever someone you thought suspicious?"

Alida shifted her feet and resituated herself in her chair. "It's hard to say because now I'm not sure what I noticed at the time or what I read about the case . . . it all sort of blends. You have to understand, for years afterward, people were coming out of the woodwork to tell you their theories. Then, fortunately, my modeling career took off and people forgot about my relationship to Susie. I was lucky; I was able to move on. But sadly for Pauline, she's always been associated with Susie's death. She has lived under a cloud of suspicion since that day in August."

"Did you ever think she did it?" Antonia asked.

Alida turned and gave her a stern look. "Not for one second. Pauline is innocent."

"Then who?" Larry asked.

"I have no idea."

Antonia eyed Alida carefully. She was clearly intelligent, extremely articulate, and well-educated. It seemed unbelievable that she would have no theory whatsoever as to who killed her friend.

"Not anyone?" Antonia asked in disbelief.

"Everyone was a suspect."

"Were you?" asked Larry.

"I probably was," she confessed. "But I had no reason to kill Susie. And I'm not a killer."

"Then who did you think did it?"

"I think it was a transient. Someone came up off the beach, or was walking around the road, maybe bike riding, and they tried to rape Susie but got spooked so they killed her."

"Brilliant," Larry said with reverence.

It was not the first time that supposition had been put forth, and Antonia felt that it was a very safe answer. But she knew that she would not be drawing anything else out of Alida Jenkins, at least not today.

12

When they were safely out of earshot and had buckled themselves into the front seats of the car, both Larry and Antonia spoke in unison.

"That wasn't as helpful as I had hoped," confessed Antonia.

"I think Alida Jenkins just solved the crime of the century," swooned Larry.

They both turned to each other with disgust on their faces and said "What?" in unison for a second time.

Once again, they talked simultaneously before Larry began shouting and Antonia became quiet. She was completely irritated. Larry was letting his libido get in the way of his brain.

"I don't know what it is with women. They are so damn competitive. Alida Jenkins basically hands us the murderer on a silver platter and you call her useless."

Antonia started to seethe. "I never called her useless."

"Whatever. 'Not helpful,' I think you said. That's just bitchy for useless."

He started the car and thrust the reverse so hard that the car jolted backwards, smashing Antonia's breasts against the seat belt. He whipped it into drive and revved the engine before taking off down the street.

"I didn't say she wasn't helpful, I said that what we learned from her wasn't helpful. Or at least as helpful as I had hoped."

Larry maneuvered the car to the left, narrowly missing two helmeted bikers in black spandex racing outfits with sponsors' advertisements all over them. One of them gave Larry the finger. In return, Larry slowed down directly in front of them and turned on his rearview windshield wipers, spraying them with cleaning liquid. They skidded to the side and narrowly missed falling off their bikes.

"You are evil."

"I hate bikers. They think they own the road. They don't stop for stop signs, don't obey the law. Ride in large packs rather than single file. I wish death upon all of them. No, you know what? I hate motorcycle people more. They can die first, then the bikers. Both spawns of Satan."

"Jeez, Larry. Tell me what you really think."

"I really think you're in a tizzy because you know that I think Alida Jenkins is the hottest woman that ever walked the earth."

Antonia noticed a small spider crawling along the dashboard and took the opportunity to squash it with her finger. It felt mean to take her anger out on a helpless insect, but she figured better the spider than Larry. Although punching him in the stubbly jaw sounded really appealing just then.

"Do you have a napkin? I have spider guts on my finger."

"In the glove compartment."

Antonia reached forward and opened the glove compartment. A cascade of Sour Patch Kids came flooding out, the various sticky neon candies spilling onto her lap and all over the floor.

"Larry, what the hell?"

"Be careful, Antonia. I suffer from low blood sugar and if I don't have the Kids to fend it off, I become pretty nasty."

Antonia tried to gather as many as she could and stuff them back into the movie-theater-sized bag. *Larry and his childish food. Well, let him die of diabetes*, she thought as she jammed the gluey pieces together.

"Please tell me why you think Alida Jenkins solved the murder."

"The bicycle rider coming in for the kill."

"You just think that because you hate bikers."

Larry ignored her. "Or the beach walker. That's who killed little Susie. Hey, do you think the person smashed Susie's skull and then said, 'Wake up, little Susie, wake up'?" Larry began to sing.

"You are so insensitive."

"Touchy."

"I think it's very convenient for Alida to put a drifter forth as a theory. Furthermore, I think Alida is withholding something from us."

"The only thing she is withholding from me is love."

"Maybe *she's* the murderer."

"No way. She's too hot. Killers are ugly. Remember that woman that Charlize Theron played in that movie *Monster*? She was hideous. No wonder she killed. I would kill too if I was that nasty-looking."

"I have absolutely no response to that," Antonia said, throwing her hands up in disgust.

Larry patted her on the knee. "Sometimes it's better to be seen and not heard."

* * * * *

"Oh, hold on a minute please, she's just walking in the door now," chirped Connie from behind the reception desk. Her ear was pressed to the phone, and she quickly placed the caller on hold. Always ebullient, Connie was the perfect front line to welcome guests to the inn. She possessed a cherubic face with dimpled cheeks and the enthusiasm of a beloved cartoon character. She turned her attention to Antonia. "Are you able to talk? This woman has called three times but refused to leave a message."

"Sure," Antonia said, taking the extension. She moved out of the way of the front door, where recent arrivals were spilling in with their luggage and took the phone to the front hall. "Hello, this is Antonia Bingham."

The voice on the other end of the phone was female and hesitant. "I wanted to ask you . . . about a guest you had. Recently. A young woman named Bridget Curtis."

"I remember her," Antonia said. She had just been thinking about her! She was such an unusual guest—always staring at Antonia, almost as if she was spying on her. And she had left the inn abruptly in the middle of the night. Antonia had even suspected Bridget of murder, but that didn't say a lot these days, when she viewed everyone as a suspect. "May I ask who's calling?"

There was a pause. "I'd rather not say."

"Okay . . . then how can I help you?"

"What did she tell you?" the caller asked, her voice stronger and more forceful.

"What do you mean?"

"Did she tell you who she was?"

Antonia was puzzled. This woman was just as strange and cagey as Bridget had been.

"I'm sorry, you're going to have to tell me what this is in regards to before I answer any questions. I don't generally give out information on my guests."

The woman sighed deeply. "I'm looking for her. It's important. Do you know where she is?"

Antonia pressed her back against the map of the East End of Long Island that adorned the front hall wall, making room for a bellboy pushing a cart laden with suitcases. "Listen, I don't feel comfortable having this conversation."

"Because of what she told you?"

"I have no idea what you're talking about. What do you mean, *what she told me*?"

The line went dead.

"Hello?" Antonia asked in vain. The woman had hung up. With a sigh, Antonia replaced the receiver and made her way to the office. She had been certain she hadn't heard the last of Bridget, and now her suspicions had been confirmed. Who was this woman who had called and what was she worried about? What could Bridget have told her? And did this have anything to do with Antonia herself or was she overthinking it?

At her desk, Antonia was excited to find an email in her in-box from her friend Sarah who owned French Presse, a gorgeous high-end linen store in Amagansett. The heading was 'Is this Elizabeth?' There was a picture attached of a pretty, dark-haired woman who looked to be in her early thirties. In the email Sarah had written that she knew this Elizabeth from yoga class and had told her she had an admirer; this Elizabeth was very excited to meet him as she had recently broken up with her boyfriend and was ready to find love. Antonia's heart beat quickly. Could she have found Giorgio Leguzzi's love? Was it only a click away on the Internet to cure someone's lonely heart?

Antonia went bounding up the steps and knocked rapidly on Mr. Leguzzi's door. If her arm could twist around her body she would be patting herself on the back. The door swung open and Mr. Leguzzi, clad in a bathrobe with shaving cream on his face and a towel wrapped around his neck stood on the threshold.

"Is everything okay?" he asked, his voice awash in concern.

"I think I found her!"

"My Elizabeth?" he exclaimed with excitement.

"Yes! Come see."

Without even bothering to change or wipe away the shaving cream, Mr. Leguzzi thundered down the steps behind Antonia. Passing guests looked askance as he followed her into her office.

"Where is she?" he mused, turning his head left and right.

"No, she's not here. But she's here, on the computer."

Antonia pointed her finger toward the screen, where she had blown up the picture of Elizabeth. Antonia beamed with pride and was flush with success. Her mind immediately went to the wedding, Elizabeth and Giorgio walking hand in hand. Maybe they'd marry at the inn. They would make a toast to Antonia, who would be embarrassed and insist she had very little to do with it and it was all fate . . .

Mr. Leguzzi squinted and then moved closer to the screen, so close his face practically touched it. He stared for what seemed like a long time before pulling back and giving Antonia a sad look.

"No. It is not her."

"What? Are you sure?"

"*Si*. This Elizabeth is very beautiful, but she is not mine."

Antonia deflated and felt acute disappointment. "Really? Are you sure? Maybe take another look."

He shook his head. "My Elizabeth's face is imprinted on my soul. I would know her in a sea of millions. This Elizabeth, while very beautiful, is not my love. I thank you for trying."

"I understand," Antonia said, more disappointed than he. She had to bite her tongue not to ask him if things didn't work out with the first Elizabeth would he be willing to meet the second one? She was very pretty. And available. But Antonia knew that would be inappropriate. "I'll keep looking."

"You have my utmost gratitude."

"I want you to have a happy ending."

13

The rest of the weekend tumbled by and disappeared as quickly as a case of Wölffer rosé at a summer ladies' night. Between the demands of the restaurant and the booked-to-capacity inn, Antonia was busy with work and had little time to devote herself to her extracurricular sleuthing. This did not please Pauline, who sent her a flurry of emails reminding her that Susie's mother's death was imminent and she didn't have time to waste. Pauline definitely knew how to push Antonia's buttons. In the other emails she gave Antonia both Dougie Marshall's contact information as well as the heads-up that her brother, Russell, was heading to town on Tuesday, and therefore she was instructed to make time to meet him on Wednesday. *Yes, ma'am*, thought Antonia after she read that one. Pauline was a woman who certainly didn't take no for an answer.

On Sunday night, after the last dinner guests had departed and the team had broken down the kitchen, Antonia checked her phone and found a message from Genevieve, instructing her—more like demanding—that she stop by Cittanuova for a drink so that she could have a chance to catch up with Victoria, Genevieve's sister, whose departure to her home in suburban Chicago was imminent. Antonia was tired to the bone, but she did want to ask Victoria about her childhood friend Holly, Russell Framingham's girlfriend. Perhaps Victoria would be able to fill in some blanks. It took all of Antonia's remaining energy to pull on a pair of white Capri pants and throw on a beaded turquoise tunic and haul herself to town.

In the past, she had been indifferent to her appearance and chose comfort over looks. But lately she found herself making more of an effort when she had to run into town. It was probably because of Nick Darrow. No, it was *definitely* because of Nick. Even though she knew he was far away, there was always the off chance that he would return to East Hampton and she would bump into him, and she wanted to at least give the appearance that she regularly made some sort of effort. Not that she was going after a married man—she would never do that. But he played an integral part in her fantasy life, and therefore she had to look the part.

Cittanuova was located on Newtown Lane and was a chic Italian-style trattoria that was open year-round and often attracted a lively bar scene. When Antonia entered, she immediately noticed Giorgio Leguzzi sitting at one of the white tables on the front patio with his back to the row of hedges that protected customers from the foot traffic. He was nursing a cappuccino, and there was a bottle of white wine cooling in crushed ice on the stand next to him. Antonia spied two wine-glasses and place settings on the table.

"Mr. Leguzzi! How are you this evening?"

He immediately stood up and gave her a little bow and kissed her on both cheeks. His appearance was equally as dapper as her previous interaction with him. He was clad in a crisp button down and a white linen blazer over pressed pants. "Hello, my friend, please call me Giorgio," he said in his thick Italian accent.

Antonia smiled. "Giorgio. It's a beautiful night. Are you enjoying your stay?"

"I am," he said. "Would you like to join me?"

"Thank you so much, but I'm actually meeting some friends. But it looks as if you are not alone. Did you find . . . er . . . Elizabeth?" Antonia asked with hope.

Mr. Leguzzi shook his head. "No. But I have not lost the confidence. I will be here every night, and I wait. She will come, I am sure of it."

"I am sure she will as well."

"And when she does, I am ready. I have the wine prepared, I have told the kitchen to prepare. They will make the dishes I have selected. It will be a beautiful night."

When Antonia maneuvered her way to the back garden to meet Genevieve and Victoria, she couldn't help be heart-ened by Giorgio's remarks. There was something so pure and innocent about his certainty. The cynical side of her wanted to shake him and tell him he had watched too many romantic comedies with magical happy endings, but the optimist in her was ecstatic. How wonderful if he was able to find this woman that he had fallen in love with at first sight. She wished there was some way she could help somehow.

"Over here!" Genevieve was waving furiously from the corner. She was sitting at a table littered with half-filled wine and cocktail glasses and semi-eaten plates of pasta and salad. Her sister, Victoria, sat on one side of her, and there was another woman at the table whose back was to Antonia.

"Hello, ladies!" Antonia said, plopping down into the empty chair.

Whereas Genevieve was statuesque and gazelle-like, Victoria was a shorter and more solid version of her sister. She possessed Genevieve's green eyes, bronzed skin, and sun-flecked brownish gold hair, but she was more wholesome-looking in appearance at first blush. Not to mention that they drastically differed in the manner in which they dressed. Genevieve's outfit tonight consisted of a very tight-fitting navy blue top with an enormous polo-playing horse trotting across her unimpressive bosom, paired with white flared bell-bottoms, six-inch heels, and a plethora of gold accessories, while Victoria wore a conservative Lilly Pulitzer dress and dainty pearl earrings.

"So good to see you!" exclaimed Victoria, leaning in for a hug. She had a warm personality that resonated when she spoke. "It's been way too long!"

"I know! How are the kids?"

"They're great. All three are at sleepaway camp this summer, just for two weeks, but that's how I was able to sneak away and see my sis!"

"So glad you did!"

"We're coming to your restaurant tomorrow—Gen said we had to save the best for last."

"Wait, I thought you were leaving tomorrow?"

Genevieve gave Antonia a guilty smile. "I had to coerce you into coming out. I told a white lie. But you can thank me later, because this is Holly."

Antonia turned and looked at the other woman seated at the table. The first thought that ran through Antonia's head was "kicked puppy." There was something inherently defensive about Holly Wender's manner, as if she had been subjected to years of mistreatment and, in turn, regarded everyone she met with suspicion and slight disdain. Antonia could imagine her dipping into chat rooms online that hosted roundtables about bullying and mean slights. She was in her early forties with shoulder-length reddish brown hair cut into an attractive shag, smooth unblemished skin, and a chin in the shape of a curvy V. Her lovely dark eyes were underlined with a skinny layer of charcoal in an attempt to mask the smallness of the feature, but eyeliner couldn't hide the sad, downward turn at the corners. And not a flicker of a smile crossed her thin lips as she scrutinized Antonia and waited for her to speak first.

"Nice to meet you," Antonia said.

"You too," she responded halfheartedly and returned to pushing arugula and watercress around on her plate. Antonia noted that she had no wedding band on her ring finger.

During the first fifteen minutes of catching up with Victoria, Antonia studied Holly out of the corner of her eye. She could see why Pauline had been less than enthused about her brother's girlfriend. It was as if instead of one chip on her shoulder she had a giant bag of Lay's. There was a petulant poutiness that resonated from her and was evident in the way she impatiently checked her phone, rudely instructed the busboy to fetch her more water—Antonia always bristled when people were unfriendly to service staff—and disinterestedly listened to Victoria's stories about her children. She did, however, seem quite aware of her body, which was clear from the way she kept shimmying in and out of her jean jacket to display her very well-sculpted biceps, shown to great effect by her tank top.

"Okay, enough catch up," Genevieve demanded. "Antonia is literally Cinderella and will be heading to bed in no time, so she needs to grill Holly on all things Pauline Framingham and murder."

"Yes, right. Holly, I understand you used to date Russell?" Antonia began.

Holly's face remained passive. "Yup."

"How did you meet him?"

"I was babysitting a kid at his club, and he hit on me."

"How long did you date for?"

"A couple of years."

This will be fun, thought Antonia. *Like pulling teeth.* "So, you also obviously knew Susie and Pauline?"

"Obviously."

"Come on, Holly. Help her out here," Victoria prompted. "Give her the skinny. Remember how we thought Pauline and her friends were so stuck-up? They all thought they were so great."

"Not really Susie," contested Holly. "It was the other two. Pauline and Alida. It's so perfect that now one is famous and the other lives in infamy. I'm sure that needles them. They were both so jealous of each other. Karma is a bitch."

Yes it is, thought Antonia. "Pauline and Alida were jealous of each other?"

"Jealous, competitive. Supposed best friends but nasty about each other behind their backs."

"But Susie was nice?"

"She wasn't nice," Holly rebuked. She gave Antonia the once-over before continuing to speak. "I said she wasn't stuck-up. She was fine, sort of blah, just there. She was kind of Pauline's toy—Russell called her Pauline's lapdog. She was around to make Pauline feel good about everything and provide constant companionship and moral support. She had very little personality."

"Harsh," Victoria scolded.

Holly shrugged. "Just because someone is dead doesn't mean they were a great person."

"Ouch," Genevieve said.

Antonia was enraged. She had begun to feel protective of Susie, and here was this little brat Holly writing her off as merely "blah." How dare she? But instead of losing her temper she chose to remain calm and professional and continue her line of inquiry.

"Do you think Susie and Pauline had a genuine friendship?"

"Susie was just happy to be along for the ride. She was the needy type, always wanting to be popular, willing to put up with Pauline's nasty little asides. And totally effusive. I don't know how Pauline didn't see through Susie, or at least get annoyed by what a phony she was. She was such a suck up, but I suppose Pauline loved that sort of fawning. Not to mention power. Russell and I used to laugh that she was Ed McMahon to Pauline's Johnny Carson. A pathetic, not-that-funny or interesting sidekick."

Again, Antonia bristled. She was liking Holly less and less. As if reading her face, Victoria interjected to give Antonia a moment to pull herself together.

"Holly, I remember you once told me that you saw Pauline tormenting Susie until she cried," Victoria added. "I think it was about some guy?"

"Oh, yeah, I forgot that," said Holly, flipping her hair out of the back of her jean jacket that she had donned again. "We were all at dinner one night, and the Framinghams were there—I mean Russell's parents. And it was this really formal dinner, and the Ambassador—we had to call him 'Ambassador'—asks Susie about her summer or something like that. And she says some obsequious thing about how grateful she is to be staying at the Framinghams', and they are the sweetest family in the world, and everything is 'amazing'—that was her favorite word, 'amazing.' She was always a sycophant.

"But then Pauline, who was clearly mad at Susie for something, starts talking about how Susie was hanging with some bad people. She said it in such a cold, calculated way, like 'Susie might have to leave. She's hanging out with a rough crowd.' And I remember, Pauline was very calm; she was cutting her steak and didn't even look up, just said it matter of fact: 'rough crowd.' And Susie was totally mortified and started to tear up, and the Framinghams—who were not at all touchy-feely people—immediately changed the topic. Any sort of display of actual human emotion was reprehensible to them. They hated it as much as they hated me. Because of course Mrs. Framingham has to add, 'we all have to be careful about the people we surround ourselves with,' and she's looking straight at Russell and I know she's referring to me. The whole thing was mortifying."

The pain was clearly just as fresh to Holly as it had been that day. Her cheeks were flushed, and she took a long drink of wine to calm herself down. Despite the fact that Antonia didn't particularly care for Holly, she felt a wave of sympathy. Obviously Holly had taken knocks through the years that had made her insecure and bitter. Antonia thought it best not to linger on that exchange, but she couldn't resist one last question.

"Who do you think the 'rough crowd' was?" Antonia asked. "There was a rumor that something went on between Dougie and Susie, like one hit on the other, and that's what prompted Pauline to snap . . ."

Holly shook her head vehemently. "No way. Dougie was so affected, he would never go for someone like Susie."

She's echoing what Alida said, Antonia thought.

"You never know what happens behind closed doors . . ." Genevieve added, wiggling her eyebrows suggestively.

"They were referring to Kevin Powers. Susie was sleeping with him."

"Kevin Powers?" Antonia remarked with surprise. "The landscaper?"

"Yeah. He supplied them with drugs, and he also supplied Susie with other things."

Antonia was stunned. "But Pauline said he was always hitting on her and they wanted him to get lost."

"Au contraire. I mean, I'm sure Pauline wanted him to disappear after she procured what she needed from him, but Susie had a real thing for him. He was her little bit of rough. She relished dipping her toe into the local Bonacker scene. I guess you could say the same for Russell dating me."

This presented an entirely different perspective on Susie's death. If she had been hooking up with Kevin and Pauline didn't approve, would that have caused Pauline to flip out at Susie and kill her? Or perhaps Kevin killed Susie in a heated lovers' quarrel?

"Are you sure of this?"

Holly rolled her eyes. "I'd see them kissing behind the guesthouse all the time. Susie thought she was so discreet, but she couldn't have been more obvious. She even made up a lie that she was mooning over Scott and that's why she hung out there, but that was all a ruse. She only had eyes for Kevin. Pauline thought it was really trashy and warned her to cut it out or she wouldn't be welcome at their house anymore."

Antonia needed time to process this information. Why had Pauline deliberately mislead her? She had called Kevin 'a spurned lover.' If Pauline knew that Kevin and Susie were having a fling, why wouldn't she straight-out tell Antonia, who she had hired to uncover the killer? Was she attempting to redirect Antonia's attention to another suspect?

"Where were you and Russell when Susie was killed?" asked Genevieve.

"We had gone to the yacht club. We went out on his boat—he had a slip there—and we went out around Gardiner's Bay and Shelter Island. Stopped somewhere to swim."

"What time were you out?" Antonia asked.

"I don't know. We left after lunch and then came back from the club around five-thirty. Then back to Russell's around six. All hell had broken loose by then."

"So you were with Russell the entire time?"

Holly gave her an impenetrable look. "Yup."

"You were totally together from around one to six?"

Holly stared at her blankly. She took an extra beat to respond. "I just said that."

"Sorry . . . I just wanted to confirm the timeline."

Holly leaned over and picked up her wineglass. She took a dainty sip. "I don't understand, I thought you were an innkeeper. Are you also a cop?"

Genevieve burst out laughing. "That would be classic! No, I told you, Antonia has a knack for solving murders. Pauline Framingham asked her to look into Susie's."

Antonia kept pressing. "Sorry to keep on at this, Holly, but did you see Dougie Marshall when you were at the yacht club?"

"No. All the newspapers said he was golfing when Susie was killed."

"Yes, don't forget, Antonia, there are several clubs in East Hampton," Genevieve interjected. "And the Framinghams were members of a few of them. The Dune Club has golf, tennis, and a beach, but then there's the Yacht Club—that's what it's called, The Yacht Club or TYC—which has sailing and water sports."

"Oh, right!" Antonia exclaimed. "I didn't make that distinction. So the Yacht Club is the one out on Gardiner's Bay? That's about twenty-five minutes away from the Framingham house, whereas the Dune Club is only about five."

"Exactly," Genevieve concurred.

That opened up the landscape entirely, Antonia realized. She had thought most of the important players had been clustered all at the same spot, but actually, Scott and Dougie were at the Dune Club, Russell and Holly at the Yacht Club, Pauline and Susie at home. And Kevin Powers was at the Framingham house mowing the lawn when he wasn't supposed to be. She wasn't sure if that mattered at all, but the width of her crime scene and potential suspects had just grown exponentially.

"Did you see Dougie or Kevin that night?"

"Nobody was allowed to come over. It was a crime scene, the police controlled access," Holly said. "Once we got there, they interviewed us briefly and then sent us away. Russell slept at my house that night."

"And what about Pauline?" Antonia asked.

"I have no idea," Holly replied.

Antonia could tell Holly was becoming tired of the third degree, but she couldn't resist one final question.

"Who do you think did it, Holly?"

Holly gave her a dismissive look. "Colonel Mustard in the library with the wrench."

"Come on, help her out," Victoria pleaded. "She needs to find this killer."

It was becoming increasingly difficult for Antonia to imagine how a nice person like Victoria could be longtime friends with someone like Holly, but then you can't really explain old friendships. People change and it was sometimes hard to remember what had brought you together in the first place. At least that's how Antonia rationalized her decision to marry her ex-husband.

"Fine," Holly conceded as if she were doing Antonia a giant favor. "It was Pauline. She's the only one who would be able to live with herself afterward. She's crazy. You really don't know what you've gotten yourself into, Antonia. It's going to end badly for you."

14

The last weeks of July in the Hamptons are like a burst piñata where all the little plastic toys and candy and confetti come tumbling out and spill over the electric green grass, and everyone is grabbing, grabbing, grabbing. Parties are everywhere. People are everywhere. Bikers, joggers, golfers, beachgoers, shoppers, tourists, landscapers, construction trucks, and luxury vehicles are everywhere and it is all *me first!* The tip of the east end of Long Island is saturated and overflowing with an abundance of people who are determined to not let anything stand in the way of what they have to do—whether it be in the quest for fun or for money.

All of the microcosms that comprise the Hamptons are fully represented. The glamorous fun-seekers cramming the restaurants and bars at night and heading to the beaches during the day with bags of food from Citarella, Round Swamp, and Red Horse Market. They stab their umbrellas into the sand and collapse in their beach chairs until the sun softens and slides down the sky and it is time to dress up and return to the whirling social scene. All over town, kids are picked up by buses that lurch off, toting them to specialized day camps. The country club folks put on their whites and head to grass courts to lob the yellow ball back and forth, competitively, but not aggressive-competitively (you could never act as if you cared if you won; way too gauche). The day-trippers slink out of their sticky Long Island Railroad seats and walk four abreast down Main Street, oblivious to other pedestrians, determined to pick up an East Hampton sweatshirt and an ice cream cone from Scoop Du Jour.

Everything is lush and dripping with color and scent. Antonia thought of this time of year as a fully ripened peach. It held so much promise, smelled so sweet, had the potential to be delicious, but ultimately had to be consumed before it began to rot. She needed to metaphorically sink her teeth into everything before it was too late.

The next morning, after helping Soyla bake pecan sticky buns for the Monday breakfast service, Antonia took a brisk walk on the beach before setting off to meet Kevin Powers at his landscaping company, Powers' Flowers and Garden Center, located on Montauk Highway near Amagansett. When she spoke with him on the phone she could tell that he was a busy man and this was not an ideal time to chat, but he acquiesced because of her friendship with his brother. She hadn't quite explained the nature of the visit; only that it was a personal matter that required some clarity.

As promised, Antonia had called Larry Lipper to invite him to the interview. It was fortuitous that he had a meeting with his editor that couldn't be changed. He asked Antonia to move her visit to Kevin's but she explained that he had little time for her and this was absolutely positively the only time he could meet. Larry grumbled but Antonia held firm. Kevin's type would probably not be candid around someone like Larry and it was better to leave him out of it. She hung up from that call with a victorious smile on her face.

When Antonia closed the door of her Saab and crunched her way over the gravel driveway toward the nineteeth-century barn that housed Kevin's offices and garden shop, she was walloped with the pungent smell of blooming flowers. Along the low boxwood hedges that bordered the building were feathery purple Russian sage, lime green zinnias, fragrant verbena, and fat pink hydrangeas. To the right were rows of overflowing flowers, bushes, and trees—a panoply of colors.

The rustic red barn doors were propped open by two enormous slate pots hosting abundant ferns. Inside, there were three women helming various desks in the large open-plan office space, one of whom kindly escorted Antonia to Kevin's work area, which was around the corner and separated by a thin wall of glass.

"Hi, Kevin, thanks for seeing me this morning," Antonia began, glancing around his immaculate work area. Everything was neatly filed and organized, and even the pens and desk paraphernalia were color-coded and aligned. Antonia would hate for him to see her office.

Kevin swiveled around in his chair before rising and presenting Antonia with one of his calloused palms for a firm handshake. Kevin Powers had the appearance of a man who had lived hard in his early years but had made an effort to clean up his act and put himself back together as best he could. In his late forties (early fifties?), he was slight of build but muscular, as if he made an effort to keep himself in shape. Antonia spied a yoga mat neatly rolled and cinched in the corner of his office; perhaps that was what kept him fit. He had leathery skin that had seen way too much sun and his black and steel hair was gelled back from his forehead. His eyes were a filmy blue, and he had deep lines springing out from the sides of them as well as firmly etched wrinkles on his forehead. He wore a landscaper's uniform of boots, faded jeans, a Carhartt button-down shirt with a pack of cigarettes in the breast pocket. There was something inherently sexy about him, Antonia recognized, although she couldn't quite pinpoint what it was. He was not her type, and yet, he had that look and insouciance of someone who was comfortable in his own skin, which was highly attractive. And yet . . . there was a mild slickness to him that caused a minor red flag to pop up in Antonia's mind.

It was odd to Antonia how little Kevin resembled his brother Len, a beefy Santa Claus–type man, who, if he wasn't a gentle giant, would be a force to be reckoned with. In fact, Antonia could believe that Len probably did scare the panties off some of the interlopers at the Dune Club, where he ran security. Funnily enough, Kevin looked a lot more like Matt, Len's son, who was an EMT and physical therapist. They had the same heart-shaped lips and small straight nose. The genes had gone somehow rogue in that family, Antonia surmised.

After the requisite small talk, Antonia got down to business and explained why she was really there, rambling on a bit about Pauline Framingham so that Kevin could digest the idea before she interrogated him. He did seem a bit taken aback when Antonia initially mentioned Susie, and she watched carefully for any clues in his body movements or facial expressions to decipher if he was in fact her killer.

Kevin remained quiet, swiveling back and forth in his armchair, as Antonia blathered, hoping that he would interject. She finally took a breath and, although she was one who definitively did not enjoy sitting in awkward silence, she forced herself to shut her trap so that Kevin would be compelled to speak.

"I'm really surprised," he finally responded, before taking another long pause.

Antonia prompted him, "That Pauline Framingham wants to find Susie's killer?"

"No . . . I'm surprised that you're involved. Why would you get yourself mixed up in all this?"

"Oh," said Antonia. "Right. I know, it's odd. It's a long story. I won't bore you with it."

"Antonia, I really think you should rethink this. I would stay away from . . . this tragedy."

There was urgency in his voice, the motive of which Antonia couldn't quite decipher. Before she could respond he continued.

"I mean, is it for the money? 'Cause I don't think it's worth it."

Antonia was offended. "No, it's not for the money. I want to find out who killed Susie. Is there a reason you don't want me to look into it?"

"I just think it's a bad idea."

"Why? Do you have something to hide?"

Kevin held her stare then finally shrugged. "No. Nothing. Ask me what you want to know."

Fueled by his resistance, and rather than be delicate, Antonia jumped right in.

"I heard you had some problems back then."

"To say the least," he said. "I was partying a lot in those days. Doing a lot of stuff I shouldn't have been. Lots of what happened is a blur because I was so stoned."

"Right. Well, I just want to cut to the chase a bit. Were you and Susie, I don't know what word to use . . . dating? Intimate?"

Kevin ran a hand through his hair. A black watch peeped out from under his sleeve. "I feel . . . I don't know, what's the word . . . indiscreet, talking about this."

"It's okay. I promise it will just be between you and me. I just need to . . . contextualize . . . what happened." She couldn't believe she had just quoted Pauline.

Kevin appeared lost in thought, his brain traveling back twenty years to when times were very different. Finally he shrugged. "I suppose it doesn't hurt to tell the truth. I mean, what difference does it make now?"

"Exactly," Antonia reassured him.

"Yeah, Susie and I . . . had a thing. I don't know what you would call it."

"How did it start?"

"I used to do the landscaping for the Framinghams, as you know. Look, I just want to say up front I'm not really proud of how I was back then. But, it is what it is. I've owned up to it. I had a legit job, but on the side I sold some weed. Pauline sussed that out right away, and soon she and her gang were my best clients. It's funny, because I don't even think Pauline smoked it. She just provided it to her friends, especially that boyfriend, Dougie. He also enjoyed the harder stuff, which I have to admit I provided for him a few times."

"A little ironic that Pauline the pharma heiress is a drug pusher," joked Antonia.

Kevin didn't smile. "I guess."

Antonia decided to resume the serious tone. "What about Susie?"

"She took the occasional toke, but not really. Those girls were all pretty clean and pure."

"Then why would Pauline want to have the drugs around?"

"Honestly? I think she liked to see everyone messed up so that she could be in control. Almost to lord it over them. But maybe that's wrong. I shouldn't be so harsh. And anyway, we were all stupid back then. She's made up for it. Who knows anything at the end of the day?"

"When did things happen between you and Susie?"

"Beginning of that summer, there was one day when Pauline was off riding and Susie was hanging by the pool, and well, we got to talking. She was always more relaxed when Pauline wasn't around, more herself. I liked her; she was funny and just . . . really positive. You don't see that a lot, people who are so upbeat. I thought it was cool. We'd talk a lot when Pauline was gone, and then one night I ran into her at the Talkhouse. Pauline was there, but she was outside on the patio, and Susie had come in to buy some drinks. I was at the bar with a buddy, and we started shooting the breeze. Then Pauline came in all mad because Dougie threw up and she wanted to go, but Susie wanted to stay, so I offered to drive her home later. Pauline was pissed, but I think she was also more pissed at Dougie at the time, so it wasn't really a scene . . . that was the beginning of it. I know it was wrong. I was older, but, as I said, I was troubled in those days."

Antonia felt a wave of tenderness toward Kevin that washed away her residual irritation from his accusing her of poking around in Susie's murder for money. It was really sweet how he genuinely had appreciated Susie. She did not sense that he had any sort of homicidal rage toward her, but then she had been wrong before, and it really was her duty to press, considering that Pauline was paying her.

"I hate to ask, but did you kill her?"

Kevin blinked twice. "You're kidding, right?"

Antonia smiled. "Yes, I mean, no. It's a box I need to check off in my investigation."

Kevin gave her a look as if she were insane. "The answer is a strong no. But, Antonia . . . I have to say there is a major flaw in your . . . investigation . . . if you think you can just ask someone and they'll confess."

"But I know they looked hard at you."

"And cleared me," he said confidently. "I didn't kill Susie. No way. Why would I kill her? Because she wouldn't sleep with me? Well, she would. Because she was going to tell the Framinghams and I would be fired? Well, they basically knew and I didn't really care if I was fired; it wasn't hard to find a landscaping job back then. Because I sold drugs and she threatened to tell the police? She didn't, but if she had, that's not something that would have worried me then. I had little thought of consequences at that age. I had no reason to kill her, and I think it's a shame she died."

Antonia let that hang in the air before her follow-up question. "First off, I didn't mean to offend you. But I can't wrap my head around this. Who do *you* think killed Susie?"

Kevin folded his hands in his lap. "I always thought it was someone in their group, you know, someone they hung around with."

"Why's that?"

"Well, there wasn't much foot traffic back then. No one rode those damn Lance Armstrong bikes, and it was early days even for roller blading. People on the street in those neighborhoods in those days stuck out. So the whole idea that someone came off the road and killed her was too random. Besides, I was there that day. I didn't see anyone come in."

"Yeah, why were you there that day?" interrupted Antonia.

Kevin stopped. "I had to mow the lawn."

"But Pauline said you weren't supposed to do it when they were there."

He shrugged. "Yeah, that was true. But I probably bailed

the day before, I don't know. Maybe I wanted to see Susie. Like I said, I was pretty drugged out."

Antonia wondered if he was being honest or if that was a clever defense. She nodded. "Yes, continue, sorry to interrupt. You were saying about someone coming off the street."

"Yeah, I think if anyone came from anywhere, they would have come up from the beach, walked through the house and down all the way to the tennis court. Pauline or the housekeeper would have seen them. And that's just strange—no one ever did that before or after. And it doesn't make sense. Why would some stranger do that, then kill Susie?"

"You're right, it doesn't make sense. But why would one of her friends kill her?"

"I don't think it was one of her *friends*. I said someone in her group."

"Like who?"

"I don't know. I thought maybe Dougie? He could get really violent and paranoid when he was all coked up. Susie told me one time he trashed Pauline's room when he thought she had cheated on him."

"When was that?"

"A few weeks before Susie died."

"But if that was the case, why kill Susie and not Pauline?"

"Exactly," conceded Kevin. "It's not a case of mistaken identity or anything."

"Did Dougie dislike Susie?"

"That's another point. I don't think he really thought of Susie. She was around but not a threat or anything. And she could be trusted to keep her mouth shut if she saw anything."

"How do you know that?"

Kevin ran his hand through his hair. "I just know. She never told anyone about our . . . us. And, also, one day we were in the yard and we'd just . . . well . . . we did what we did and said goodbye and I went one way through the back paths and she went the other way toward the house and we hadn't gone ten feet when there was a noise. We both froze. And it was that girl, I forget her name but she's a local who grew up in Springs—Russell's girlfriend."

"Holly Wender?" Antonia offered.

"Yeah, that's it. I've seen her around. Okay, now that you know her, I feel like it's not appropriate to say . . ." His voice faded.

"You have to tell me," prompted Antonia with urgency. "Come on, what did you see?"

He shook his head. "You know what? I take back what I said before. You're really good at this, you know? Getting stuff out of people?"

"Thank you," Antonia beamed. "All for the greater good. So tell me what you saw."

With reluctance he continued. "I guess it can't hurt now . . . Well, Holly was with that tennis pro who lived in the guest-house. They looked very *familiar* . . . if you catch my drift. But neither Susie nor I ever spoke of it."

"Holly and Scott were having an affair?"

"I didn't say *that*. But they were talking in a way, I don't know . . . It felt very personal. I felt uncomfortable 'cause I knew she was Russell's girlfriend. I was glad Susie never mentioned it."

"And Holly didn't see either of you?"

"She definitely didn't see me."

"What about Susie?"

"I'm not sure. Susie was on the other side. I don't think so but I can't be sure."

Antonia was intrigued at the new twist. Holly had implied that she had been devastated by the Framinghams' rejection of her and intimated that it had been the cause of the demise of her relationship with Russell. But if she had been cheating on him? That was a whole other story entirely. Maybe she had seen Susie that day and killed her so she didn't tell Russell. But she had an alibi for the time Susie was killed.

"Was there anyone else in their group that you suspected?" Antonia asked.

Kevin shook his head. "It's strange. It was a pretty violent murder, so despite what the press said about it being Pauline, I never thought she would be so aggressive and bash her best friend's head in."

"Sounds like there's a but?"

He gave her a shrug. "I just remember feeling, well, girls at that age, they fight like hell with each other. Only a girl would get that mad. And I think whoever killed her was mad, really mad. It was very violent . . . But what am I saying? Pauline had nothing to do with it."

"How can you be so sure?" asked Antonia.

He shook his head. "Wasn't her."

Antonia felt there was something strange about his response, how he had quickly changed his tune. She continued to press him. "You were there that day. Tell me what happened."

"Yeah, I was there. I was mowing the lawn, and I wore earplugs and headphones to block out the noise from the mower. I didn't hear anything. It wasn't until I saw a cop car pull in the driveway that I even knew anything had happened."

"There were no screams or anything before from Pauline?"

"May have been. But I couldn't hear. The cop car comes, and at first, I don't even dismount my lawn mower. Just thought it was a safety check or something. But when another car came, I stopped the machine and headed down to the court, where they were converging. That's when I saw her . . ."

He stopped, remembering. Antonia could see sorrow in his face. "Yeah, so, she was lying there. Her head was all bloodied. It's funny the things you think, but I remember I kept thinking that it was a shame that her hair was all bloody, because she had really nice hair. Isn't that an odd thing to think?"

"No. It's sad."

"Yeah, it was sad."

They were silent. After a few minutes they descended into small talk before Antonia rose and made her way toward the exit. Kevin escorted her out and they discussed some of the plants that were on sale by the entrance. Antonia promised to send Hector, her landscaper, over to pick some out for the backyard. As she was about to leave, she turned and asked a final question.

"Just one more thing, Kevin," she said as she opened her car door. "Do you remember what Pauline was doing when the police arrived? How did she appear?"

"Honestly? I don't even remember seeing her. She must have been there, but I was only looking at Susie. Poor Susie."

15

Antonia was stopped at the crosswalk on Main Street in East Hampton for the throngs of people to meander their way across when she glanced over at White's Apothecary and a figure caught her eye. She only saw the back of him flash by before he entered, but she could have sworn it was Nick Darrow. Could it be? Wasn't he in Australia filming a movie? Antonia's heart quickened. Perhaps he was already back! She was suddenly seized by a gust of emotions: hope, anticipation, excitement. How was it possible that against all of her better judgment she continued to harbor a crush on this man? This married man. This married celebrity man. She was a self-destructive idiot.

The crosswalk cleared and Antonia pressed on the gas pedal. She had planned on heading straight, directly back to the inn, but then she slowed and quickly put on her blinker to turn into the town parking lot. If Nick Darrow was back in

East Hampton, she had to know. But her decision backfired, and before she was able to turn, another car crashed into her bumper. Antonia was thrust forward with a jerk. Great. Just what she needed.

"I am so sorry!" exclaimed the female driver, after she extricated herself from her car and ran over to Antonia. "Are you okay?"

"I'm fine, I'm fine."

"I thought you were going straight, I didn't see the blinker, I am so sorry!"

"It's my fault, really. I decided to turn at the last minute."

The driver was an attractive middle-aged brunette, petite, trim, and well-dressed in a gray sleeveless sheath dress. Her face was friendly, but her expression was tortured with guilt and worry. She moved aside as Antonia exited her car and went to survey the damage.

Antonia walked to the back of her Saab and leaned over the bumper to assess the damage. For such a strong hit, there were only a few scratches, and Antonia couldn't honestly be certain that they had not been there before. She and her car had been through a lot together, and both of them had the wear and tear to prove it.

"I am really sorry, I can't believe it. I've never been in an accident," the woman rambled on, her solemn eyes troubled.

"Me neither." Antonia looked at her again. "You seem like the law-and-order type."

"I am," insisted the woman. "I've never even gotten a speeding ticket! Oh dear, so how do we do this? We exchange insurance cards. Oh look, here comes a policeman. We can ask him."

"Don't worry, please. It was my fault."

"But it's always the fault of the person who bumps into you."

"Not if the first one is a bad driver. Look, don't worry about it. There's barely a scratch."

The officer walked over to them. He looked about fifteen years old and had chubby cheeks that his grandmother probably still squeezed and hair like a Boy Scout. "What seems to be the problem, ladies?"

Antonia could imagine that he probably practiced that line in a mirror every night before he went to bed. Where did they find these kids every summer to patrol the village? Starting Memorial Day it was like some hive burst open and spawned all of these teenagers running around in fake police outfits, handing out parking tickets and attempting to control traffic. There were just too many, and they were mostly clueless.

"We're fine," Antonia said to the cop. His nametag said C. HORTON. "Just a little tap, Officer Horton."

Antonia could see his face deflate and his childish blue eyes turn down on the corners. He had probably been dreaming of writing up an accident report. Well, he could save his ink.

"Are you sure?" the woman asked. She bent down to look at the bumper of Antonia's car. "There's no damage? I felt a thrust."

"My car is fine."

"Okay, ladies, we need to file a report," the officer insisted, eager to interject himself and his authority into the conversation.

"No need, we'll be on our way," Antonia replied.

"Here's my contact information, in case you change your mind," she said, thrusting a crisp business card into Antonia's hand. "Thank you so much for being so understanding."

"And thank *you* for being understanding," Antonia said. She shoved the card into her handbag and turned to look once again at White's, just in case.

*   *   *   *   *

"I heard you were out here," Antonia said as she walked through the garden to the Adirondack chair where Joseph sat reading a book. "No library today?"

He took off his reading glasses and laid them on the arm of his chair. "The weather is too beautiful. I couldn't bear to lock myself up and miss this glorious day."

He motioned toward the turquoise sky, where thin puffs of white cloud streamed like smoke from a small pipe. The sun was shining hard, and the air was warm and enveloping. Everything from the trees to the grass and flowers seemed to shimmer.

Antonia plopped into the chair next to him. "I know what you mean. Sometimes I forget to stop and appreciate all this beauty."

Joseph gave her a long sideways glance. He tucked his bookmark into his book and laid it aside. "Everything okay?"

She nodded. "I'm a little rattled. I just got into a fender

bender." She put her hand up to prevent him from speaking. "I'm fine. The woman was nice, not even a dent on my car. I made a snap decision to go right, she didn't see my blinker, it was basically just an accident in every sense of the word."

"But you're okay?"

She smiled. "Yes, just mad at myself." She turned and looked at him. "I was being silly. Chasing a ghost. I have to really remember not to make bad decisions."

Joseph did not know about her crush on Nick Darrow, but he was astute enough to understand that she was referencing her kamikaze love life. "As long as you're okay."

"I am," she shrugged.

They sat in silence for a minute before Antonia finally broke it and updated him on her meeting with Kevin Powers.

Joseph listened carefully, peppering her with questions after she was done, and providing information of his own. "I did have a chance to go through the archives and look up all the press surrounding Susie's murder. I made copies and left them for you in your in-box."

"Thank you! That's so helpful. Anything interesting?"

"Not really. Mostly the lack of progress on the case. So much was initially written on the murder—it was covered in all of the New York papers—but then it fizzled out."

"People lose interest."

Joseph cocked his head. "Sometimes," he conceded. "But I believe there is a voracious appetite for any small detail when it is such a high-profile and salacious murder, as this was. Usually there is a trajectory as the discovery continues. The police release bits and pieces to encourage witnesses to come forward and also to warn the killer that he or she hasn't quite gotten away with it. But that didn't really happen here. Every article was a rehash of the information that was initially dispensed. It's as if the police had no idea which way the investigation was going."

"Maybe they were keeping their cards close to their vests?"

"I would doubt it. There was such a wave of criticism against them as it was, that it would not have been worth it. People were calling the police completely inept; there were editorials deriding them."

"But how could it be that they didn't discover anything? Surely the killer left clues? What about forensic evidence such as footprints and bent grass or something of the sort?"

"Nothing was ever mentioned. Pauline Framingham found the body, so her lawyer argued that any sort of DNA or evidence linking her to the victim was inadmissible on those grounds. Pauline and Russell Framingham both entertained frequently at the tennis courts, so you have a location that saw a lot of people coming and going. Kevin Powers had just weeded the courts that morning, so the presence of his DNA could be explained. Overall, I believe the biggest conundrum to the case was motive. Why did someone kill Susie? No one has been able to answer that question. And until you have the motive, you are unable to find the killer."

Antonia sighed. "It's true. I've talked to several people now and everyone seemed to like Susie. Pauline and Alida were her best friends. Kevin Powers was dating her. They all liked her.

Only Holly was less than a fan, but I'm not sure Holly likes very many people. The question is, did she have a big enough beef with Susie to kill her? Was she worried Susie would tell Russell that Holly was having an affair with the tennis pro? Which we haven't even confirmed but, so far, she's the best I've got."

"You still have a few more people to meet with. The brother, Russell; the boyfriend, Dougie; the tennis pro, Scott . . . am I forgetting anyone?"

"I don't think so. Ugh, so much to do and so little time!"

"Any word on Susie's mother?"

Antonia shook her head. "But I feel like it's imminent, because Pauline's emails have a sense of urgency. It's so sad."

"Just keep plugging along. You're doing the best you can."

"Let's hope that one of the people I interview this week is the killer."

Suddenly, the absurdity of her statement became clear to both of them and Joseph and Antonia descended into fits of giggles. It was so crazy that they were immersed in a world of crime and murder. If they had been asked two years prior if they thought there was a chance they would be in the midst of solving *murder* cases, they would have looked askance at the person asking them.

Antonia finally rose and wiped the corners of her eyes where tears of mirth had sprouted. "I have to start dinner service."

"What's on the menu for this evening?" Joseph asked. He adored hearing about all of Antonia's delectable dishes, which changed often depending on season and availability of produce and proteins. Antonia relied on local farms, fishermen, and butchers to source the products for her kitchen.

"We have a tasty sautéed chicken liver appetizer. Very delicious—the chickens are from Iacona of course, and Balsam provided the onions. I think you'll enjoy that one."

"Sounds divine."

"There's a lovely golden and red beet salad with both pickled and roasted beets matched with a lemony goat cheese and sugared walnuts. I have a peppered tuna tartar with wontons and avocado as well as a very nice kale Caesar, but I know you've not bought into that food trend yet."

"Kale is for farm animals!" protested Joseph.

"Some day I will convert you," laughed Antonia. "But in the meantime, for dinner I have maple syrup–coated pork chops with mashed purple potatoes, homemade cavatelli pasta with wild mushroom ragout, and steak frites. But I'm sure you'll love the swordfish entrée. I prepared it Sicilian style with onions, capers, and tomatoes."

"Done. And how will you satisfy my sweet tooth tonight?"

"Caramelized figs with local honey and mascarpone on a puff pastry crust? Or maybe homemade strawberry rhubarb pie with vanilla bean ice cream."

"I can't wait. Diet be damned." He motioned to the vegetable garden next to them. "And start thinking of zucchini recipes! Another bumper crop this year!"

"Oh dear! Maybe we need to rent some rabbits!"

16

The conversation had been brief, the instructions simple: "Meet me at the club at two."

Although she was now hip to the fact that there were many clubs in East Hampton, Antonia assumed Dougie meant the Dune Club. By all accounts, that was where he spent most of his time in the summer, and now Antonia had been invited to join him.

She had just sunk herself into a marvelously creamy coconut milk bath on Monday night—even going so far as to light candles, pour herself a glass of wine, and prop her computer on the ledge so that she could watch a cozy mystery serial from the Hallmark Channel that was now streaming—when her cell phone rang and she finally connected with Dougie. She never allowed her phone to go to voice mail; it was a luxury an innkeeper could not afford. Not to mention that she looked after two houses as a caretaker and, despite the fact that the owners were in residence for the summer and she did not have to make her weekly stops to check on them as she did in the off-season, she still considered herself responsible for their care and felt she had to be available lest they needed anything.

"Dougie Marshall here," he had said. "Pauline says I need to talk to you. Let's meet tomorrow," he commanded before designating the appointed time.

That was how Antonia found herself driving on Tuesday afternoon toward the stately Dune Club. Whereas Southampton's "South of the Highway" was mostly cleared of dense trees and consisted of houses and hedges, East Hampton was woodsier and dense with foliage and evergreens, with very little real estate south of the highway. That was why it was such a surprise when the Dune Club majestically appeared at the end of Dunemere Lane before it curved into Further Lane. Almost abruptly, the shadowy trees parted and gave way to a broad expanse of sky as the undulating hills of the championship golf course spread out on both sides of the road. Hook Pond, always a shiny azure hue (although recently plagued by a serious algae problem), unfurled between several holes of the course with only small wooden bridges spanning it to link the swaths of manicured grass.

In the distance, hovering on the edge of the dunes, was the grand clubhouse, a structure built in the style of an English manor. It was an impressive building, large and looming, with tangles of ivy crawling up toward its third floor and a circular driveway making a sweeping entrance. As Antonia drove closer, she felt as if she were heading toward Downton Abbey. She had been to the Dune Club before, but only in the dead of winter when it was closed for the season. Len Powers, who headed security, had given her a tour, and even though he worked there and had every right to escort her around, it had felt illicit, as if she were breaking some rule. Perhaps it was because the club itself was so out of her league. The members included not only the wealthiest but also the most pedigreed Americans, and there was even a former president who was a member.

Antonia parked her car in the upstairs lot designated for guests and walked down the small path by the honeysuckle bushes toward the stairs. Since Dougie had given her no explicit details as to where to meet she had called Len that morning and asked if he had any idea and could clarify. He told her to meet Dougie at "the pit," otherwise known as the snack bar area, and gave her directions. Because of Larry Lipper's tactless behavior she decided she would exclude him from this interview as well. She didn't trust him to behave himself in a fancy club. She would find some way to defend her decision when she told him.

Antonia hoped that she had dressed appropriately. She had donned her preppiest outfit—a navy and pink dress that she had bought on a whim when it was on sale—and accessorized with pearl earrings and gold flats. She had been told that there was a somewhat standard uniform of Roberta Roller Rabbit shifts and Jack Roger sandals for the ladies but since she owned neither this would have to do. The few female members who passed her on her walk were wearing golf shoes, skorts, and visors, so she figured she was safe.

The top of the stairs afforded a sweeping vista of the club and the Atlantic Ocean. Below, there was an Olympic-sized pool surrounded by clusters of chaises. Enveloping the pool and stretching out along the dunes were rows of weathered gray cabanas with yellow, blue, and white awnings. Each cabana bore a faded plaque with the name of the member who owned it. Beyond the pool on the edge of the beach was a giant yellow tent with blue tables and yellow chairs for dining. There was also an extended patio where diners could eat in the sun. That, Antonia surmised, must be the pit.

It was a gloriously sunny day, and most of the members appeared to be on the beach or in the ocean, where the surf afforded boogie boarders the chance to ride the waves. Antonia walked down the steps, clutching the silver-painted banister tensely, and scanned the crowd. Mothers were hovering over their toddlers in a small baby pool that was to the left of the larger pool, where older kids frolicked and splashed one another. Groups of women sat on chaises, chatting easily. Anyone who looked her way offered her a small smile as she passed and seemed friendly. She wasn't sure but she felt as if they knew she didn't belong, although maybe that was her own imagination. That was the thing about clubs, you felt as if you stood out if you didn't belong.

When Antonia was closer to the snack bar she stopped and glanced around. There a few tables filled with women dining off of blue plastic trays. At the front tables, children were stationed, licking ice cream cones, leaving globs of rainbow sprinkles splattered on the tabletops. There was a foursome of men who looked as if they had just stepped off the golf course. It was actually pretty quiet for a summer afternoon, which amazed Antonia. Wouldn't there be crowds of people lining up to use all these spectacular amenities? Where else would they be?

She waited at the entrance, hoping that someone would either approach her or arrest her for trespassing, but no one did. (Where was Len when she needed him? Perhaps she was wrong to not bring Larry. She was paying for her arrogance.) She walked along the edge of the tent, craning her neck to see if anyone could be Dougie. Problem was she had no idea what he looked like.

On the far end of the tent there was a bar with a deck and a few tables. She saw a man with a thick thatch of dark hair, in his mid-forties, who was deep in an animated conversation with two other men. He was the right age, she thought, but he was clearly not on the lookout for a guest. Just as she was about to turn away from him, he held up his arm as if he was hailing a cab. Antonia caught his eye.

"Dougie?" she mouthed, because there was no way she was shouting his name across the entire club. He nodded then went back to his conversation with his friends. Antonia waded slowly through the various tables, to allow herself to assess Dougie as much as possible before they met.

He was not an unattractive man. On the contrary, there was something appealing about him in an overgrown frat boy kind of way. He held himself in that insouciant and confident manner that so many men of privilege do. He was still fairly fit, although when he waved his arms to gesticulate a point, Antonia noted that there was a slight protrusion in the stomach area of his striped polo shirt, but nothing repellent, especially since he was broad shouldered and his arms were toned and tanned.

When Antonia finally approached, Dougie did nothing to acknowledge her, and she was immediately thrust into awkward social limbo. His two friends glanced up at her curiously, but Dougie seemed determined to finish the anecdote he was regaling them with and it wasn't until it came to its natural conclusion ("You can see Rochester from here! *Hahaha!*") that he finally turned his attention to his invited guest.

"You must be Antonia," he said.

"Yes."

His eyes looked as if they had seen a million hangovers and were now a glassy bloodshot hue with remnants of blue and gray peeking through the red. The reddened eyes were countered by his fiercely dark and thick eyebrows, arched in alertness. There was a softness around his chin and a few days' worth of stubble, but he had a sharp and brazen look about him that many women probably found dashing.

There were introductions to the friends who immediately excused themselves and an offer of a beverage or lunch for Antonia, which she resisted until pressed several times when she finally acquiesced with a request for an Arnold Palmer. There was no waiter service so he disappeared briefly to the bar to fetch her drink and a beer for himself, before returning and placing both drinks on the table, as well as a dish of Ritz crackers and a plastic container of orange cheese in the most alarming Cheeto color she had ever seen.

"In case you're hungry," he proposed.

"Thanks."

Dougie took a large swig of his beer before pulling off the sunglasses that had been hanging on the lapel of his shirt and blowing on them. He grabbed the edge of his shirt to wipe them before wrapping them around his eyes.

"It's bright today."

"Yes," Antonia concurred. "Not a cloud in the sky."

"I love summer. Best time of the year," he said, leaning back in his chair and crossing his legs.

"It's great, but I also love fall. The colors are spectacular."

"Yeah, I suppose." He leaned forward, selected a cracker and smeared a glob of the neon cheese across it. Antonia caught a whiff of his aftershave, which smelled of peppermint. "Everyone leaves in the fall and everything dies, so I'd rather summer."

"True."

Just as Antonia wondered how long they would have to make this inane small talk, Dougie got down to business.

"So, Susie Whitaker, huh?" he asked rhetorically, before popping the cracker in his mouth. He rubbed his hands together to disperse any renegade crumbs.

"Yes. Pauline asked me to look into it."

He shook his head and cocked an eyebrow. "She just loves to stir things up, doesn't she?"

"What do you mean?"

"Ah, you know Pauline."

"Actually, I don't really . . ."

He rolled his eyes. "She gets bored. Or she's pissed at someone. Then she causes a scene. But she's always very clever about how she orchestrates it. Has others do her bidding and then sits back and acts as if she had nothing to do with it. But she loves to make people squirm. It's a shame, you know. She would have been a good CEO. She's Machiavellian."

Antonia was surprised. Not by his assessment of Pauline but by how candidly forthcoming he was. She had expected someone more reticent and less voluble. But Dougie appeared completely blasé about sharing all of his thoughts.

"So it's your opinion that she's having me look into Susie's murder because she's bored or angry at someone?"

He shrugged. "I don't know particulars, but I know that Pauline relishes drama and attention. Always has, always will. She's a total narcissist."

Before Antonia could press him, Dougie waved at a friend who was passing on his way down to the beach and exchanged some passing chitchat. Antonia took a sip of her drink, which was surprisingly bad, though she was unclear as to what country club fare should taste like. She was a bit disarmed by Dougie's statements, and unsure how to proceed. She was working for Pauline, and he was Pauline's friend—ex-boyfriend—so she felt odd allowing him to bash her, but on the other hand, there were things she had to find out.

"Tell me about Susie and Pauline's friendship," Antonia inquired when Dougie's friend had departed down the walkway to the water.

"That was a long time ago."

"Well, how about you describe what you can remember about Pauline and her friends back then?"

"Lots of drama. Girl drama. Not only with Susie and Pauline but also with Alida and all their other friends. Girls that age fight all the time and are best friends the next minute. You know, Susie was a nice girl, actually. She tried very hard to be a good friend to Pauline. And she was. But I think toward the end she kind of got fed up. You can only be someone's whipping boy—or girl—sorry, so much. And Pauline could be harsh to her. Pauline is high maintenance and was a total bitch that summer. We actually broke up a few times."

He stopped to take a sip of his beer.

"Did you break up because she was high maintenance or was there another reason?"

He chuckled. "Well, for one, I thought she was cheating on me. In fact, I'm pretty certain. But whatever, it was a long time ago."

"Who do you think she was cheating with?"

"That tennis pro, Scott whatever. All the girls loved him. Very convenient because he was shacking up in Pauline's guesthouse. I caught her coming back from there more than once. She denied it, said she was just retrieving a tennis ball that went over the fence, but I don't buy it. I actually asked Susie about it."

"And?" Antonia asked eagerly.

"One night, a bunch of us were down at the cabanas having a bonfire and we were all hammered, and Pauline and I started going at it. And I called her on her bull—told her I knew she was cheating. I said I was sure Susie knew and asked her to confirm. Yeah, kind of bad that I dragged Susie into it, but I was drunk and pissed, and Susie looked scared. She didn't deny it right away, and Pauline went crazy on her, calling her a liar and a white trash chaser."

"White trash chaser?"

"Yeah, she was always ragging on Susie's boyfriends. I don't even know if they were boyfriends, I never met them, but the guys she hooked up with."

Kevin Powers, Antonia thought. "And then what happened?"

"Pauline told Susie she had to find somewhere else to sleep that night and left."

"Where did Susie sleep that night?"

"No idea. Probably Alida's or somewhere. I took off."

"And how long was it before Susie was murdered."

"A couple of weeks maybe. Definitely August. Things are always crazy in August."

"What do you mean?"

"You know, people have been together all summer—boozing too much, partying, playing eighteen holes a day—total hedonism. Don't get me wrong—I love it. But let's be honest, that can make people look for problems where they shouldn't, and if they don't find them, they cause them. My mother has this saying, that at the end of the summer, it's time to drain the bathtub. When you arrive in East Hampton in June, the bathtub is empty. You have no worries, no petty feuds, no problems. But slowly all summer the bathtub starts to fill up, and by Labor Day it's time to drain it. That's when everyone takes off. Then it's time to go down to Palm Beach and start filling up that tub until we hit Aspen."

Antonia nodded, musing about what it would be like to have a life that was a constant migration from one wealthy enclave to another, the only worry being your back becoming sore from carrying around your golf bag.

"That's a good metaphor. Do you think someone took it a little too far and 'drained the bathtub' by killing Susie?"

Dougie smiled. "Interesting theory. Not sure."

"There were rumors that you killed Susie. Or that Pauline killed Susie because you were having an affair with her."

He laughed. "Yeah, I heard that."

When he didn't respond further, Antonia pushed. "Any truth to that?"

"Did I kill Susie? No."

"Were you having an affair with her?"

He looked at Antonia askance. "Did you see a picture of her?"

"Yes."

He shrugged. "Not my type. Hey, listen, do you want a glass of wine? I have a bottle of rosé in daycare."

"What?"

He motioned toward the bar. "Daycare. It means I opened one yesterday and they hold it and look after it for me until I need it."

"That's okay," Antonia said. She realized every time they became close to a serious question, Dougie changed the subject. She couldn't let him. "Who do you think killed Susie?"

"That's the million-dollar question. I wish I knew. But I was playing golf that day."

"Do you think it was Pauline?"

He sighed. "I don't know. Pauline, yeah, she could freak out. She trashed my room one time when she thought I kissed Alida."

"Alida?" Antonia asked, her eyes widening. "Did you?"

He waved his hand in the air. "Yeah, once, but we were both drunk."

"And that means it didn't matter?"

"In my book. It was one of those things."

"How did Pauline find out?"

"You know, not sure. Funny, Susie was there that night. Maybe she was a snitch after all."

"Would that have been enough for Pauline to kill her?"

Dougie put both elbows on the table and leaned toward Antonia. "I'd love to say no, but I'm not sure. As I said, Pauline enjoys drama and power. She thrives on messing with people. It would be just like Pauline to hire you to investigate Susie's murder when she did it herself. And I bet you signed all these legal documents saying that if it was her you couldn't do anything about it."

Antonia's face drained of color. Dougie noticed. "Oh, jeez. She did have you sign a bunch of stuff, didn't she?"

Antonia nodded. She fervently wished she had at least glanced at the small print, but Pauline had been so insistent.

"You have to be careful with Pauline. She loves her lawyer, Schultz; the guy is her best friend. She always has people signing nondisclosures and stuff like that. Bummer. Question is, why is she messing with you? Did you double-cross her or something? Steal her guy?"

All Antonia could do was take a deep breath. "I accused her of murder."

Dougie laughed. "Of Susie's murder?"

Antonia shook her head. "No. Someone else's . . . oh boy, I'm a total idiot."

"Don't worry about it. Take a number, you are only the latest Pauline Framingham plaything."

"Would she really go to all this trouble to seek revenge?"

"What else does she have to do? As I said, she's bored. No husband, no kids, no job, and too much money. It works for some people—hey, I shouldn't talk, people in glass houses and all—but Pauline is pretty smart. She should use her brain for something other than riding her horse. Maybe she is."

"Why do you think she never married?"

He leaned back in his chair. "That's been the subject of much speculation. She definitely had guys banging down her door. And no way is she a lesbian—I know that idea was floated, but I would know."

"Because you dated her?"

"Yeah. She's not," he said brusquely.

"So . . . she's just celibate?"

"Or very discreet."

"What do you mean?"

"Maybe she got all hot in the pants about Susie having a white trash guy because she had one too."

"Scott? You think they're still together?"

Dougie smiled. "He's still around. Teaches tennis at that club on the highway that anyone can get into. Cove Hollow Club. He had a good gig here, and he blew it up with his drinking. How the mighty have fallen. Karma."

It was strange to Antonia that Dougie had used the word "karma" in connection with Scott as Holly had in connection with Pauline. Maybe there was something to it.

17

Antonia had been tempted to head straight to the Cove Hollow Club to find Scott Stewart, but the practicalities of her full-time job as an innkeeper and chef could not be ignored. Already she had been remiss in her duties, leaving Kendra, Marty, and Soyla to fend for themselves in the kitchen, and Jonathan to manage any potential disruptions at the inn. In general, she was very fortunate to have a stellar staff who were entirely capable of performing without her, but the summer was very busy and there were still executive decisions that she needed to tend to. In order to do that, she had to push aside all replays of the conversation she'd had with Dougie and focus on dinner service.

When she made it back to the inn, Connie informed her that the new custom bedsheets had arrived from Matouk, and Jonathan was upstairs in the recently vacated room eight, fitting them on the queen-sized bed. He had requested Antonia's attendance as soon as she arrived.

It had been an utter and complete pleasure for Antonia to decorate the bedrooms at the inn. She appreciated softness, cleanliness, and comfort above all else. The walls were a pale robin's egg blue, the fabrics on the upholstered chairs and bench at the foot of the bed a mix of cream and periwinkle patterns and stripes. White billowy curtains (with blackout liners) adorned the windows and, unlined, framed the bedposts in an elegant canopy. The wood floors were mostly covered by a thick, white plush rug that guests could sink their bare feet into. She had decided not to clutter the rooms, instead leaving the side tables and dresser bare except for lamps and a charging dock, so that guests would have plenty of space to spread out their belongings. Owing to the antique nature of the inn, each room was a different size and shape, contributing to a quirky individuality.

"Oh, they look beautiful!" exclaimed Antonia when she entered the room. Jonathan and one of their housekeepers, Rosita, were fluffing the new duvet over the new floral-printed sheets.

"Brilliant, right?" Jonathan asked, rhetorically, in his soft British accent.

"Pretty," Rosita agreed.

"I just love it. Well done," Antonia said. "Now all I want to do is collapse on the bed and take a long nap."

"I know the feeling."

After spending a solid ten minutes admiring the sheets with Jonathan, Antonia exited the room on her way back to the kitchen. As she started to walk down the stairs she glanced into room six where the door was ajar. She could see Giorgio Leguzzi sitting on the edge of his bed, staring into space. Normally she didn't bother her guests—oh, who was she kidding, she always interfered with everything and everyone—but she couldn't stop herself from gently knocking on the door.

"Hi, Mr. Leguzzi—Giorgio, I just wanted to check in and make sure everything is okay."

He jumped up abruptly and did a little bow. "*Si, si,* thank you for asking."

His face smiled, but Antonia could see sorrow in his eyes.

"I'm sorry about the false alarm the other day."

He waved his hand in the air. "I am grateful you are helping me."

"I still haven't heard back from some friends, maybe they know her."

He shook his head sadly. "I have not lost hope . . . but . . . I wisha I could meet her soon."

Antonia nodded. "Do you know anything about her other than that she's here in the summer? Where she works maybe?"

He shook his head again. "We talked only little about work . . . that was the nice experience for me. At home, everyone wants to talk to me about work . . . I'm a . . . I don't like to boastful . . . but I'm a big man in my city. With Elizabeth, she didn't know who I was. We talked of films and theater and sunsets and travel. And architecture. *Si,* lots of architecture and design. She said she worked with design of the home, I think. But I am not sure. I did not want to spend time on profession, more on her as a person."

"So she's possibly a decorator?"

"I think possibly. But I looked at the computer, and I didn't find her. There are many Elizabeths . . . Perhaps she is not."

"Now that I know she's a decorator, I can reach out to some friends in that field . . ."

Giorgio's eyes grew bright. "Thank you."

"It's no problem. I am not sure how much I can find out, but it's worth a try."

"I would be most grateful."

Antonia turned to exit when he spoke once more.

"You must think I'm crazy. But you see . . . my wife died. She died during the birth of our son twenty years ago. And I never thought I would feel love in my heart again. I never hoped I could *see* love. When I met Elizabeth, I knew I could feel again. That's why I need to find her."

* * * * *

Giorgio's words stayed with Antonia the rest of the day. She robotically worked her way through dinner service, ignoring Marty and Kendra's bickering. (Kendra had started fooling around with filters on Instagram, and it was a whole new time suck.) It felt relaxing to methodically peel and simmer and plate and immerse herself in her culinary endeavors. This was how she used to escape when she was married to her monster ex-husband Philip. She was so fortunate that she'd had a catering business while she was married. She could push all of her problems aside and focus entirely on creating delicious food. It provided her with both a release and immense satisfaction.

It was heartening to hear someone speak of love like Giorgio Leguzzi did. Love for his wife who had died and the prospect of new love. Antonia did not know if she would ever have that. She wished she would. It would be amazing to have that fluttery feeling about someone solid and available. It was the sensation she experienced when she was around Nick Darrow. If only she could rid herself of that and focus on someone else. She had met a cute chef named Sam earlier in the summer. But although she was attracted to him, it wasn't the same as it was with Nick. With Nick, there was passion. That was enticing to Antonia. But, unfortunately, totally impractical.

That night, there was a message waiting for Antonia on her landline when she returned to her pink-walled ground-floor apartment. She pressed play and an almost indecipherable voice came warbling out.

"Antonia. It's Barbara Whitaker . . . I want to say thank you so much for helping find Susan's killer . . . It's been my wish to have closure before I die. I don't have much time, and now you're my only hope. I thank you, dear. Now, no need to call back, Pauline said you are very busy and I don't want to take you away from all your work. I cannot thank you enough."

Antonia shuddered. She was almost relieved that she hadn't been home to take the call because she would have collapsed when she heard the sad elderly voice begging for assistance. She sat down on her sofa and pulled out the picture of Susie again.

Tears splashed down onto her face and Antonia brushed them away. What had she promised? Could she deliver before it was too late?

It was hours before Antonia finally fell into her enormous sleigh bed only to find herself unable to sleep. She had tried doing a crossword puzzle, which usually helped lull her into slumber, but that night it only bored her. Afterward, she attempted to read one of her favorite cozy mysteries, but her mind felt agitated, and she was having difficulty following the plot. At one a.m., after over an hour of restlessness, she forced herself to turn off her light and lie unblinking, focused on the ceiling. Images of Susie rolled through her mind. After tossing and turning, she found herself staring glassy-eyed at the framed Henri Matisse poster that hung on the wall near the bathroom. It was one of Matisse's most famous works—titled *Dance*—and portrayed five naked dancing figures, painted in a vibrant red, set against a dark green and blue landscape. Antonia had researched the painting. It was said to reflect Matisse's fascination with primitive art. In addition, the dancing nudes were meant to convey the feeling of liberation and hedonism. But instead of leaving a joyful impression on the viewer, Antonia felt there was a violence depicted in the painting and a sense of struggle. The dance didn't appear effortless for all of the five figures. One had her head upright and was standing erect with her leg flung out. The man opposite her stood tall but was contorted uncomfortably. Two of the dancers had their heads down and arms awkwardly stretched. And the dancer at the bottom—a woman—looked as if she had been dragged by the others until she had fallen down.

In her sleepy haze, Antonia conjured up the image of Pauline Framingham's circle of friends. Pauline would be the one in control—yanking her friends in the direction she wished. Alida and Dougie would be the two with their heads down, going along with whatever Pauline wanted. Susie was the one who had fallen down; she couldn't keep up with the dancers. But then who was the fifth figure? Who was the man holding up the other side of the circle? Was he indeed a man in Pauline's world? And was he the killer?

* * * * *

"This is my brother," Pauline said matter-of-factly. "Russell, this is Antonia Bingham."

They had converged in the front hall of the Framingham house and stood in front of an antique breakfront that hosted several bowls of shells of varying sizes and colors. Antonia quickly assessed her new acquaintance. Russell was a large man—perhaps six foot four, weighing about 250 pounds. His face was round and his head mostly bald in the middle, with the remaining brownish-gray hair shaved down to a quarter inch on each side. What were unique were his eyes. They were blue, unblinking, and extremely alert—as if an ophthalmologist had recently placed drops in them and they had transformed into the shape of cartoon saucers. His expression was both inquisitive and suspicious, his manner awkward and formal, and as Antonia would learn the more she conversed with him, he was without any social pleasantries. He was a strange combination of pompous, turgid, and offensive, and as blunt as a Dutchman.

"I've just been told that I am supposed to describe to you the murder that occurred at our home twenty-seven years ago despite the fact that you have no professional credentials or legitimate experience in the crime-solving profession. That my sister has chosen to hire an amateur sleuth is her business, but I would prefer that you know up front that I find your presence in this investigation absurd," Russell announced after shaking Antonia's hand.

"Russell . . ." Pauline began with exasperation.

Antonia waved her off. "No, no, he's correct. I am an amateur sleuth, I'll own it."

Her attempt to deflect her anxiety with lightheartedness fell spectacularly flat.

"I'm glad."

"Russell, we've been over this," Pauline said tersely. "The police have done nothing. The private detectives did nothing . . ."

He turned and addressed her curtly. "They were encouraged to not do anything."

A look passed between brother and sister, and a tension filled the air. Antonia wanted to prompt Russell to elaborate, but she thought it best to bite her tongue.

"Don't be foolish, Russell," Pauline said. "Of course our family did everything they could to solve the murder."

Russell scoffed. "They did everything in their power to make it go away . . . but, that said, I have no problem with that. It was a terrible bore."

Antonia raised her eyebrows. She had heard murder called many things but "a terrible bore"? That was a first.

"Look, Russell. Darling. I need ten minutes of your time to tell Antonia what happened. Then she can check you off her list and you can go on your merry way," Pauline said in the same tone a teacher would address a naughty preschooler.

"Very well, then. Since my sister has an interest in the macabre, why don't you accompany me down to the actual scene of the crime: the location where our innocent victim met her untimely demise. I have a tennis game in half an hour and I have allotted this time to practice my serve."

"That sounds fine to me."

Antonia followed brother and sister as they stepped off the porch and crossed the circular part of the driveway by the entrance. Antonia's dusty old Saab was parked next to a vintage convertible Mercedes and a sleek black BMW. She gave her car a little tap on the hood as she passed it—her way of telling it to hang in there and hold its own amongst the fancier automobiles. She had an unnatural love for her car.

Once they had crossed the driveway, the large expanse of lawn spread out in front of them for about two acres, framed by privet hedges on both sides. Antonia marveled at the consistency of the dark green turf. In her yard at the inn, everywhere she looked there were patches of different grasses and weeds sprouting up in little leafy tufts. She had about twenty different varieties of grass competing for dominance. But at the Framinghams' there was complete cohesion in every blade and every interloping scrabbly turfgrass or fescue rejected. *Kevin Powers must have loved mowing this stuff back in the day,* she thought idly.

The trio veered left toward the faded stone path that trickled through the thicket of beech trees running in a loose diagonal to the privet hedge on the western side of the property. It was a bright day, but as soon as they stepped on the path they were thrust into a shadowy darkness. Meager slats of light broke through the leafy branches that sloped downward toward them. They walked in silence, Russell leading the way. Antonia noticed that his tennis shorts were much smaller than was the current fashion, and his white polo shirt had sunblock stains around the collar. She surmised that he had probably owned this outfit for several decades. Pauline was dressed in her riding outfit, which complemented her fit and athletic figure.

The path came to an end at the tennis court, which was enclosed by a large chain-link fence covered in ivy. The door squeaked when Pauline opened it and they followed her inside, but not before Antonia glanced around at the area outside the court. There were large dense bushes—a tangled mass of branches and weeds—surrounding the entire court. When she peered to the right of the court, she could just make out the roof of the guesthouse. The impression she garnered was that despite being so close to the main house and the road, this area was quite isolated by virtue of the intense vegetation. There were little pockets where people could hide between trees and bushes. Places for a murderer to lurk.

"Russell, please stop and talk for a minute," Pauline commanded when Antonia stepped inside the court.

"Wait," he snapped. He walked over to the back edge

where there was a ball machine, and began dragging it toward the base line.

"You can see why I don't enjoy having him around," Pauline said.

Antonia didn't respond. She'd never had a sibling, so she had no experience with internal familial squabbling. But she did know that it was smart to stay out of family fights, because blood is definitely thicker than water. While Russell set up his machine, Antonia took the time to walk around and examine the court. The hard court surface was paved a slate green, outlined by washed-out pale white lines. On the far end of the court was the gate that was close to the street. It was fastened by a thick padlock on an impenetrable chain.

"Fine," Russell announced with exasperation. "I can talk for approximately four minutes."

He marched over to where Antonia and Pauline stood and folded his arms like a petulant child.

"Thank you. I appreciate your taking the time—" Antonia began before he cut her off.

"No small talk. Waste of time. Begin."

Antonia glanced at Pauline who rolled her eyes. "Okay, where were you when Susie was killed?"

"On my boat."

"Alone?"

He sighed deeply. "Did you even bother to read the police reports? This is ridiculous . . ."

He began to protest, during which time Pauline began berating him. A fight ensued, and Pauline escorted her brother off to the side of the court. They argued heatedly, but finally he agreed to talk.

"Okay," he said flatly. "What was your question?"

"Who were you with on the boat?"

"My girlfriend, Holly Wender."

"I actually just met Holly," Antonia said.

Antonia thought Russell's expression might change or maybe he would show some sort of reaction, but instead he remained stone-faced, so Antonia pressed on. "She said she was with you the entire day. But was there a time you were separated that day? Maybe she took off or you did?"

"I cannot recall with accuracy, but my memory is that we were together all day."

Antonia cocked her head to the side, thinking. It was difficult to interview such a reluctant witness, and it was also awkward to do it with Pauline standing and watching with her arms folded and her faced contorted with irritation. It rattled Antonia. Not to mention that there was a ticking clock, which was emphasized by the fact that Russell kept glancing at his wristwatch. It reminded Antonia of the one time she had tried speed dating. She just had to jump in there and lay it all on the line.

"Who do you think killed Susie?"

Russell's face remained unmoved. "I think it was Scott Stewart, the tennis pro."

Antonia could barely hide her surprise. "Really?"

"Oh, Russell," exclaimed Pauline. "Why would Scott kill her?"

"Don't interrupt, Pauline," Russell commanded.

This time, Antonia had to agree. "Perhaps it's better if I interview Russell alone? In the interest of time . . ."

Pauline was about to say something but stopped. She walked down to the other side of the court, out of earshot. Antonia returned her attention to Russell.

"Why did you think Scott did it?"

"It was someone who knew Susie. It's ludicrous to think that some stranger broke in and killed her. This is not a homicidal town. Or at least it wasn't back in the good old days. The person who killed Susie wanted to kill Susie, intended to kill Susie, and waited for the opportune moment to kill Susie. The person who killed Susie wanted to frame my sister for killing Susie. It was not a fluke that she became the leading suspect in Susie's murder. That is what the killer desired. Your investigation should not focus on who hated Susie. It should focus on who hated my sister."

"And why did Scott Stewart hate your sister?"

"She rebuffed him. He made overtures, and she wasn't interested. In retaliation, he watched from his perch in our guesthouse for the opportune moment to seize revenge. Kill Susie, blame Pauline. Susie was collateral damage. My sister's the true victim. I do not say that with any form of sentiment by the way, it's merely a factual statement."

"But what about the witnesses that can attest that Scott was teaching at the time of the murder? I heard women at the Dune Club vouched for his presence."

"They interviewed two women who swore he was there at the time. One of them is a known slut who had been having an affair with Scott. He pressured her to give him an alibi so he wouldn't tell her husband. The other woman was there, but she had an incontinence problem and had fled to the bathroom for twenty minutes. I know that because a friend of mine was in the ladies' locker room at the same time and said the scene was vile. The woman was washing her underwear in the sink and then using the blow dryer on her panties. It took twenty minutes. That's all the time Scott needed to zip over here and make his kill."

"Oh. Wow. Still, it seems a little bold . . ."

"Pauline was only gone long enough to fetch lemonade. How long does it take to go up to the house, retrieve the lemonade, bring it down? Five, ten minutes? That's all you need."

"I suppose you're right."

"Ah, here is my tennis date. Now our conversation has come to a close."

Antonia glanced over at a scantily clad blond who had entered the tennis court shyly. Her breasts were the size of watermelons and bursting out of her tiny Lululemon tennis outfit. She was garish and tacky, and Antonia could see Pauline bristle at the sight of her. It didn't make sense to Antonia. How did Russell attract these women? He was so unappealing. *Ah yes,* Antonia remembered. Money was always an aphrodisiac.

*   *   *   *   *

"I know Russell is very rude, but you seem like you can handle that behavior," Pauline said as she escorted Antonia to her car. Antonia surmised this was Pauline's version of an apology.

"He was fine."

"What did he tell you?" she asked with curiosity.

"He said he thinks Scott did it because you rebuffed him."

"He's always thought that."

"Is it true?"

"That I rebuffed him? No. We were friends, that's all."

Antonia eyed her carefully. They were still walking so she only saw Pauline's expression in profile, making it hard to read. "Some people have told me you had a relationship with him."

Pauline laughed. "Never. Scott wasn't my type."

"Can I ask, who is your type?"

"What do you mean?"

"I mean . . . I know you were dating Dougie. But some people suggested that you were not, let's say, madly in love with him. And maybe you were seeing someone else?"

"Who are these 'some people' that are saying that?"

"I don't know if I should say."

"I'm paying you to say."

"True . . ."

Pauline shook her head. "You know what? Don't tell me. I can guess who it was. It's not significant. Dougie was my boyfriend, but we were teenagers and neither of us was very faithful. But there was nothing of consequence to report. Dougie thought he was very discreet, but it's impossible to pull the wool over my eyes. I knew what he was up to."

"Did he have a fling with Susie?"

Pauline smiled slightly. "No. Never."

"Was Susie dating anyone?"

"No."

Antonia stopped walking and stared at her. "Would you tell me the truth? I am, after all, working for you, trying to solve this murder . . ."

"Of course I would tell you the truth," Pauline insisted. "This is not a game for me. Do you think it is? Would I really take the time to go to my lawyer and have him draw up legal papers?"

"I guess not," Antonia said with uncertainty. She didn't want to contradict Pauline, but she knew Pauline was lying. Pauline knew Susie was dating Kevin Powers.

Pauline squinted. "I think it's time that the person who did this pays. Someone got away with murder. And that person is probably toying with someone else right now. Manipulating them. Maybe the killer hasn't *killed* again, but the killer could be inflicting damage and pain on other victims. And having fun with it."

"And you still think that person is Kevin Powers?"

Pauline shrugged. "Kevin Powers?"

"Yes, the other day you said it was Kevin Powers."

"I don't recall saying that."

"You said your parents thought that."

"I don't recall that."

Antonia thought she was going crazy. Fortunately, she had her phone in her pocket. She pulled it out and clicked on the voice recordings. She had marked Pauline's interview but, oddly, she could not find it.

"Let's hear it."

"Um . . . that's so strange, I can't find your interview."

Pauline nodded. "I thought so."

"That's so weird . . ."

"I don't know what you were talking about."

Antonia was confused. Had she accidentally erased the recording after she listened to it with Joseph? She didn't think so. But truthfully, she couldn't rule it out. She didn't want to think that someone had picked up her phone and toyed with it. She didn't even have a passcode, so it would be easy enough to do. But would someone really do that? She was actually quite careless with her phone and didn't have it on her at all times, especially when she was in the kitchen. But this was bizarre.

"Well, in any event, was it Kevin?"

"Probably not."

"Okay, well then, who?"

"I hired you for a reason, didn't I? You need to find out."

"Right," Antonia conceded. "By the way, Mrs. Whitaker left me a message last night. Thanking me for helping but begging me to hurry."

"I told you, Antonia. We have very little time left."

"It was depressing. I can't imagine her pain."

"We've all been suffering. This is what I imagine purgatory is like—a suspended reality, a holding place. I need the truth to come out. I need to move forward with my life."

"I know. I'm doing my best."

"You need to do better than that," she said sternly.

"Do you think you could give me Mrs. Whitaker's number? I'd love to call her back."

"The woman is literally on her deathbed, there's no way," Pauline protested, before adding in a softer tone. "I have something for you in the front hall. I think you'll find it interesting."

18

Susie's pink-and-white-striped diary burned a hole in Antonia's purse the entire drive home. She felt as if she had just been endowed with the Pentagon Papers or some explosive documents that would shake up the world. How the hell did Pauline have Susie's diary? Was that even legal? And could the clue to Susie's murder be written in this long-forgotten girlish tome? Antonia sure as hell hoped so.

That said, the police probably would have confiscated it if it held anything of substance. Maybe it was only filled with scribbles and immature daydreams. (If it was anything like Antonia's diary from age seventeen it would have a whole lot of games of "Hangman" and pages devoted to her love of boy bands.) Pauline had the strangest look on her face when she handed it over to Antonia and had only provided a vague answer as to why it was in her possession. She demurred when Antonia asked if the police had ever seen it, and Antonia decided not to press lest Pauline suddenly have a change of heart and decide now was the time to march it down to the police station and surrender it to Officer Flanagan.

After turning off her car, Antonia bounded out of the parking lot and headed toward the back entrance of the inn. Before she checked in at the kitchen or asked how things were going at the front desk, she was determined to stop by her apartment for at least half an hour to skim the diary. She skirted past the dining room and was about to veer left toward the back hall that led to her apartment when a voice stopped her from behind.

"There you are, you cheating skunk! I *knew* you were avoiding me. Coming in the back entrance so I wouldn't see you? Sneaking around behind my back? We had a deal, Bingham. And you are blowing it."

Guiltily, Antonia slowly turned around. "Hello, Larry."

He stood in the middle of the main hallway with his hands on his hips. "*Hello, Larry?* Really? That's all you can say."

Antonia sighed deeply. "What's wrong now, Larry?"

"Oh, you know what's wrong. We had a deal, lady. A deal. And I find out from one of my very hot sources that you were at the Dune Club interviewing Dougie Marshall? Um, hello? We agreed that we would conduct all interviews together. This is a total breach of everything."

Antonia smiled beatifically and gripped her handbag closer to her chest. Susie's diary was deep in the bowels of the messy bag, no doubt camouflaged by all of the junk she carried around—lip gloss, tissues, compact mirror, Altoids, pens, keys, pepper spray (a recent necessity), as well as credit cards and cash—but she hoped to hell that Larry would not guess that she had something like that in her bag or he would rip it from her in the same manner a bear attacks his prey.

"We said *some* interviews."

"That won't cut it. You are going to sit down with me right now and walk me through everything you have learned so far or I won't share with you the mega information I discovered. And I want every detail. Hell hath no fury like a reporter scorned."

It took half an hour to tell Larry everything she'd discovered in her interviews. She had initially tried to condense her reports, but Larry was having none of it and pressed her for more details. When they had exhausted the topic, and Antonia had completely missed her window to look through Susie's diary, Larry finally stopped firing questions at her.

"Okay, now tell me this so-called mega information you discovered," Antonia commanded.

"Only because I believe that you have fully come clean with everything you know, I will share with you."

"You're too kind," she said sarcastically.

Larry smiled beatifically. "I know."

"What is it?"

"Barbara Whitaker—Susie's mother—died four years ago."

Antonia felt the blood drain from her face. "What? That's not possible."

"Very possible. She's a full-on ground monkey now. In fact, it wasn't even hard to find out. A quick Google search and the obituary popped right up."

Antonia was stunned. "Then . . . why would Pauline say she was on her deathbed? And who left me a message?"

"She's playing you. She knew that if there was a ticking clock you'd get moving on your investigation."

"That's so strange . . ." Antonia opened and closed her mouth as if she wanted to say more but she was too shocked. What kind of a psychopath was she dealing with? "Pauline and I literally just talked about the message Barbara left me not two hours ago."

"She probably left you the message herself."

Antonia retrieved the receiver of her landline and played the message on speaker. Now that she knew it was an imposter, the voice sounded phony.

"Not even a good actress," Larry added.

"I can't believe it. What else has she lied to me about?"

"Probably everything. The good news is I talked to Officer Flanagan . . ."

"Larry! I was planning on talking to him."

"I know, that's why I had to get there first. I told him all about how we're working together . . ."

Antonia's blood began to boil. She crossed her arms and scowled at Larry. "I just hope you didn't mess it up."

"I didn't. But you're focusing on the wrong thing. Don't you want to know what he said?"

"Yes. Tell me."

"He was young at the time and so wasn't a very important person on the force or big in the investigation. But he recalled that they had interviewed Susie's parents, who said something had been going on between Susie and Pauline at the time. They were fighting, and Susie would call home crying a lot. They kept telling her to come home, but she didn't want to."

"That makes sense. She didn't want to leave because she was dating Kevin Powers, but Pauline was giving her a hard time about it."

"Right. But the parents also said that Susie told them that . . ." Larry took a minute to whip out his leather-bound notebook and flip through it to find a certain page. "She told them that she 'may have gone too far.' That's a direct quote. 'May have gone too far.'"

"What does they mean?"

"The cops think she did something to piss off Pauline so Pauline offed her. Susie's parents suggested that she was agitated and afraid, particularly the night before she was killed. She told them she felt alone, that she had done something she shouldn't have. And she was paranoid, because she called them from the Dune Club and said she was scared to use the phone at the Framinghams' because 'they may be listening.' The point is, Susie had done something that made someone, most likely Pauline, pretty mad. She regretted it because she knew it made Pauline homicidal, and next thing, she's dead."

Antonia sat still, all of the information coming at her from a thousand different points in her head. "But it doesn't make sense, why would Pauline hire me to find Susie's murderer? Why open this all up again?"

Larry threw up his hands. "It's what everyone has been

telling you! Pauline is having fun. She enjoys manipulating people. Oh, Antonia. When are you going to start to see the bad in people?"

* * * * *

Everything went like clockwork in the back of the house that night: the restaurant turned tables quickly, Kendra's Instagram photos were all submitted so now it was a waiting game, and the receipts had been good. Antonia left the crew to shut down the kitchen while she changed out of her whites before wandering into the dining room where there were a few stragglers. She glanced around the room and then froze as her heart leapt into her mouth.

Nick Darrow was sitting at the bar nursing a drink. He was tapping the bar with a straw, and his foot jogged along on the bottom of the barstool. Even from a distance he had a commandingly powerful presence that made him riveting. As Antonia approached, she saw that he had a few days' stubble of beard on his tanned face, giving him a rugged look that he sometimes had in his films. The closer she came to him, the more she smelled his particular scent—that familiar masculine aroma of saddle soap and leather that made her weak in the knees. He turned and looked up at her and smiled and she felt as if her life was happening in slow motion. Why hadn't she prepared herself for his return? She wanted to be casual but all she felt was unsteady.

"Hey! You're back," she said mustering as casual and cheerful a tone as possible. It seemed to her as if her voice came out in a shaky, warbly tone similar to when they slow down a film and the actors' voices become distorted.

He stood up and firmly gripped her arms with his large, warm hands. They looked into each other's eyes before he leaned in for a strong kiss on her cheek. His lips were soft to the touch and didn't merely graze her cheek but pressed against it. She felt slightly weak in her knees.

"Antonia, you look great."

"Thank you," she responded softly. "So . . . you're back?"

"Yes, I came back earlier this week."

"That's great."

"But only for a little while, I still have to head back."

Disappointment coursed through her body and she slid herself onto the stool next to him. "How was it? Did you have a good time in Australia?"

He waved his hand in the air. "I'm sure you heard everything."

She became immediately alarmed. "No, what happened?"

"Melanie and I broke up. I thought you'd have seen it, it's been all over the press."

"No. I don't really read that sort of press."

"Good for you," he said with gratitude. "It's been awful. For me, for Finn. A long time coming."

"I'm sorry to hear that," she said, although that wasn't entirely true.

He frowned. "She's so dramatic and selfish. She can't be reasonable. Jealous of everything and everyone. Thought I was having an affair with Daphne Jennings . . ." When he saw Antonia's blank look he clarified. "That's my costar. It's not relevant. It wasn't true. But Melanie is so damn paranoid she can talk herself into anything. She became furious and took off. Without a word—didn't even tell the sitter or me or Finn where she was going. Returned three days later just as I was about to send out a private detective. She took Finn and came back here, saying she needed time. I had to leave the set to deal with this. That's why I'm back, to see him. I don't know for how long."

Antonia nodded. There was so much she wanted to say, but she wasn't sure what was best. Her honest advice might be clouded by the fact that she had a giant crush on him. Should she tell him to do everything he could to work it out with Melanie? Probably. But could she say that genuinely? No. What she really wanted to say was *okay, now marry me!* Melanie had her chance—their marriage had always been contentious. Let Antonia take over! *Why be with a gorgeous movie star when you can be with a chubby chef? Albeit a chef who would love you more than anyone in the world could.*

"I hope everything works out for the best."

He nodded. "We'll see. But how are you?" His eyes slid over her body. "You look great. I see you're all recovered."

"I'm no longer hobbling around on a cane at least."

"I'm glad. Although I bet you rocked the cane."

"How can someone 'rock a cane'?"

"You know what I mean. You're an elegant woman, I'm sure you inspired a trend. Now I'll walk down Main Street and see all the fashionable young women using canes."

Antonia laughed. "Hardly. But it was actually slightly fun in the beginning. Then it became inconvenient."

"And how's business? This place looks like it's going gangbusters."

"We're having a great summer."

"I'm really glad."

He stopped speaking but looked as if he had more to say. He stared at her face, running his eyes all over it. "It's good to be back."

"It's good to have you back."

Something was passing between them, but Antonia had no idea what. This wasn't the time or place to say anything more . . . and besides, could she really? He stared at her intensely before downing the rest of his drink.

"Listen, I'm beat and have to be up early tomorrow. Any chance we can have dinner this week?"

"Sure. Tomorrow?" She didn't want to appear too eager, but she couldn't help herself.

"Yeah . . . no, wait. I have to go to the city tomorrow for a few days. Let's do Sunday night."

"Sunday," she said, nodding. "Sure. Sounds good."

He pulled out his wallet and placed a twenty on the bar. "We'll talk more. We have a lot to discuss."

"Great."

Before he left, he hugged her goodbye and whispered in her hair, "I missed you."

Antonia felt again the rush of weakness and swimming

giddiness that Nick incited in her. It was as if every compliment he extended toward her was an ember that warmed her body and soul. Antonia knew attraction and lust were fleeting, but connections were lasting and what she shared with Nick was an undeniable connection.

She tossed and turned in her bed that night trying to decipher the meaning of that statement: "I missed you." His words echoed over and over again in her ears. Should she take them at face value? Or was there something more there? What was it about Nick that brought her to her knees? Antonia had to be careful. She hadn't felt this way since . . . well, if she had to admit it to herself, it was since she'd met her ex-husband, Philip. She dragged her mind away from Nick and forced herself to rethink her past in an effort to avoid the same mistakes.

In retrospect, it was so hard for her to even imagine what she had seen in Philip, now that she knew what a violent and manipulative man he was. And he was in no way her type, physically or personality-wise. Previously she had only dated soulful poets, dreamers who were as penniless as they were cerebral. Then one day she was catering a Fourth of July picnic for the police department. It was before she had her own company—she was still young—but she had been charged with making most of the meal as the owner of the company had come down with a stomach bug and relinquished many of her duties to Antonia. Antonia was totally in the weeds—running around like a chicken with her head cut off—when this clean-cut attractive cop swaggered up to her station. Philip introduced himself, told her she made the best fried chicken he had ever eaten, and informed her that he was taking her to dinner that Friday and he wouldn't take no for an answer.

Antonia was young enough to be dazzled by this handsome authority figure who exuded confidence and control. Little did she know how controlling he actually was. Everything that had initially attracted her ended up repelling her. What was it about Antonia that gravitated toward him? It was certainly something about her character that she could not understand. Particularly since her parents had been such fabulous role models—good people with a loving marriage. Was she self-destructive? Was this "flirting with danger" (to put it very mildly) the same inclination that had her running around chasing killers? All she had to do was go about her happy life in her cozy inn with her incredible friends and restaurant, and yet, here she was: skidding around town trying to find out who killed Susie Whitaker decades ago. Human nature was impossible to understand. And self-awareness was even more daunting. Antonia drifted off to a fitful slumber, with images of darkness dancing through her dreams.

19

Dear Diary,

Pauline is so mad at me! I don't know what to do. I think she is being totally irrational. I am her BEST friend, I only have her BEST interests at heart. The problem is she thinks she can do anything and there will be no consequences. She has always gotten her way. But I think what she is doing is wrong on so many levels. And she just won't listen to me. Call me what she wants—prude, snitch, nerd—I don't care. But I have MORALS. She DOESN'T. And you know what? Who will she come crying to when this is all over? ME. Okay, maybe not crying—she never cries—but she will be like, all upset. And if she would just listen to me, she could totally avoid this situation. You know, that's the problem with her. She thinks she is so mature and grown up and knows everything, but she is still young—we both are. That's why she has to be careful. You can't get yourself into these situations.

Everybody gets super mad. If there was only a rational person that she trusted that she would listen to, but her parents are clueless and she doesn't listen to anyone. But this time I won't back down! She has to listen to me.

August 20

Dear Diary,

I totally am going to hide you in the most secret place because I am REALLY SCARED and if anyone reads you, it's DISASTER. I think Pauline has gone off the deep end. She is in over her head. This guy is scary and controlling. She thinks she can handle it, but she can't. She's all like, "He's awesome, what are you talking about?"And she pretends that she's in charge, but he is so manipulative. And I KNOW he left me that note to back off. Pauline was like, "What note?" she said. And the worst is she says in front of him that I am against them being together and he laughs and thinks it's funny but then I see him giving me these really creepy mean looks like he hates me. He scares the hell out of me. But so does Pauline if I am honest. She's my best friend but there is a weird part of her that likes to be mean to me. I think she takes pleasure when I cry. She is really testing me. I am so tempted to say something to her father when he gets back but he has that terrible temper, and I've seen him shoot the messenger.

Dear Diary,

It's so annoying but Alida totally takes Pauline's side and tells me to grow up and stay out of it. She pretends she doesn't but she totally worships/is scared of Pauline. I tried to talk to her but she blew me off and made me seem like I was crazy. I would totally leave if I didn't have my crush, he is literally the only reason I'm here. I tried to talk about it with him, but he thinks it's all girl fights and doesn't care, but it's not. He also thinks Pauline is a total snob and she rules me and treats me like garbage. The thing is, Alida and Pauline are banded together and they make me into the whiny third wheel, which I'm not. Even the other day Russell's girlfriend Holly said they were jerks to me and why do I put up with them. Maybe I should tell Holly about what's going on. She's weird, but I need to know if I'm paranoid or if someone is really following me/harassing me. It just seems like there are too many coincidences. Should I tell the Framinghams????? Maybe when they get back I will.

Those were the last three entries in Susie's diary. Antonia had read them again and again and was now waiting for Joseph to finish and provide his assessment. They were sitting on the front porch of the inn, watching the cars speed by on their way to the beach or work. The backdrop of the Wednesday-morning hustle and bustle was a strong contrast to the plaintive missives of a diary written by a girl buried so long ago.

"Wow," Joseph sighed as he put the diary down on his lap. "Harrowing stuff."

"I know. Not to mention heartbreaking, depressing, and everything else. It really makes you want to head back in time and tell Susie to run for the hills! It's sad that she knew someone was following her and yet she felt too alone to talk to anyone."

"How does Pauline still have possession of this diary? Shouldn't it be with the police? Or her family?"

"She told me she didn't find it until years later—Susie had hidden it very well in the floorboards of the bedroom she slept in. Pauline had decided the police were useless at that point and never even told them she found it. But now that I know Pauline is a confirmed liar I have no idea if that's at all true. She probably hid it herself."

"Did she say anything about the contents?"

Antonia shook her head. "She was very blasé, like, 'Oh, here, this might be of interest.' And obviously it's so strange because of what Susie wrote! It's incriminating. But Pauline handed it off to me without even clarifying or trying to defend herself. It's all a game to her."

"Entitled and bored. The dangerous consequences of possessing extreme wealth and receiving everything she ever wanted. People like her look for entertainment in the most devious ways . . . Do you think the boyfriend that Susie is referring to is Dougie Marshall?"

"That's who Pauline was dating. But people have suggested Pauline was fooling around on him so perhaps it was someone else . . . This all brings me back to square one. I'm going to have to interview everyone all over again. Not to mention check off all the other boxes."

Joseph nodded. "No one said it would be easy."

"I know. At least I have a little more time now that I know that Barbara Whitaker is already dead."

"True."

"By the way, I went through those clips you sourced for me, thank you again, but there was really nothing."

"Agreed. As I said it's the absence of evidence and leads that I find most intriguing with this case."

"As if they didn't care."

"Or if the people who cared had the money to silence it."

*   *   *   *   *

"Scott Stewart?"

The tall man in the tennis whites turned around and smiled at Antonia. He was probably in his early fifties, and the years were evident on his face. He had handsome features and blond-ish shaggy hair peeking out from under his baseball hat. His skin was raisin brown and freckled from the sun, and his body was taut and muscular, as was to be expected from someone who made his living on a tennis court.

"I'm Antonia Bingham," she said, thrusting her hand toward him.

"Nice to meet you. I don't think you're my next lesson, seeing as you're not wearing sneakers . . ."

"No." Antonia chuckled. "I'm afraid I don't play. Tried my hand at it when I was young, but I am sadly uncoordinated. It was not pretty."

"Don't sell yourself short. I'm a pretty good teacher."

"I'm sure you are. But that's not why I'm here, actually."

"What can I do you for?" he asked in a folksy manner, as he dumped yellow balls into a basket.

"I'm actually here because . . . well, Pauline Framingham asked me to look into the murder of Susie Whitaker . . ."

Before Antonia even finished, a flash of darkness crossed Scott's face.

"I don't want to talk about that." He bent down and picked up more balls with his racket.

"I understand it might be painful . . . but Pauline is looking for closure . . ."

"Are you a detective?"

"No, I'm actually an innkeeper. I own the Windmill Inn . . ."

He interrupted her. "Listen, I don't mean to be rude, but I am not interested in talking about that."

He started walking toward the other side of the court where there was a pile of balls. Antonia trotted alongside him.

"I'm sure it was a terrible time, but I think it would be great for everyone to have closure . . ."

He laughed to himself. "Yeah, right."

"This is obviously a very difficult topic for you."

"You got that right."

"I'm sorry. I didn't mean to upset you."

He stopped abruptly and stared at Antonia. "Look, I'm

sure you mean no harm, but I'm done with this. I don't want to talk about that time at all. And if I can offer you some advice it would be to stay away. Nothing good will come out of this for you. I don't care how much money she's paying you. It won't be worth the sacrifice."

He walked off the court, slamming the gate behind him.

"He didn't want to talk about it, did he?"

Antonia swung around and came face-to-face with Holly Wender. She was clad in a short tennis dress, with her hair up in a ponytail under a visor and her eyes obscured by dark sunglasses.

"Holly! What a surprise."

"Not really," Holly replied.

"Oh right. Yes, it's a small town. Actually, I'm glad I ran into you because I have a few questions for you. Do you have a sec?"

Holly glanced at her Fitbit and then shrugged. "Sure. My lesson isn't for ten minutes."

"Do you have a lesson with Scott?"

"No."

"He really doesn't want to say anything about Susie."

"Of course not. Everyone was burned by what happened."

"How so?"

"Living under the cloud of suspicion, people gave you strange looks and treated you like dog poop. Not to mention, if you tried to say anything the Framinghams would sue you."

"It sounds terrible."

"It is terrible. Pauline derives pleasure from it, that's why she asked you to look into it again. The Framinghams enjoy manipulating people."

"Listen, I recently came across some information that Susie was afraid before her death. She felt someone was harassing her. And it seems as if the person who was harassing her was in a relationship with Pauline, possibly. It could be Dougie Marshall, or perhaps not. Did Susie reach out to you at all and discuss this with you?"

Holly sneered. "Me? No. Those girls didn't even glance my way."

"But I think . . . I *know* Susie was considering talking to you about it. It sounded as if she needed a friend, and although you might think she didn't like you, it sounded as if she did."

"I never got that vibe."

"Do you have any idea who Susie was referring to? Who was Pauline seeing?"

"I only know that idiot Dougie. I'm sure she screwed around on him, but I never saw her with anyone."

"Was there any other man lurking around at that time? Anyone following the girls."

"No one I noticed."

"I don't mean someone that was unfamiliar to them, I'm suggesting someone they knew but who didn't like Susie?"

"Everyone kind of thought she was annoying."

It was arduous for Antonia. She decided to try a new tactic. "That last week, who do you remember being at the house?"

"Well . . . Russell, Pauline, Susie, me . . . Alida and Dougie . . . Scott and Kevin . . . the housekeepers . . . Ambassador Framingham."

Antonia perked up. "Ambassador Framingham was there? I was told he was in Europe."

Holly looked perplexed. "I'm pretty sure he was out that week . . . he met with his lawyer."

"Are you sure?"

Holly nodded. "Yes. I totally remember now. The day before Susie was killed, Russell and I were searching for the badminton net. I went into the front hall closet next to Ambassador Framingham's office and I heard him with that Schultz guy."

"Are you sure?"

"Yes."

"That's strange . . . I wonder why he said he was out of town."

"Everyone lies."

"It's starting to feel that way. But you don't think Ambassador Framingham would have killed Susie?"

"Who knows? He was a jerk."

Antonia wasn't sure what to say next.

"Can I go now?" Holly asked impatiently.

"Sure." Antonia began to walk toward the exit. "So, you and Scott are still in touch?"

"Yeah, we live together."

Antonia froze. "You didn't mention that before."

"You didn't ask."

"How long have you been together?"

She smiled slightly. "Seems like forever."

20

Antonia returned home to the inn to find Kendra slumped on the back steps by the kitchen, wiping tears from her face.

"Is everything okay?"

"I'm fine," she said, brushing away the teardrops with the back of her hand. "Don't worry."

Antonia sat down and patted her on the back. "Did Marty finally go too far? Just tell me and I'll read him the riot act."

"It's not that. It's stupid."

Antonia dug through her bag and found a small packet of tissues. She handed Kendra one. "I'm sure it's not stupid."

"It's just that . . . I lost the Instagram contest. I know, so dumb that I care. But I really thought I had a shot. People were voting like crazy on my pictures and then, at the last minute, this other chef signed on and he got about a million hits and won."

"That's disappointing. I'm sorry to hear that."

"Everyone loved his picture of shrimp and grits. Shrimp and grits—I can make that with my eyes closed! He added some peculiar variable like pickled something and *bam*! He wins."

"Kendra, your pictures were incredible and your food is incredible."

"Just not incredible enough."

"Hey, I bet that other chef has a celebrity following or is paying off a ton of people or something. Don't worry."

"Actually, what stinks is that he's a nice guy. You know him."

"Who?"

"It's that guy Sam Wilson. Remember him?"

Did she remember him? Antonia felt the blood rise to her cheeks. Of course she did. He had arrived last spring and complimented her on her food and then one thing led to another and they had a brief affair. She had liked him, until she accused him of being a murderer. But what really broke it up was that he could see that her feelings for Nick were stronger than her feelings for him. It had been awkward. She still thought of him a lot, wondering if she had made a mistake in ending their relationship.

"Well, at least it went to a good guy. And hey, maybe you can win next year? Or at least place?"

"Oh, I did place. I came in second."

"Kendra! That's great! Congratulations."

"I guess. I'm a sore loser, I know. I don't even want to go to the photo op that we need to take on Tuesday for the *East Hampton Star*."

"Come on, you have to go."

"Will you go with me?"

"Where?"

"To the photo shoot? It's at Wölffer Vineyard. I'd feel so much more comfortable if you were there."

"Um . . . I don't know. What time is it?"

Antonia was hedging because she really didn't want to see Sam again. She was embarrassed at how she'd behaved, and there was actually nothing that appealed to her less.

"It's Tuesday at ten. It won't take that long, please?"

Kendra peered up at her with the pleading eyes of a child. Antonia swallowed and then said with fake cheer, "Of course I'll be there!"

*   *   *   *   *

"Thank you for coming to me. I would have been more than happy to meet you at your house again."

"No worries. I was on my way back from The Salon in Amagansett, so it was only a small detour."

Antonia was in the library of the inn, sitting across from Alida Jenkins, who was clad in a spectacular white sheath dress that was a beautiful contrast to her dark skin. As soon as Antonia had returned home she had called both Alida and Dougie to arrange a meeting. Dougie asked her to swing by after his golf game at five p.m. the next day (of course right in the middle of her crunch time for dinner service) and Alida was completely amenable and was at her inn within fifteen minutes. For someone who had world-class fame and an international career, she was surprisingly available.

"I won't waste your time. I've recently learned that Susie was upset with the person Pauline was seeing. She found him menacing, controlling, and felt Pauline didn't know what she was up against. Do you know anything about this?" Antonia asked.

"I know that Susie and Dougie were not on the best of terms."

"Why's that?"

"Maybe I misspoke. It's not that they fought or there was contention—he paid very little attention to her, she was quite inconsequential to him, and that ruffled her."

"But was he menacing toward Susie?"

"I doubt that very much."

"Was Dougie threatening?"

Alida waved her hand in the air dismissively. "Absolutely not. Dougie . . . he's a party boy. He's not anyone you take seriously."

"Was Pauline seeing anyone else? Someone who scared Susie?"

If Antonia had to swear on a Bible, she would assert that she saw a glimmer pass behind Alida's eyes. She knew something.

"Well . . ."

Before Alida could answer, Soyla entered the library with a tray of tea and macaroons.

"Sorry to bother, I thought you might want something to drink," Soyla said sheepishly.

"Thank you very much. That's so nice."

They waited in silence for Soyla to set up the tea tray. Alida's phone buzzed, and she glanced at the screen. Antonia watched as Alida's expression changed. As soon as Soyla left, Alida jumped up.

"I'm so sorry but I have to go."

"Is everything okay?" Antonia asked, rising.

Alida gave her a small, tense smile. "Yes. I just have to be somewhere."

"I'll walk you out. Do you mind telling me what you were about to say?"

"I don't quite remember," Alida said as she strode through the library door toward the entrance.

"It looked to me as if you knew the person Pauline was seeing? Someone who scared Susie?"

Alida kept walking and didn't look Antonia in the eye. She demurred. "No, I don't know a thing about it."

"Are you sure?" Antonia pressed.

Alida opened the front door and began walking down the steps. Antonia jogged along next to her, feeling dwarfed by the tall supermodel.

"Yes, I know nothing about this," insisted Alida.

"Don't worry; if you're concerned about telling me anything that might be compromising to Pauline, I have her full coop-eration on this. She wants very much to solve Susie's murder."

Alida stopped and emitted an acerbic laugh. She put her hand on Antonia's shoulder. "Oh dear. You really think that, don't you? You haven't figured it out at all. I bet she told you that she needed to find out on behalf of Susie's father who is on his deathbed."

Antonia gulped. "She said it was her mother."

Alida gave a fake laugh. "Of course. Listen, Antonia, I'd be careful if I were you. I think you might want to walk away before things get out of hand."

"They already have."

Alida shook her head. "You ain't seen nothing yet."

She turned and headed toward her car, passing Joseph along the way. He turned and gave Alida the once-over before revving the engine of his scooter and zipping up the ramp leading to the front door.

"I saw that," Antonia said, wagging her finger at him.

"My dear, I have never been immune to the beauty of women. And that creature is a rare specimen."

"Agreed. And that beauty of a woman just basically warned me that I should end this investigation. Told me to walk away."

Joseph shook his head. "Hmmm . . . something to consider. She would know. In fact, I bring to you some interesting information about her."

"Really? Well then, step into my office."

As some guests had wandered in and planted themselves in the library, Antonia and Joseph really did need to meet in her office, which was a spectacularly untidy and overstuffed room off the lobby. There was barely enough space for Joseph to squeeze his scooter in, and the effort to orient him caused a number of overflowing mail trays to be overturned.

"Oh, dear, I really have to organize this. I'm sorry."

"No worries. I suppose it is good news that we have to gather in here. It means business is booming and the inn is alive."

"I suppose so. Would you like a sweet?"

Antonia offered him a plate of peanut caramel clusters that Soyla had baked for her that afternoon and left on her desk. Joseph took one and Antonia bit into hers. She had to admit that the protégée was beginning to overtake the master.

"Yum, these are amazing," Antonia moaned.

"Delicious."

"Probably my last supper, if I read into what Alida was hinting at."

"Oh no!"

"Tell me what you have on her."

Joseph retrieved a folder from the basket of his scooter. He opened it and flipped through the pages. Finding the one that interested him, he handed Antonia the sheet. It was a copy of an article from *Women's Wear Daily*. There was a picture of a much younger Alida Jenkins alongside the headline: FABRICANT FRAGRANCE CHOOSES NEW FACE. The accompanying article was about how an "unknown young seventeen-year-old model" had been chosen to be the exclusive spokesmodel for the venerable makeup company.

"I'm not following," Antonia said. "We knew Alida was famous."

"Do you know who owns Fabricant Fragrance?"

"No."

"Framingham Industries."

"Really!"

"Yes. And look at the date of the article—it's two days after Susie's murder."

"You think they gave her the contract in order to shut her up?"

"I think it's possible."

"But Alida is a beautiful girl. She even had you swooning. Surely she would have received a contract on her own."

"Perhaps. But there are a lot of beautiful girls out there. And while I don't want to diminish her exquisiteness, there is something of luck involved with attaining a career like she has."

"This deal could have been in the works for a while."

"It's possible. But I think the timeline is too coincidental. And, in fact, I researched other similar announcements of fragrance spokesmodels around the same time. They were done with much more fanfare than this—there were launch parties and television interviews. A mention in a trade paper, while important, seems a bit hasty and under the radar. Especially considering how prominent a role she played in the advertising campaign over the next few decades. I believe, to date, she is still the face of Fabricant Fragrance. Which is awfully rare. And one can intimate that she received her contract because of her close friendship with Pauline Framingham, but let's be realistic. Friendship can only do so much for so long."

Antonia paused, thinking. "Do you think she blackmailed them for it? Maybe she knew Pauline did it and, to keep her quiet, they offered her this? Or do you think they just handed it to her as a reward for silence?"

"A very good question. I have not had the opportunity to talk to Ms. Jenkins. Did she appear to be a devious person? It would take some gumption to blackmail someone at age seventeen."

"True."

"Then you'll have to believe it was used to silence her."

"And maybe she could be bought off, but Susie couldn't . . ." Antonia trailed off. She took the opportunity to tuck into another cookie. One absolutely could not be expected to only sample one cookie off a cookie plate. That was absurd. She pushed the tray toward Joseph.

"I can't," he demurred.

"You have more willpower than I do."

"It's not that. Soyla told me that strawberry shortcake was on the menu. That is something I simply cannot refuse, so I will abstain from ingesting any more of those dollops of paradise."

Antonia smiled. "They are so good, aren't they?"

"The ratio of caramel to peanuts is heavenly. But I digress. Let me show you something else I discovered as I perused back issues of the *East Hampton Star*."

Joseph selected another printout from his folder and handed it to Antonia. It was a large spread on the Hampton Classic, one of the leading horse shows in the world, not to mention one of the largest. It had been held for the past three decades in Bridgehampton and attracted serious horsemen and women from around the globe. This current article dated back approximately ten years. Antonia scanned the pictures and found two of Pauline Framingham. In one, she was atop a chestnut-colored horse named Jasper, jumping over a large white fence. They had apparently leapt to victory because the notation under the picture said that she had placed first in the open jumper class.

It took Antonia longer to find the second picture of Pauline, but she located it on the bottom right corner. In a blurred photo, Pauline was sitting in the bleachers of the Classic, chatting with a dapper-looking older man with a mustache. He was standing next to her, looking very regal in a suit. Pauline was gazing up at him with a friendly grin.

"I don't recognize him. Should I?" Antonia asked.

"Who?"

Antonia pointed at the man with the mustache.

"Him? Oh, Redmond something or other. But that's not important. I wanted you to look at the man sitting next to her."

Antonia's eyes swiveled toward the other side of Pauline. Sitting ever-so-close to her was none other than Kevin Powers. He also wore a smile on his face and appeared quite at ease despite the class warfare that had plagued them years prior.

"I don't understand. I thought she hated Kevin Powers. Called him trash."

"If you read the article, it mentions that Powers' Garden Center was awarded the contract to provide flowers to the VIP tents at the Classic. Per the suggestion of executive board member Pauline Framingham."

"But this makes no sense . . ."

"Another payoff, my dear. Pauline put her ducks in a row."

"But why would she have waited ten years? Susie was killed way before this picture."

"Didn't you tell me that Kevin had a substance abuse problem? I think his sister-in-law Sylvia—who is not known for her discretion, I might add—once told me that Kevin had been in and out of rehabilitation centers for years and just when they had finally given up on him, he became sober. Became sober, somehow opened the garden center, and very quickly landed the contract with the Classic."

Antonia put down the paper. "She really owns these people, doesn't she?"

"It would appear that way . . . although, perhaps they own her?"

21

The bright sun flooded Antonia's room at six the next morning, leaving her no choice but to haul herself to the beach for her morning walk. She grumpily pulled on sweatpants and Crocs and ran a brush through her tangled mop of hair. Her eyes were puffy from sleep, and the coffee she guzzled did little to rouse her from her drowsiness. In her mind she asked why it mattered for her to walk along the beach when a few more hours of sleep would be more beneficial. It was always a negotiation and usually a coin toss as to whether laziness or fitness prevailed. With the added work of an investigation, Antonia felt she was entitled to a little extra lounging. Especially since Nick Darrow was in the city for the next couple of days and she had no chance of running into him there.

Yet as soon as Antonia pulled her car into the Georgica Beach parking lot, a wave of joy washed over her and she was so glad she had come. Why was it that the idea of exercise was so much worse than the actual exercise? And to be honest, a walk on the beach was hardly a jog or a run. All she had to do was walk down to the jetty and back, and as it was a glorious golden morning with the sun's rays bouncing off the water it could not have been a more pleasurable foray. She waved to passing joggers and dog walkers with the type of enthusiasm usually reserved for residents and neighbors on Sesame Street.

The sand was already warm under Antonia's feet and she found herself walking briskly, reveling in the soft breeze coming in off the ocean. She passed Pauline's house with nary a glance, determined to focus on the other aspects of her life besides murder. When she was young, her mother told her to take time every week to count her blessings. This week, the top blessing on her list would be that Nick Darrow was back in town. (She decided to remove the circumstances from her mind—focus on the positive.) Other blessings were that the inn was fully booked for the summer, her restaurant was doing well, she had her health as did the people closest to her, and the weather was nice.

In the distance, Antonia thought she saw that jogger who approached her on the beach and told her that Pauline was evil. Was it a coincidence? Did the woman just know Pauline's reputation? Or was she legitimately warning her? Antonia set off briskly trying to catch up with her to find out. But after about a minute of running, Antonia found herself heaving and collapsing from the exertion. Note to self, Antonia: get in shape. She glanced at her watch and realized that she was running late to assist with breakfast service so she quickly veered around to change directions. Just as she did so, she heard a light snap in her damaged knee.

"Sugar!" Antonia exclaimed. Her knee suddenly felt hot. She was still able to walk—but it was more of a hobble—toward her car. When she plopped herself in the driver's seat, she yanked up her pants to stare at her pale knee. It appeared slightly swollen to her untrained eye, but nothing very serious. She knew she should probably rest it, but hopefully an ice pack would help alleviate the swelling. She had to confess, she had been remiss in doing the exercises that Matt Powers, her physical therapist, had prescribed her. She was also due to visit him. Maybe now was the best time, since she could probe him about his uncle Kevin. She dialed his number.

Fortunately Matt had a cancellation, so at ten o'clock that morning, Antonia found herself at his office at East Hampton Sports Medicine, which was located in a large aluminum-sided building just off Route 114 toward the airport. Antonia had an innate aversion to the place as she did to any location that had a whiff of sports equipment and exertion. The athletic paraphernalia scattered around the windowless space—stairmasters, free weights, treadmills, and jump ropes—coupled with the scent of sweat and hardy determination conjured up vomit in Antonia's throat. To her knee's detriment, she avoided the place like the plague. But today, she sucked it up and allowed Matt to manipulate her leg into positions he must have learned about in some medieval torture manual, while she focused on eliciting information about Kevin.

"I just saw your uncle the other day," Antonia said with feigned casualness.

"Frank?"

"No—who's Frank?"

"My uncle," Matt said flatly. He was a stunningly attractive man in his late twenties who was as humorless and conceited as he was good-looking. Antonia believed that the only reason he was still single was that the girls who were pretty enough to secure him were quickly bored by him. He was what one would call a hot nerd.

"I meant your other uncle. Kevin."

"Oh, yeah. He's my father's half-brother. Does this hurt?" he asked as he twisted Antonia's leg to the left.

She found herself sinking into the thin, plastic-covered mattress on the table. "Yes," she was able to warble. "I didn't realize they're half-brothers. It explains why they don't look that much alike."

"Are you doing your exercises? Because there should be way more mobility by now."

"Sort of," admitted Antonia. "When I have time."

Matt frowned, then rubbed his hands together before pulling down on Antonia's leg. "It's really important that you do your strengthening . . ."

Antonia zoned out while Matt lectured her. She watched his mouth move, but the words flooded over her without any meaning. She noticed that he had perfectly straight teeth, and she wondered if they were capped. It was so funny how his features were so dainty when his parents had such thick and fleshy faces and bodies. She waited for him to finish before she returned to her desired topic.

"Are you and Kevin close?"

"Not really. He wasn't around much when I was young."

"Oh really? I thought he always lived here."

Matt shrugged. "Technically."

"What does that mean?"

Matt was pressing down on Antonia's leg so hard tears sprang into her eyes. She had to bite her lip to keep from scream-crying.

"Kevin had some issues so he went away for a while."

"Oh, right. He told me all about that."

"Really? I didn't think he talked about it."

"Drug and alcohol addiction is a serious disease. It's nothing to be ashamed of. The more we talk about it, the more awareness there is."

A strange look came across Matt's face. "Oh that. Right . . ."

Antonia sat up. "What were *you* referring to?"

Matt shook his head. "Nothing."

"We're probably talking about the same thing. He was extremely candid with me," fibbed Antonia. She was going straight to hell in a handbasket.

"You mean you talked about Kimberly?"

"Of course we talked about Kimberly. He told me all about her. What ever happened to her?"

"I'm not sure. I think she moved away. I see her mom from time to time when I'm at Hampton Market Place. She still works there."

"Right, what's her name again?"

"Sally."

"Right." Antonia could not believe how much she was bluffing. Could Matt really not tell? "So what was your take on what happened with Kimberly and Kevin?"

"I was pretty young. I just remember my parents looking really worried. There was a lot of whispering, and even as a kid I could sense something was wrong. But it was a he-said-she-said thing, according to them. I remember my step-grandmother— Kevin's mom—saying, 'If you have a toxic relationship, things escalate. It's both people's fault.' But my parents never really bought that. That's sort of why I didn't see much of Kevin. They were wary of him and they didn't trust him. But his mother would hear none of it; he could do no wrong in her eyes. He was always mixed up with bad things."

Antonia sat bolt upright. "Wait, what? He was physically abusive to Kimberly?"

Kevin gave her an odd look. "The fight . . . you said you knew."

"I didn't realize he hit her." Antonia felt sick.

"He threw a bottle at her. That's why he went to prison."

"Prison?" sputtered Antonia.

Matt squinted at her. "I thought that's what we were talking about."

"It is, it is," she said, not wanting to let on that she didn't know. "I just . . . I don't refer to it as 'prison.' That seems so . . . pejorative. I like to call it the Big House. In a Big House, people are awarded second chances."

"Sometimes they don't deserve them."

"Agreed. What did Kevin do exactly?"

"From what I understand, he messed Kimberly up pretty bad. He claims that he didn't mean for the bottle to hit her, but it did. Who throws a bottle at a woman, no matter how drugged out or drunk you are? Their fighting was apparently legendary. But maybe they just brought out the devil in each other. There are people who do that. They bring out the devil in each other—the worst possible version of themselves. Have you ever come across that?"

"Yes." Antonia nodded, distaste and contempt growing inside her. "Unfortunately, I have."

22

As it was on her way back to the inn, Antonia made a detour to stop by Hampton Market Place to ask Sally about her daughter and Kevin Powers. Antonia had pretended to Matt that she knew Sally but, to the best of her knowledge, she had never laid eyes on the woman. Antonia was truly shocked by the idea of Kevin as a violent person. He had acknowledged his past transgressions, but Antonia had never assumed that they included violence toward women. This was disgusting and changed everything, and she needed to know more. Her case might have just solved itself.

Antonia chided herself for having been too quick to exonerate Kevin in Susie's murder. Maybe it did have something to do with him being a local and the fact that she knew his family? Could that have been what persuaded the police to look the other way too? And although it was disgusting to admit—there was something more . . . well, exciting was the wrong word, but interesting? Intoxicating? Righteous? Whatever the word—something *better* about believing that Susie's murderer was one of the rich and famous folk that she kept company with.

And if Antonia were to be perfectly honest with herself, it had been there all along for her to see—Susie dated men who her friends thought were unfit for her. Antonia had assumed Susie's friends were snobs, and that they disapproved of the men because they were from the wrong side of the tracks, so to speak. But perhaps the friends disapproved because the men were dangerous.

She was mad at herself for her own biases (pro-local, pro-underdog, pro-cute guy!), and she was mad at herself for not seeing the real Kevin. He had seemed so mild and soft-spoken. No one else had indicated that he could be violent. He even had a yoga mat in his office! Could a man who does yoga be violent? Of course it was a stereotype that yogis were peaceniks, but still. Antonia had to wrap her head around it. *Darn it, Bingham!* she scolded herself. *Wake up and do your job!*

Hampton Market Place wasn't far from the train station and housed in a building that had undergone many metamorphoses in recent decades. For years it was called the Chicken House, and it was where everyone in town procured beer kegs and the tastiest fried chicken around, according to those who had sampled it. But that was before Antonia's time. It was Schmidt's for a while, and then after a fire, it had reemerged as Hampton Market Place, with a deli counter that was in strong demand as well as a salad bar and then a variety of Irish packaged snacks and expensive organic foods that didn't seem to jibe with the clientele. A young woman at the counter directed Antonia to Sally who agreed, somewhat nervously, to take a break and chat with Antonia outside.

Sally was a hefty woman in her early sixties with a messy mop of dirty blond hair held together with bobby pins. She had a warm smile but was meek and tentative, and Antonia couldn't help but feel as if she was a teacher leading an errant student to the principal's office.

"What's this about, can I ask?" Sally inquired nervously. She had the gravelly voice of a smoker.

"No, nothing bad. Well, bad, but long ago bad . . . I've been asked to look into the murder of Susie Whitaker."

Antonia could see recognition in Sally's eyes. She quickly pulled out a pack of cigarettes and lit one. "I remember that."

"Yes, I'm sure you do. I wanted to ask you about Kevin Powers. As I'm sure you know he was a suspect in that murder."

Sally released a long stream of smoke before biting her nail. "I know."

"And I only recently learned that he had an issue with your daughter, Kimberly."

"The police knew all about that," Sally said quickly.

"I'm sure they did."

"Kimberly's fine now. Married and living down in Florida."

"I'm really happy to hear that."

"Got two grandbabies. Cheryl and Brandon."

Sally pulled out her phone and showed Antonia her screen-saver. Two tow-headed children missing various front teeth beamed from the screen.

"Adorable."

"I don't get to see them enough. Hopefully she'll make it up for Christmas. Although it's hard to leave the warm weather when it's so dark and cold around here. We'll see. Maybe I can make it down there."

"That would be wonderful," Antonia agreed. "So, Sally. I'm sorry if I'm being indelicate, it's just that I need to clarify some things. Do you mind telling me exactly what happened between Kevin and Kimberly?"

Sally took another drag on her cigarette. "That was a bad time."

"I'm sure."

"It was about . . . I don't know, let's see . . . Kimberly is thirty-one, so she was about nineteen when it happened. Let's see, that's twelve years ago. But she was dating Kevin for a year or so. Maybe longer, I'm not sure. We're out in Montauk and she would take off, you know, her and her friends. I knew she was seeing someone but wasn't sure she was steady. It took her a few months or so to bring him around. I thought Kevin was nice enough. He was older, for sure, in his thirties, and Kimberly was only a teenager, but she was very mature, you know. Very mature. I never worried about her. She helped me out a lot with her younger brothers . . ."

Antonia was shocked by the age difference but she nodded along, not wanting to interrupt. "Sure," she murmured.

"Well, you know how it is when you don't pay attention and then something happens and you realize you were a big dummy and it was in front of you all along? One time, Kimberly went out to meet Kevin and she was in a real short skirt. Now, maybe I shouldn't have let her out of the house like that, but it was the fashion, she told me, and all her girlfriends were dressing like that, so who was I to say? I don't follow fashion or read up on the magazines, so I said okay. She made her own money at her job at Gosman's, and she bought her own clothes. As I said, I'm not the fashion police.

"Well, someone said that Kevin didn't really like that outfit, and he thought she was really being a bit too friendly with one of the other guys. It was a guy from Kimberly's class at high school. Now, they've known each other since they were little, and nothing was going on, but he was—Kevin that is—thinking she was two-timing him. Of course she was not. But he was apparently experimenting with drugs then, and it made him paranoid. And so when he saw Kimberly talking to her friend, they started to fight, and he threw a bottle. Now, whether or not it was meant to hit her is up for dispute, but it did. And she got a great big gash on the side of her head. The police were called. Now, it ain't right at all. And I am mad as hell that he took advantage of the trust Kimberly's dad and I had in him. He was too old to be behaving that way. And Kimberly's friends said it was not the first time but before he had been lucky. The cops came and they sent him away for a while. And that was that."

"Did Kimberly date him after prison?"

"Naw, she moved on. Funnily enough, she did start dating the young man that Kevin was all worked up about. That's the reason she moved to Florida; he was going to college down there. But that didn't work out. Now she's married to Larry. He's a contractor down there. It's a good job; they're building up everywhere apparently. According to Kimberly."

"Do you ever see Kevin?"

"Well, you know, when he got back, he came over here to see me. I've been here for years, since it was the Chicken House. And you know, he was all remorseful. He asked for my forgiveness and told me he had been all messed up on drugs and didn't remember a thing, but he wanted me and my husband and Kimberly to know that he was deeply sorry and if he could take it back he would."

"That was nice. But still doesn't make up for what happened."

Sally took the last drag of her cigarette before flicking it to the ground and squashing it with her sandal. "It doesn't. No excuses. But I blame it on the drugs, really. I think he's sorted himself out now. Would like to leave the past behind him."

Antonia nodded. "You think people can change like that?"

"I've seen it happen before."

"I hope you're right," said Antonia truthfully. "Do you remember him ever talking about the murder of Susie Whitaker? Did he say anything to you or Kimberly about it?"

"That was the rich girl killed out by the ocean?"

"Yes."

"I know that he told Kimberly that he dated her. Frankly, I think her death is what sent him into his drug spiral. I know he dabbled before, but he didn't hit the hard stuff until that girl got murdered. I think it made him crazy that everyone thought it was him. He told Kimberly they all knew who did it but they couldn't say."

Antonia's blood pressure shot up. "Really? Who did he say did it?"

Sally smiled. "I don't know that he ever said. He just said they knew."

"Then why wouldn't they tell the police?"

"I'm not sure. I think Kimberly said they were scared. It wasn't worth it or something, because the person would just get away with it."

Antonia thought about the picture of Kevin with Pauline Framingham at the Hampton Classic. They appeared awfully friendly in that picture. "Do you think anyone . . . rewarded him . . . for not saying anything?"

"You mean how can he afford that fancy garden center?" laughed Sally. "I think of that sometimes when I pass it on the way home. It's pretty fancy. Although maybe he got a loan . . ."

"Maybe. Is it easy to obtain a loan when you're a convict? Not sure."

"Maybe he had a fairy godmother."

"Why do you say that?"

"I don't know . . . Kimberly always said that. Kevin had a fairy godmother. I don't know what she meant."

Could it be Pauline? Antonia wondered. What would be the incentive? Silence?

"Did Kimberly ever meet Pauline Framingham?"

"I don't know who that is."

"The girl whose house it was where Susie Whitaker died."

"Oh yeah. No, I don't think so. I'm pretty sure Kevin avoided that place. Too many bad memories."

"Sally," Antonia asked with urgency. "Do you think Kevin killed Susie?"

She sighed deeply. "I'd be surprised. I know what happened with my daughter, but he just didn't strike me as the type to kill anyone. But then again, I would have never said that he would get physical with my daughter, and he did. Just shows you, people always surprise you. And not for the better."

"Yes. Unfortunately they do."

23

When Antonia returned home, she went to her apartment to read over Susie's diary once again. She had primarily focused on the last few pages in the days leading up to Susie's death, but perhaps she needed to revisit the early entries, especially since she knew that Kevin had been violent with a subsequent girlfriend. Had he ever laid a hand on Susie? Would she have written about it? If Kevin Powers had gotten away with murder, Antonia was going to bring him down and destroy him. How dare he?

Antonia paged through the diary with renewed intensity and realized there were few things more mundane than the musings of a teenager. With all apologies to the dead, teenagers are self-involved, petty, and tedious. Sadly, Susie was no different. It was also incredible how much her emotions and opinions oscillated. One minute she was "obsessed" with something and the next minute it was "totally dorky." But still, Antonia felt so much compassion for her, recognizing that even her childish musings were tragic due to Susie's early demise. It was heartbreaking to read of someone's hopes and dreams and to know that they never had a chance to realize them.

Antonia was about to discard the diary when the entry from July 5 caught her eye.

OMG. Really worried. We snuck out last night and Ambassador is P.O.'d like you never would believe. Normally I didn't think he cared about that stuff, there is, like, no curfew here really but earlier in the night at dinner Pauline said we were going to the fireworks party, and he said it's not for kids, and she was like, "We're invited" and he said, "You cannot go." I have no idea why, but he was really strict about it. Then they went out and we snuck out and I had no idea but they were at the same party and saw us! We tried to hide but when we got home Ambassador called Pauline into his office and was like, "I do not like the company you are keeping . . . bad influence . . ." I know he's talking about me but it was not my idea to go to the party! Pauline wanted to. I even said we shouldn't go. I hope this isn't major and will blow over because I really don't want to go back to Connecticut for the summer, it is SOOOO boring there. Ugh, so upset. Not to mention Pauline is mad at me, says her dad saw me at the party and if I had just followed her to the other side of the house he would never know. This sucks. Her dad is so scary and Pauline is just like him when she's mad. I also wonder . . . her dad was talking pretty closely to that woman at the party and it looked . . . very intense. Maybe that's why he didn't want us to go?

Antonia put the diary down. There were too many loose ends surrounding Ambassador Framingham. She needed clarity before she continued her investigation and that would entail a visit to Pauline's house. She had been avoiding Pauline since she learned that she had flat out lied about Susie's mother. How would she confront her? She needed help. Antonia reached for the phone.

* * * * *

"You're the bad cop, I'm the good cop, got it?"

"Relax, Bingham. You know I love role-playing."

"Ha ha."

"No, in all seriousness, I have no problem grilling this woman about her lying ways. I'm here to help."

Antonia and Larry were seated in Pauline's sunroom awaiting her arrival. She was apparently showering after a swim in the ocean. The visit had been unplanned, therefore they had to wait. Antonia had brought Larry to unleash on Pauline, allowing him to ask all of the controversial questions, so that she could come off smelling like roses, both professional and nice. She had apprised him of the latest revelations about Kevin while they were waiting.

"Sorry to have kept you," Pauline announced as she strolled into the room, her hair still damp from the shower.

"It's not a problem. I apologize for stopping by, but there were some pressing questions. This is my friend . . ."

"Larry Lipper," he said, standing and jutting out his hand. Pauline took it with a skeptical look.

"Larry writes the crime column for *The Star*. I thought he could be useful, and he has been assisting me with his contacts."

"Interesting," Pauline said before sitting down. "So what was so urgent?"

Antonia started to speak at the same time as Larry, but for once she allowed him to take the lead.

"Well, first off we found out that Susie Whitaker's mother is dead. So unless you are a psychic it's not clear why you dragged her into this."

Pauline squinted before responding. "I wanted Antonia to have urgency in solving this crime."

"Why? What's the rush?"

Pauline shrugged. "I'm tired of it. Ready to get closure and move on."

Larry stared at her in a manner that would have Antonia squirming if she was on the receiving end. But Pauline returned his gaze without a flicker of emotion.

"There are a few more inconsistencies we want to clear up," he said, whipping out his notebook and flipping through it. "You are one hell of an unreliable narrator! First of all, you said your parents were not home the week of the murder. We recently learned that your father was here the day before Susie was killed."

Pauline shook her head. "Not true. My parents were in Europe."

Larry raised his eyebrow and looked askance. "Miss Framingham, we have it on very good authority that he was here."

"I don't know who that authority was, but they are apparently not as good as you think. My father was abroad. I can produce his travel records in a few hours. All I need to do is phone the company."

Larry held her gaze a beat. "All right, we'll leave that for now. Seems as if Susie was terrified of your father."

"He could be quite intimidating."

"How so?"

"He was cold and harsh and a man of power."

"Was he menacing? Did he ever get physical?" asked Larry.

"His weapons of choice were silence and withholding love."

"Nothing else?"

Antonia watched without blinking as Pauline and Larry continued their question and answer session. It was similar to watching two champion tennis players volley at net.

"My father was a jerk, but not that sort of jerk."

"You mean he didn't hit you?"

"He didn't hit anyone as far as I know."

"Pauline, I'm sorry if this is indelicate . . . but was your father having an affair?" Antonia interjected.

Pauline swiveled her eyes away from Larry to glance at Antonia.

"Probably."

"Really? With whom?"

"I have no idea. He was an attractive man."

"Do you remember the fireworks party you snuck out to that summer?" asked Antonia. "I read about it in Susie's diary."

"Yes. That was a lot of fun."

"But your father was mad you went there," Larry insisted.

Pauline returned her gaze to him. "I wasn't supposed to sneak out. He didn't want me at that party."

"Why not?" Larry asked.

Pauline shrugged. "He enjoyed making demands of his children now and then. His reasons were usually arbitrary."

"Susie wrote that he was talking to a specific woman and perhaps he was mad you had both seen him?" asked Antonia.

"I don't know about that. Maybe a lover."

"Would he be worried Susie would tell your mother?" asked Larry.

"Ha, no. My mother and father were not possessive of one another. In fact, I have no doubt she was consorting with her best friend's husband."

Antonia was surprised at the turn this conversation was taking. If being rich was all about infidelity and your kids not liking you, then no thanks.

"Speaking of the diary," Larry continued, "who were you having an affair with that had Susie all riled up?"

Pauline gave him an amused look. "You're quite direct, aren't you, Mr. Lipper?"

"It's been the key to my success."

"Undoubtedly."

Pauline stared without speaking, holding Larry's stare.

"So, who was it?" he prompted.

"I think we all know I was dating Dougie Marshall."

"Yes, we all know that. But were you seeing someone else in addition?"

Pauline refolded her legs. "I had other relationships on the side. Neither Dougie nor I were what you would call faithful. We were teenagers, after all."

"And was there anyone in particular you were seeing that might have scared Susie?"

"Susie was frightened by a lot of people."

"Yes, but in the diary you gave to Antonia, she specifically writes about one guy in particular who Susie believed had written her a note, who 'scared the hell out of her.'"

"Does anyone scare you, Mr. Lipper?"

Larry appeared flummoxed. "Me? No."

"Interesting," Pauline said.

"But we're not talking about me. We're talking about Susie."

"Yes, I know we are. But we are also talking about fear in general. What makes people afraid? What pushes their buttons? For example, I know that Antonia is scared of her ex-husband."

Antonia's jaw literally dropped. Like, to the floor. She had no idea Pauline knew about her ex-husband. A wave of fear swelled inside her.

"How do you know about him?" she managed to squeak out.

Pauline turned her eyes from Larry to Antonia. "I don't just hire people willy-nilly without a background check."

Antonia swallowed. "I guess that makes sense, but . . ."

Larry turned and gave Antonia a quizzical look. He started to say something, but Pauline spoke.

"He does terrify you, doesn't he, Antonia? Your former husband."

Antonia nodded. "Yes."

"And what about you, Mr. Lipper? What scares you? And please don't say nothing because it is only a tiny bit of legwork for me to find out."

Larry didn't blink. "I'm scared of the dark."

"You can't be serious."

"I am. Since I was a kid. I don't like blackness at all. Still need a nightlight. I have a Mickey Mouse one that I plug in next to my bed."

"What about death, are you scared of that?"

"I think everyone is. But once again, Miss Framingham. This is all very fun, and I am loving this get-to-know-ya. In fact, maybe one day we can all come here late at night and have a séance. I'll bring the Ouija board. We can try and conjure up your old friend Susie and ask her what she was afraid of. But right now, I'm on deadline for an important piece I'm doing, and I don't have time for games. Could you please tell me who Susie was afraid of?"

Pauline smiled but didn't say anything. Something about her expression made Antonia shudder.

There was tension in the room. Antonia couldn't take it, so she spoke. "Why were you and Kevin Powers looking friendly at the Hampton Classic a few years ago? I understand you disliked him and didn't think he was good enough to date your friend Susie."

"Kevin was a druggie back then. He's cleaned up his act and has a successful garden center."

"Did you invest in his garden center?" Larry asked.

"My family owns various buildings all over the Hamptons."

"You didn't answer my question."

"I prefer not to talk about my business. There are too many copycats out there. I really hate copycats. So if I say I invested, then everyone else will invest in a garden center and there will be too much competition."

"There are already a ton of garden centers out here. It's hardly unique," Larry said with a chuckle.

Pauline gave him a look. "True. I may need to diversify my portfolio. Invest in newspapers or inns."

Antonia ignored the comment. It felt like a subtle threat. She had more serious concerns.

"I only recently found out that Kevin had gone to prison for violence against his ex-girlfriend," Antonia said. "Is that why you thought he might have killed Susie? Was he violent with her?"

"Not to my knowledge."

"It just seems strange that you would enter into a business relationship with a felon who you suspected of murder," Antonia pressed.

"I didn't say I was in business with him . . ."

"Was it some kind of payoff for something?" Larry asked.

They were interrupted by the French doors opening. A man in a coat and tie appeared on the threshold. He had steel-gray hair slicked back from his forehead, and he appeared to be in his early sixties. He wore a look of frustration and contempt on his face.

"I have to interrupt. I'm Tom Schultz, the Framinghams'

family attorney. I would prefer to put an end to this conversation right now." He strode into the room with an air of authority and planted his briefcase on the coffee table.

Pauline looked annoyed. "Mr. Schultz, really. I can handle this myself."

He didn't even glance at her and kept staring at Larry and Antonia in a menacing manner. "Ms. Framingham is one of the largest shareholders in a publicly traded company. It does not behoove her or the other family members and shareholders to continue this dialogue. Those closest to her have decided to put an end to this endeavor."

"But Pauline hired me to look into this . . ." Antonia protested.

"I'm sorry she has wasted your time."

"Mr. Schultz . . ." Pauline sighed with irritation.

"I think Ms. Framingham can speak for herself. She's a grown-up," Larry said, turning toward Pauline. "Do you want to finish this conversation?"

The lawyer swiveled around and gave Pauline a seething look.

She spoke to Antonia while her eyes remained fixed on her lawyer, giving him a contemptuous sneer. "I suppose we can wrap this up for today."

"We are wrapping it up indefinitely," Mr. Schultz said sternly. "We will remit payment to you and thank you for your time. Please consider the case closed."

"I don't know about that . . ." Pauline said, squinting at her lawyer. "What incentive do I have to end this?"

"Your loved ones have asked you to end this."

"Do I really owe them anything?"

Her lawyer appeared irritated. "They are willing to work with you and ensure your personal demands are met."

"Loved ones," interjected Larry. "I thought you just had a brother."

"There's my mother as well," Pauline said.

"What? I thought your parents were dead," exclaimed Antonia.

"My father is. My mother is in assisted living in Massachusetts. Waiting for death and remaining a burden until it comes."

"Is she there with Barbara Whitaker?" sneered Larry. "Is this another one of your lies?"

Pauline scowled. "You can ask Tom."

"Her mother is alive," he said impatiently. "And now Miss Framingham, let's end this."

"All right then." Pauline stood up. "That will be all, Antonia."

Antonia stood up. "Pauline? What do you mean?"

"It was fun while it lasted."

Antonia was stunned. This was not the ending she expected. "So that's it? You don't want me to continue investigating?"

"It sounds as if my lawyer has good reason to shut this down."

He cleared his throat. "I trust, Miss Bingham, that you will adhere to the nondisclosure documents that you signed, and that the discoveries made during your investigation will remain confidential. That goes for you as well, Mr. Lipper. If we read anything about this in your newspaper, you will face litigation for the rest of your natural-born days."

After that, Larry and Antonia were bum-rushed out of the house.

24

"I can't believe it's over, just like that," Antonia sighed as she and Larry zipped out of the driveway in his sporty little car.

"Hang on, Bingham. It ain't over until the fat lady sings."

"Do you want me to start singing now?"

He glanced over at her. "You're not fat. You have a dangerous future ahead of you if you don't watch out, but you look okay to me right now. And I'm pretty critical."

"Gee, thanks."

"Don't involve me in your weight self-esteem drama and then criticize me for it."

"Fair enough. Okay, why don't you think it's over?"

"Basically we've narrowed it down. It's either Dougie, Ambassador Framingham, or the guy that Pauline was sleeping with."

"Or Holly, or Scott, or Alida . . ."

Larry shook his head. "No."

"What about Pauline? Turns out she's totally bonkers."

"Let's go see Dougie Marshall."

*　*　*　*　*

Dougie lived in the guesthouse of his parents' large estate on Middle Lane. Antonia wondered if he had squandered most of his inheritance, forcing him to move back in with his parents. Or perhaps he was a freeloader. Although, to be fair, the cost of houses in the Hamptons had risen so precipitously that if you had access to a fully functioning gratis bungalow, why not take advantage?

There was a fork in the driveway, one prong of which directed traffic to the main house on the right. It was called Spring Cottage according to the white sign with the embossed black font. The fork to the left had a small wood sign inscribed D. MARSHALL in shaky black spray paint. As they drove toward the guesthouse, Spring Cottage loomed in their peripheral vision. Antonia wondered how anyone could describe a house that big as a mere "cottage."

Dougie's house was a neatly kept affair, two-stories, small, shingled, and adorned with green shutters. A brick path led to the front door, which was flanked by two slate planters full of straggly white geraniums. Despite a new red convertible Mercedes parked close to the entrance of the guesthouse, no one answered the door when Larry and Antonia knocked.

"This is a joke," said Larry. "Didn't you have an agreed upon time?"

"Maybe he's in the shower? He said he was playing golf . . ."

"You don't sweat when you play golf, Bingham. You drive around in those little carts with the wind in your face, and then you get out and swing a club at a tiny little ball."

"Maybe he walked the course?"

"He's avoiding us."

"Larry, you think the worst of people."

"And I'm usually right."

Larry leaned on the doorbell. They stood a moment and waited for someone to open it, but no one appeared.

"I guess we should leave."

"Hang on." Larry cupped his hands and glanced through the window of the door. There was no movement. He walked along the side of the house, peering in the windows.

"I don't feel so hot about this. Let's go."

"Not yet."

Antonia did not want to add trespassing to her résumé so she walked back to the car as Larry made his way around the circumference of the house. She leaned against the passenger door and glanced up at the second story, her eyes skimming the windows. Suddenly she saw movement. Dougie's face was in the window, and he was peering down at her. He quickly jumped back as soon as she saw him.

"Larry!" she said in a stage whisper.

"What?"

"Come quick."

"Hang on."

Antonia rushed over to him. "Listen, I see Dougie upstairs. He knows we're here and he's not answering."

"See! I told you! Listen to me, Bingham. I'm always right."

Larry walked backwards, his head extended so he had a view of the second floor. "Which window?"

"That one." Antonia pointed.

Larry picked up a pebble from the driveway and hurled it at the window.

"Larry!"

"What?"

"You could break it."

"I won't break it if he comes down," he said, whilst scooping another pile of pebbles into his hand. He threw yet another, which snapped off the window. Then another. Antonia noted that he had surprisingly good aim for someone who did not appear to be athletic in the least. The next pebble ricocheted off the window onto the eave that hung over the front door with a clatter. Finally, Dougie opened his window and thrust his head out.

"What the hell?"

"Sorry, Dougie . . . we wanted to see if you were home," offered Antonia lamely.

"We need to talk to you," Larry demanded with a force Antonia was unfamiliar with.

"I can't talk now, I'm busy," Dougie said, his eyes scanning the yard.

At the same time as Antonia said, "It's okay," as she opened her car door, Larry yelled, "We won't take no for an answer."

"Who the hell are you?" Dougie asked.

"I'm your worst nightmare. Let me in."

Dougie gave one more furtive look around before slamming the window shut. Antonia was convinced she had seen the last of him when the front door opened and he ushered them inside.

"Quickly, come on. Hurry."

He pressed the door closed behind them. The cottage smelled slightly of mold, cigar smoke, and air freshener and was host to a random assortment of discarded antiques, miscellaneous furniture and wall hangings, and other decorative touches that had no doubt been liberated from the attic of the main house.

Dougie walked over to the front windows and closed the curtains. He motioned for them to sit down.

"What's going on, man?" asked Larry.

Dougie turned to Antonia. "Is this the newspaper reporter?"

She nodded. "Larry Lipper."

"Why all the cloak and dagger?" Larry asked, plopping himself on a tired sofa. He picked up a small bronze of an elephant that was on the coffee table and then, after scrutinizing it, replaced it.

"I've been told not to talk to you."

"Who told you that?" Antonia asked.

Dougie ran his hand through his hair. He appeared different from the previous time she'd met him. He was jumpy and wired. She liked to think the best of everyone, but it almost seemed as if he was on drugs. Was there something about Susie and her death that drove everyone around her into a life of debauchery?

"Pauline and Russell's people. They want this shut down. You all don't understand . . . there are bigger things going on here. They're pretty powerful."

"But why now?" Antonia asked. "Why involve me then decide to end it?"

Dougie walked over to a bar cart on the side of the room and poured himself a large tumbler of bourbon. "Want some?" he asked feebly but both Larry and Antonia demurred.

"It's Pauline. She enjoys playing games. You have to understand—she's a sick person. I tried to hint to you the other day. She likes to manipulate people. But then she always has someone come in and clean up her mess or stop her."

"Did Pauline kill Susie?" Larry asked.

Dougie finished his bourbon and put it down to refill. "Either she did or . . ." He trailed off.

Antonia and Larry both leaned in and said in unison. "Or?"

Dougie slumped down in a chair. "The thing is . . . everything is all lies. It was all orchestrated to confuse everyone. They made it seem as if they were protecting all of us, but they weren't. We all signed on for a life of misery."

"What are you talking about, Dougie?" Antonia asked.

"None of us were where we said we were. I did play golf with my dad that day, but I bailed after the thirteenth hole and headed over to Pauline's. When I drove in, I saw Susie on the court, she was talking to Alida. I drove up and went in the back by the kitchen. I saw Pauline getting the lemonade. She had the refrigerator door open. I was about to walk over and put my hands over her eyes and surprise her when I heard her talking to someone. A guy. I couldn't see his face, because it was obstructed by the refrigerator door, but I saw his legs. He was wearing shorts and tennis sneakers. I didn't think it was strange until I heard her call him 'darling.' Then I froze and listened. She said, 'Darling, we have nothing to worry about. Susie's fine.'"

"Who was the guy?" asked Antonia.

"I don't know. I got the hell out of there. Got in my car and drove away. I thought they hadn't seen me, but she must have heard my car because later she told me she knew I was there, and that I had lied to the police. But man, I was scared."

"Did you ask her who it was?"

"Yes, but she didn't answer. Just wanted to make it clear she knew I was there. She . . . she implied that she thought I had killed Susie. But I don't know if she really thought that. I think she just wanted to lord it over me. And every time this comes up, her mother sends her lawyer after me . . ."

"Wait a minute, her mother?" asked Antonia.

"Yeah. They have a laundry list of my transgressions. Yes, I'm not perfect. But it's stuff I don't want released, so they have me by the balls."

"Murder?" Larry asked.

"No! Nothing like that. Let's just say activities that would not go well with my ex-wife. The Framinghams—they're very thorough. They have eyes and ears everywhere. Not sure why I'm telling you this."

"Did they threaten you today? You seem awfully nervous."

"Let's just say I was warned to keep out of it."

"I want to get back to Mrs. Framingham for a second, what is she like?"

"Bitch."

"You don't mince words, do you, buddy?" Larry asked.

"It's true."

"Hey, call a spade a spade, I get it."

"But she's not well as I understand," said Antonia.

"She's been in assisted living for years, but that didn't do anything to her brain. She's still the evil powerhouse she always was, sending all of us injunctions and legal documents whenever she catches wind of something she doesn't like. Rumor is that Pauline had her declared mentally incompetent and shoved her away, made everyone believe she's totally gaga and has dementia. But, you ask me, she seems totally lucid."

"You think she knows who the murderer is?" asked Antonia.

"I think she must or why else does she want everyone to shut up about it?"

"Dougie, did you kill Susie?" asked Larry.

He glared at Larry with rage in his eyes. "Of course not!"

"Then who do you think did?" Antonia asked gently. "You're skirting the question."

Dougie took another swig. His eyes shifted all over the room, consumed with worry and fear. "It could have been anyone. She set us all up. We are all suspects."

"Was it Kevin Powers?" Antonia pressed.

"I don't know . . . I'm not sure. But there is one thing I know."

Larry and Antonia leaned in closer as he paused. "Yes?" Antonia prompted.

"Whoever killed Susie did it because of, or for, Pauline. All roads lead back to her. And the sickest part is, she loves it. But that's all I'm going to say now. You have to leave. I've already said too much."

* * * * *

"All right, let's go through this again," Antonia said when they were back in the car. "Pauline asked me to look into this murder, then her lawyer shuts it down because her family is upset. Which family? Her dad is dead, her mom is in a home, but turns out she's still meddling in everything. And then there's Russell. He's awkward and strange and people give him a get-out-of-jail-free card for that, but maybe they shouldn't?"

"Everyone seems to think Pauline had something to do with the murder. Not to mention, Pauline has something on all of her friends and acquaintances so that they do what she wants," Larry said.

"True. And there are sinister elements enough to scare Dougie. He stops talking. Scott the tennis pro won't talk, and we know that he had a rough few years with alcohol that some people have suggested were a result of Susie's death. Ditto Kevin. We need to look hard at Kevin, I think I exonerated him too early. Kevin was dating Susie and has a violent past."

"Now we know why the cops liked him. But the thing is, if they liked him so much, why didn't they nail him? Everyone was gunning for him but they didn't have enough evidence."

"Protecting their own? He probably grew up with people on the force."

"You have such a cynical view of the cops."

"Once bitten, twice shy."

"I don't know any guys like that. And I knew Tubby Walters, the chief. He was under heat. He would have nailed Kevin. What about the guy in the kitchen with Pauline? Do you think it was Scott?"

"Or maybe her brother Russell . . . 'I heard her call him darling' . . . I mean, heck, we know now Alida was there. Maybe it was her . . ."

"Alida? Are you crazy?" Larry asked. "No way would that knockout kill anyone. Just wipe her off the list."

"But why did she lie about being there?"

Larry shook his head frantically. "I won't even entertain that thought."

"Blinded by lust," Antonia murmured.

"Listen, Bingham. The good news is this: we are closer. The fact that they want to end it means we are on to something."

"Yes, but I have to figure out what."

"*We* have to figure it out."

Antonia didn't respond. Something was bothering her, but she couldn't quite put her finger on it.

25

That night at the inn, Genevieve came by to talk to Antonia. She waited patiently in the library until Antonia could take a break from dinner service, and when Antonia was finally liberated from the kitchen she found Genevieve more serious than usual. It was actually this Genevieve that Antonia preferred. It was great when she was fun and goofy, but she was also a person of true substance even though she often chose to hide that fact. She was capable of being an incredible sounding board and a loyal and brave friend and had been so helpful to Antonia when Antonia was trying to extricate herself from her ex-husband. But Genevieve too often chose to be topical or superficial, as if she didn't want to challenge herself or be serious. There was an infantilism in her that Genevieve couldn't seem to totally relinquish.

"How's it going?" Antonia asked before planting herself in the sea of cushions on the sofa.

Genevieve put down the magazine she had been flipping through. "I wanted to talk."

"Uh-oh. Boy trouble?"

"No, I actually wanted to talk about Holly."

"Oh?" said Antonia. "What's going on?"

"I think she's hiding something."

"Well, she recently informed me that she was living with Scott Stewart, the tennis pro who lived in the Framinghams' guesthouse. Is it that? She did it in such an odd, roundabout way. I wonder why she didn't confide in me when we were all at Cittanuova."

Genevieve nodded. "I know, that was strange. Maybe she just assumed I told you? The thing is, I didn't make the connection that "her Scott" was the same guy until later. But it's not that . . ."

"Then what is it?"

"I hadn't seen much of Holly in recent years, and we only really reconnected after Victoria was here. One day they came into the store and she went gaga over these adorable sandals. Dark blue with gold piping, can be worn during the day but also could work for casual dinners and cocktail parties if worn with the right outfit. They finally went on sale, and I used my store discount to help her buy them so they were a total steal. I should get you some by the way, but they would probably sit in your closet getting dusty like every other decent pair of shoes or clothing that I have given you. Meanwhile you wear those god-awful Crocs . . ."

"Let's not go there, please continue."

"Okay but you simply must stop the avoidance of a wardrobe upgrade. If there is one thing in my life I need to do it's make you dress better . . ."

"Back to Holly," commanded Antonia.

"Okay, so I call her and tell her and she says can I bring them by and stay for dinner, so I head over after work. We're hanging out, she tries the sandals on, and shows me this cute dress she bought online—it's A-line striped black and blue—then the front door opens. There's this tall guy there and Holly instantly gets this annoyed look on her face, and then so does he. He's like, 'Who's she?' and Holly says, 'Don't worry about it. My friend Genevieve.' At this point I stand up and say 'Hi, I'm Genevieve,' and he doesn't even shake my hand or nod or anything. He just walks to the kitchen as if he's been there a bunch and it's totally okay to make himself at home. Holly tells me to wait a minute and then follows him. I hear them talking but can't hear what they're saying so I peer around the corner and I see him hand Holly a wad of cash. After that he leaves and he doesn't even say a word."

"Who do you think he was?"

"It was Russell Framingham."

Antonia felt her interest piqued. "Russell? Why was he giving Holly cash?"

"I don't know. I asked her who he was, and she kept changing the subject and then finally I cornered her and she admitted it was Russell. And I asked what he was doing there and she said 'Taking care of business.' I tried to ask about the money, like, 'Did I see him hand you a wad of cash?' and Holly didn't even answer, totally ignored the question."

"Was it a payoff?"

"I have no idea, like I said. I just thought it was bizarre. And Holly was so strange about it. And then all of the things Holly has said over the years about the Framinghams came floating back to me . . . like they can buy anyone, they get whatever they want, people are disposable to them. And then I wondered if it was some sort of hush money? Maybe Russell did murder Susie and he's paying Holly off to be his alibi."

"It could be. At this point, I wouldn't put anything past these people."

"Okay, then later on, Scott comes home, we're all in the kitchen cooking—nothing like you make, just pasta and meatballs and some salad. And Scott goes to open a drawer to get a can opener and quickly slams it and looks at Holly. I figure that's where Holly stashed the cash from Russell because Scott says, 'So he finally came?' Holly says, 'It only took ten phone calls and some serious threats.' Then Scott says, and this part I was like, WOW! Scott says, 'He really thinks he can take things from everyone and get away with it.'"

"Oh my gosh!" exclaimed Antonia. "What did you say?" She pulled her hair out of a ponytail and readjusted it into a bun as she waited.

"I said, 'Are you talking about Russell?' and neither Scott nor Holly answered. So I repeated the question. Holly rolls her eyes and says 'Yes, he's such a spoiled brat,' but she doesn't want to spend one more minute on this topic because it is an extremely sore subject. Well, I'm not going to let it go this easy, so then I ask, 'Why's he paying you off? Hush money?' and Scott says 'Services rendered.'"

"What services?"

"I was about to ask that but then their friend Barry showed up and we were interrupted. By the way, turns out they were totally trying to set me up with Barry, I had no idea. He's kind of cute, but recently divorced and has three young kids. I'm not sure I'm quite willing to take that on. Although he did have a hot body. He says he works out at the rec center every day. I didn't love his outfit, but with my store discount I could definitely find him some cute pants and a nice shirt . . ."

"Genevieve!" interrupted Antonia. "Back to Russell. Was that all? Any other details?"

"Nothing else."

"Do you think you could straight out ask Holly why he gave her money?"

"Oh, that's the last part I forgot. So, we're all done with dinner, just sitting there drinking some wine. Not Scott, though. He doesn't drink anymore. I try and turn the conversation to Russell one last time. And Holly, who's well into her cups now, says Russell owes Scott big time. And then she makes a whacking gesture like this."

Genevieve held up her arm and swung it.

"Oh no."

"I know," Genevieve said quietly.

Antonia's mind raced. "The trouble is, Pauline Framingham dismissed me from investigating the case today."

"Why?"

"Her family is apparently against it."

"You can't stop now! I feel like you're really on to something."

"So do I."

"You're not going to listen to her, are you? I mean, what's the worst thing that can happen?"

"I don't want to imagine that. But I'm so close, I know it. If I can do a little more legwork, I'll have this case wrapped up."

"You know you will, girlfriend! You are my hometown Miss Marple."

26

Antonia incorporated the knocking into her dream. She was back in California and knocking on the door of her father's house, which was locked for some reason. That was peculiar, as her father never locked his back door. Her father wasn't expecting her. She was knocking and knocking, but he wouldn't come to the door. When she glanced through the window in the kitchen she saw him with a woman in an embrace. They were smiling and gazing at each other as if they were in love. Antonia remembered feeling both anger and confusion. She began tapping on the window, knocking and knocking, but neither of them looked at her. In fact, they were oblivious. She knocked harder.

"Antonia!"

She shot up in bed. It had been a dream, alas, but it felt so real, almost as if it were a memory. But now someone was knocking on her apartment door.

"One second," she called, as she slipped on her bathrobe.

A glance at the alarm clock next to her bed told her that it was 2:24 in the morning.

"It's me, Antonia. Jonathan."

Antonia slid the lock open and found the manager of the inn standing on her threshold. Jonathan looked tired and a bit disheveled, unlike his usual immaculate self.

"Jonathan, what's wrong?"

"There's been an accident. Looks like a car was turning into the driveway of the inn and another car crashed into it. Hit and run."

"Oh no! Is anyone hurt?"

"The driver is in pretty bad shape. A helicopter is landing on the town green to take him to Stony Brook."

"Is he a guest of the inn?"

Jonathan shook his head. "The car is not in our registry, so I don't think so. It's a red convertible."

The blood instantly drained from Antonia's face. "A Mercedes?"

"Yes, I believe so."

"That's Dougie Marshall's car."

"Oh no, is he a friend?"

Antonia shook her head. "No. An acquaintance."

Jonathan went back outside while Antonia quickly dressed. Why had Dougie been coming to the inn? He must have wanted to tell Antonia something. He had been so shaken and paranoid that afternoon, and now it was clear that he'd had reason to be. Antonia had never heard of a hit-and-run in East Hampton. It seemed very purposeful.

The scene at the end of the driveway was dramatic. The entire driver's side of Dougie's car had been hit head-on and pushed into the streetlight. The front window was cracked, the airbag had exploded, and the door was crumpled. It was a mess of broken metal and smashed glass. Several emergency vehicles were parked around the car, including an ambulance where a team of paramedics was hovering over a stretcher. Antonia could make out Dougie's feet, which were shoeless, but couldn't see his face as the paramedics were administering oxygen and other lifesaving measures.

Officer Flanagan, the cop that Antonia had worked with on her last investigation, saw her and approached. Despite the fact that it was the middle of the night, his suit was neatly pressed and his dark cropped hair was brushed. Antonia was cagey with all police officers because of her past experience, but she had begrudgingly grown to like Officer Flanagan and certainly admired him. He was extremely astute, very accurate and professional, and meticulous about himself and his work.

"You were able to sleep through the big bang?" he asked.

"Like a baby. But I must have heard something because I was having the most unsettling dream," Antonia confessed.

"I think a lot of your guests will be sleeping in tomorrow."

He gestured up to the windows of the inn, where many guests had turned on their lights and were peering out at the action below.

"Oh dear," Antonia said.

"Yeah, we're going to have to talk to some of them. See if they saw anything."

"The car just took off? Were there no witnesses?"

"There was another driver who witnessed the accident, said it was a dark sedan, but he was focused on assisting the victim and didn't take time to note the plates."

"It probably never occurred to him that the driver would leave the scene of the crime."

"That's for sure. Do you have any surveillance cameras that might have captured the accident?"

Antonia silently cursed herself. After the last incident at the inn both Joseph and her insurance agent had implored her to install cameras, both for safety and liability issues. She had not possessed the extra cash in her budget to do it at that time, and then even when Jonathan found less expensive cameras she had delayed it as she had been busy with other things. It was her nature to be a Luddite and eschew anything technical, she wasn't quite sure why. Now she was regretting it.

"Unfortunately no."

"That's okay. Didn't think so. The library has them so we'll check their feed. Maybe some of the neighbors."

"It's Dougie Marshall who was hit, right? I mean, that's his car."

"The car is registered to Dougie Marshall. I cannot identify him . . ."

"It's okay," Antonia said quickly. "I know it's him. Will he be okay?"

"They're working hard on him."

"I hope so. I didn't really take him seriously."

Officer Flanagan gave Antonia a quizzical look and then

sighed. "I should have known you had something to do with this."

Antonia bristled. "Me? I had nothing to do with this. Although I do believe that it's possible that Dougie might have been coming to tell me something."

"About?" Officer Flanagan said with an arched eyebrow.

"About a case I'm working on . . ."

He took out his notebook and flipped it open. "Let's start from the beginning."

* * * * *

It was several hours before Antonia returned to bed. The parlor of the inn had become something of a meeting center for the emergency responders and the police, who were interviewing any witnesses and guests who might have seen or heard something. Jonathan had put on pots of coffee and brought out the cookies and cakes that were leftover from dessert the previous evening. Joseph had come down to sit with Antonia as she attempted to make sense of what had happened. They could only conjecture about who they thought had hit Dougie with the car. But their first choice was Pauline Framingham. Antonia had wanted to rush over to her house and see if she had a black sedan that looked like it had gone through the meat grinder, but Officer Flanagan dissuaded her and, in fact, made her promise not to bother Pauline. He and his own officers would head over to talk with her.

After a fitful two hours catching up on her sleep, Antonia rose and helped Soyla with the breakfast service. She then headed to her office to field any calls and troubleshoot any potential problems with the sleep-deprived and no doubt grumpy guests.

"Good morning, get me some coffee as soon as possible," commanded a rumpled Larry Lipper as he stood at her doorway.

He had arrived at the scene of the accident last night almost as soon as Antonia and had remained at the inn to pester the police for information. Antonia had informed Officer Flanagan that Larry was privy to as much information as she was about Dougie, and persuaded Flanagan to hound him instead of her. (She was very pleased with her chance to deflect attention away from herself and cause Larry to squirm.) Antonia had been careful in what she told the police, and was not as candid as she would normally be. This was mostly because she had signed all of those nondisclosures and feared that Pauline's lawyers would come after her, but partially because she always instinctively held something back from cops. Larry was also cagey about what he knew, but mostly because he wanted to keep the information to himself so he could personally solve the crime and then write a best-selling book and sell the rights to Hollywood and have Nick Darrow play him.

"Good morning, Larry. Didn't make it home?" Antonia asked, pouring Larry a steaming mug of coffee from her pot.

"No, I didn't make it home. Some people have to work for a living, Bingham. I have to be on the scene at all times. It's a demanding job, you know. I'm not like you—curling up and heading to bed with my teddy bear. Although I did try to get into your apartment but you had locked the door."

"I always lock the door. Only Joseph has the key."

"No wonder you have no love life." He slumped into the seat across from her. "You have way too many pillows drowning your sofa, Bingham. I had to throw them all on the floor."

"I hope you retrieved them."

He leaned over and snatched a pastry off the tray Soyla had brought in earlier. Antonia watched as he sank his tiny teeth into the cherry Danish and hungrily ripped off an oversized piece that flapped from his lips as he chewed. Larry's manners left a lot to be desired.

"You think we go first to see Pauline or head to Stonybrook to see Dougie? It'll be a nightmare traffic situation heading up island with all the summer traffic. Will take all day. So probably Pauline first."

"Officer Flanagan warned us to stay away from her . . ." Antonia said.

"Whatever. Free country. Let's go see her. Why don't you ask your kitchen to fire me up a bacon, egg, and cheese sandwich so I can operate on a full fuel tank while I hit the john then we'll head out."

"How about a 'please'?"

"Don't push it, Bingham."

Antonia picked up the intercom to ask Soyla for Larry's sandwich. When he returned, he picked up the stack of articles about the case that Joseph had copied for her. He started flicking through them, leaving jelly stains as he discarded them.

"They could have used a reporter like me back then. None of these reports have any information or revelations whatsoever."

"I know."

He bit another chunk of the pastry. "They were too in awe of the family. My, how things have changed. Back then, they wanted to protect the rich and powerful. Now they want to take them down and destroy them."

"Perhaps if they hadn't use kid gloves on the rich, Susie's killer would have been brought to justice."

"Not sure. You got a shark lawyer like that Schultz guy and the cops don't have a chance. I know those lawyer types—they're an impenetrable wall that stands between authority and their loaded clients."

"True. Intimidation and a law degree work magic."

"Hey, this is interesting," Larry sat up in his chair. "Listen to this Letter to the Editor. It's from someone named Kitty Overwood who describes herself as a good friend of Susie's."

"I haven't heard her name mentioned."

"Didn't you read this?"

"I scanned it. Thought it was just someone expressing her condolences. Why, what does it say?"

"It says: *Susie was a kind and generous friend whose only fault was that she always chose to look for the good in people. She never should have done that with Pauline Framingham, who is a cunning and manipulative person. Sadly, Susie realized that too late. I was a counselor at a camp in Maine this summer and wish I could have been more help. In the last frantic letter I received from Susie it said only one line: If I die, it's because I know their secret and they don't want it to get out. I have no idea who she was talking about but I can guess. Of course I can't write it because of libel, but we all know who I'm talking about.*"

"Wow," Antonia exclaimed. "We need to track her down."

"Yes, but it's obvious she's talking about Pauline. Pauline and an accomplice."

"Time to go."

"First, my sandwich."

27

There was no sign of life at the Framingham house. Larry sat on the buzzer but no one answered, not even the house-keeper. The driveway was also empty.

"Maybe they took her down to the station?" Antonia suggested.

"Could be. That's perfect for us. I want you to show me the tennis court."

"I don't know, Larry . . ."

"Come on, don't poop out on me now."

Antonia reluctantly led the way down the path to the court. There was a slight breeze that morning that ruffled the leaves on the trees, causing the jagged shadows to jump around on the ground. Antonia glanced up at the sky where several seagulls were taking flight toward the beach. The mood in the air was ominous and Antonia couldn't help but feel that she was walking toward something very bad. She knew that it was only because this was the spot where Susie was killed so long ago, but that didn't lessen the ominous feeling she was experiencing.

When they reached the court, Larry opened the squeaky metal door and they stepped in.

"Where was she found?" he asked gruffly.

Antonia pointed to the corner. Larry walked over to the spot as Antonia glanced around at the empty court. What had Susie felt like as she waited here for Pauline to bring the lemonade? It was a day not unlike today, sunny and beautiful. Summer days when you're a teenager are full of hope and excitement, which Susie no doubt felt. She was in the throes of a romance with Kevin Powers. She had fun parties to attend with her friends. But at the same time, she was worried. Someone made her feel scared and intimidated. Did she feel that way when she was waiting for Pauline?

Antonia suddenly remembered that Dougie had said that he had seen Alida talking to Susie on the court before she died. What were they talking about? Why had Alida always denied that she was there?

"Bingham! Come here," barked Larry.

Antonia slowly strode over to him.

"You know, I'm looking around and I have to confess, I have a hard time buying the fact that some lunatic came off the street to kill Susie."

"No one ever bought that, Larry."

"I thought Alida Jenkins had some insight . . ."

"You weren't thinking with your head."

He ignored her response. "The hedge is too thick by the

gate that abuts the street. Now, it might not have been at that time but if you look, you will see that it opens from the outside. Even if there was no hedge there was still a fence there that would have obstructed anyone from entering. Only the tiniest anorexic—and I mean superhuman skinny—could have entered."

He demonstrated by attempting to open the gate. It was impossible to open more than five inches.

"I'm sure the police thought about that and that's why they debunked that idea. You only entertained it because your crush suggested it."

"Oh, Bingham, it is so cute when you're jealous."

"It also begs the question of how Alida entered and what she was doing here."

"I'm not going there."

"You may have to."

Larry grew pensive and walked around the circumference of the court. He tilted his head up and down, examining the height of the fence. A puffy cloud floated past the sun, and the sky suddenly darkened. Antonia shuddered.

"Let's go."

"Hang on."

"No, Larry. We're trespassing now."

"Fine."

They walked to the end of the court and opened the gate, stepping into the dim path now shrouded in patchy darkness. Antonia exited first and waited for Larry to turn and lock the gate. She watched him slide the bolt into the lock. They both turned around to walk back toward the house when they stopped abruptly and emitted squeals. The small wizened gardener that Antonia had seen on her first visit was standing in front of them on the path, a large set of tree clippers in his hand.

"You scared the hell out of me!" exclaimed Larry.

"Oh my goodness, we didn't see you," said Antonia.

The gardener, who was balding and wrinkled and appeared to be in his eighties looked quizzically at the two trespassers.

"Came down to see who was here," he said in a low deep voice.

"We . . . were just . . ." Antonia fumbled to answer.

"We were looking at the murder site. Is Miss Framingham back yet?" Larry asked.

The man stared at them unblinking. There was something strange about him that made Antonia uncomfortable.

"Miss Framingham left a couple of days ago."

"She did?" Antonia asked with surprise.

"Where did she go?" Larry probed.

"Don't know, she didn't tell me."

"Well, is anyone at the house?"

"Mr. Russell was there yesterday but wasn't there today when I got here."

"What's your name?" Larry inquired.

"Name's Eddie."

"Have you worked for the Framinghams for long?"

"I'd say . . . about twenty years."

"So you didn't work for them when Susie Whitaker was killed."

"Can't say that I did."

Larry immediately became disinterested. "Okay, let's go, Bingham."

Antonia noticed a funny look pass across Eddie's face. "Hang on a second, Larry." She turned to Eddie. "You didn't work for the Framinghams at the time, but did you know them?"

Eddie's fingers tightened their grip on the tree clippers, and he switched them from his left hand to his right. "Knew them on sight, but didn't know them personally. Didn't start work here until 1995."

"Where did you work before?" Antonia asked.

"Across the street. At the Miners'. They've since passed."

"Were you there at their house the day that Susie Whitaker was killed?"

"Yes, ma'am."

Larry turned toward the man, suddenly intrigued. "Did you see anything? Or hear anything?"

"I was mostly working in their vegetable garden in the back. Wouldn't have heard anything. Besides, the Powers boy was mowing the lawn over here, one of those old loud, noisy contraptions."

"And you saw no one?"

"When I brought the wagon to the side compost, I saw some cars go in and out, but nothing unusual."

"No one hanging around the street?" Larry probed.

"Nope. Dead quiet back then."

"Dead being the operative word," Larry said, before turning to Antonia. "Let's beat it."

"Hang on. Eddie, do you have any thought as to who killed Susie?"

"No one's ever asked me that."

"Well she's asking you now," Larry sneered, becoming impatient.

"In my opinion, it was Pauline's fellow that did it. I used to hear them arguing when I was clipping the front hedges. They'd be up in that guesthouse going at it really hard. Screaming and yelling. Those two just love a good fight. I imagine they still go at it. Saw him storm out of there two days ago."

"Dougie Marshall?" asked Antonia, incredulous.

"Don't know his name. The fellow from the country club."

"I think he means Scott Stewart. The tennis pro," said Larry. "He's the one who lived in the guesthouse."

"But he doesn't live there anymore," said Antonia. "He lives near the IGA."

"What guy are you talking about?" Larry asked the gardener.

"Don't know his name."

"Why do you think he did it?" asked Antonia.

"From the screaming around that time it was something about his job being in jeopardy if anyone found out. I told Tubby Walters all this, but he didn't want to listen. Ask me, he was hell bent on putting it on Kevin Powers."

"Thanks, Eddie. You've been very helpful," said Antonia.

"Unexpectedly," confirmed Larry. "Who knew, old men *do* add value."

* * * * *

"It makes sense," Antonia said as she buckled herself into Larry's car. "Scott was totally reluctant to talk to me. There was something fishy about the whole thing. And the fact that he's dating Holly and she didn't mention that at all? It was strange. It could be why Russell is paying them off. Maybe he's doing it on behalf of his sister."

"But you think Scott is still banging Pauline on the side?"

"Okay, hate the word choice. But yes, maybe that's why Holly is so bitter. She wants him but knows he can't be faithful."

"Let's hit the tennis club and ambush him."

"Larry, that's not going to work at all."

"Why do you say that?" he asked. He pressed firmly on the gas and navigated the car out of its parking space and down the driveway. Antonia could already feel herself becoming carsick.

"Because he will just refuse to talk to us. He has no reason to whatsoever. And do you truly think he will 'break' under our questioning and confess?"

"Maybe he's tired of keeping the secret. It's tearing him up inside. He wants to 'fess up."

"Unlikely. Here's another question: do we think it was Scott who was harassing Dougie? Was he the one who crashed his car into Dougie last night?"

"One way to find out."

Larry gunned the motor and floored it, forcing Antonia to start saying her Hail Marys.

* * * * *

"Didn't come in today, called in sick," said the bubbly blond behind the counter of the pro shop at the Cove Hollow Club. She was no more than twenty-one and wore an extremely tight baby blue tank top and tennis skirt that had rendered Larry a giddy mess right from the get-go.

"Does he do that a lot?" Antonia asked while she waited for Larry to pick his tongue up off the floor.

"I've only been here this summer, so not sure about the past. But this is the first time this year. He said he had a stomach bug," she responded with a giant smile as if reporting that Scott Stewart had recently won the lottery.

"What's your name?" Larry asked.

"Brittany?" she responded, more as a question than answer.

"Beautiful name," Larry said. "Listen, I've been thinking of taking up tennis. Do you teach?"

"No, sorry. We have some great teachers who I can hook you up with?" she said brightly.

Larry leaned across the counter toward her.

"But I want to hook up with you. Do you think you could make an exception?"

Brittany's long fake eyelashes batted flirtatiously. She was no doubt very used to being hit on, Antonia surmised, and was completely unfazed by Larry's advances. "I would teach you, but I don't know how to play myself!"

Brittany erupted in giggles. Larry joined in.

"Then why the tennis outfit?" Antonia asked with irritation.

"Oh, well, that's my uniform. Kinda like if I worked at say,

McDonald's and had to wear a uniform. Although this is much cuter."

"Yes, it is," Larry confirmed.

"My big goal is to work at Lululemon. They have the most rocking clothes."

"And I bet you would look sensational in them," Larry added. "Or you could work at Victoria's Secret."

Antonia cleared her throat. "Can we return to business?"

"What do you want, Bingham? Can't we chat a little with Brittany?"

"I'm sure she's busy and has other customers," Antonia said tersely.

"Oh, it's okay. It gets pretty boring in here. People just come in and sign in and then maybe buy a can of balls, but usually they just leave. I'm happy to talk."

"See Antonia?" Larry said accusatorily. "She is *happy* to talk."

"Okay, well, tell us more about Scott Stewart. What kind of car does he drive?" Antonia asked.

"One of those boring kinds. Japanese or something."

"I drive a BMW," Larry said. "Want to go for a spin sometime?"

Brittany found this hilarious and devolved into another round of giggles. "You are too funny!"

Antonia was losing patience. "What color is his car?"

"Whose?"

"*Scott's*," Antonia said firmly.

"Oh. Black or blue. Something like that."

"Would you say it's a dark sedan?"

"Yeah."

"Larry, are you catching this?"

Larry's eyes were glued to Brittany's breasts. "Yes, I get it, Antonia. Same color and type of car as crashed into Dougie."

"Was Scott acting strangely yesterday or over the past few days?" Antonia asked.

"Not really, I mean, we don't talk a lot. But he did get into a big fight with his girlfriend."

This finally caught Larry's attention. "What kind of fight? Will you break it all down for us, sweetie?"

"I mean, I didn't want to eavesdrop, but they were right outside. She came in to get some balls and find out which court she was on and then when she went outside he met her and they started arguing. It got pretty loud so I did overhear some things . . . like she said she didn't want him to keep going there, it was wrong, and couldn't he just stay away . . ."

"Going where?" Antonia and Larry inquired, practically in unison.

Brittany became nervous and bit her puffy pink lip. "I don't know . . . why? Maybe I shouldn't tell you this. I don't even know who you are."

"I'm Larry and this is Antonia. I'm with *the newspaper*, so you technically do have to tell me this."

"Oh, okay. Well, I don't really remember. It sounded like some friend or something."

"Did they say a last name at all?"

Brittany glanced up as if the answer might be in the sky. "This is really hard . . . I'm trying to remember."

"Take your time," Larry said, placing one of his small hands on top of hers and pressing. "We have all the time in the world. We want you to get this right."

"Me too . . ." she said, still staring at the ceiling. "They did say some name . . ."

"Was it Framingham?" asked Larry.

Brittany beamed. "Yes! I think it was. Framingham."

"Larry, you can't just feed her the name. That's entrapment," chided Antonia.

Larry ignored her. "Good girl, Brittany!"

"Did I do well?" she asked eagerly.

"Extremely! In fact, you win!"

"Oh! What do I win?"

"Dinner with me," Larry said. "And I'm taking you to her fancy restaurant in town, where Antonia will personally cook us anything our hearts desire."

Brittany clapped her hands together and jumped up and down. "Yay! So cool."

"I know, isn't it?" Larry said with the grin of a Cheshire cat.

"Can I bring my boyfriend?" Brittany asked. "Oh, and maybe we can make it a foursome. My mom is single and about your age! What do you say, double date?"

28

Larry dropped Antonia at the inn. He was heading over to Scott Stewart's house to see if he could glean if there was any damage to the car. As much as Antonia was desperate to join him, she absolutely had to return to the inn and check in on the guests and the kitchen. Her behavior had been downright reckless and she was astounded that she had been so carried away with the investigation that she had totally ignored her duties at work. It was beyond irresponsible—something she would have lectured Genevieve about at length if the shoe were on the other foot. But she had become so consumed with the entire affair that she had ignored all reason. And the crazy part was she wasn't even on the case anymore! She had been dismissed and paid in full for the rooms in February, which gave her no excuse to carry on.

Larry promised he would report back anything he discovered, although knowing him it would take many phone calls from her to find anything out. That was okay. She was also planning on placing a call to the hospital to find out how Dougie Marshall was doing. She prayed he would pull through; it would be awful to have something happen to him that had been indirectly caused by her. Maybe there was truth to what everyone said—that they were all just playthings being manipulated by Pauline to amuse her. *What a sad life she has at the end of the day,* thought Antonia. *Alone, rich, and bored—a toxic combination.*

"Anything going on, Connie? Any fires to put out?" Antonia asked her receptionist.

"Actually, surprisingly all is well," Connie responded. "But Joseph is waiting for you in the library."

Antonia was certain Joseph was eager for her to download all of her recent findings, but she really didn't have time right now. Just as she hesitated, Joseph scootered out of the library.

"Antonia, I think you need to come in here, please."

His tone was strange.

Antonia followed him without a word. The library was empty except for a woman with dark hair standing by the window, glancing outside, her back to the room. She wore a long floral dress reminiscent of the kind women wore in the 1940s, with puffy sleeves, which looked very chic. Joseph cleared his throat and she turned around.

It was Bridget Curtis, the young woman who had recently been a visitor to the inn. She was extremely attractive, with long dark hair and big bright eyes, but there was something tense and skittish about her that made Antonia nervous. In fact, at one point she had considered that Bridget might be a killer. And the fact that she checked out of the inn in the middle of the night on her previous visit had only added to her mysterious demeanor. It was also strange that Antonia had recently received a phone call inquiring about what Bridget had told her.

"Hello, nice to see you again," Antonia said pleasantly. Rule number one as an innkeeper was to make everyone feel welcome, no matter how strange or awkward the person or situation.

"You too," Bridget responded brusquely. Then she turned toward Joseph and gave him an imploring look.

"Why don't you both sit down. I'm at an unfair advantage in my scooter," he said, adopting a lighthearted tone.

Antonia did as she was told. Bridget hesitated for a split second and then followed suit.

"Are you back in town for long?" Antonia inquired.

Bridget shook her head and folded her hands nervously. "No."

She turned toward Joseph. Antonia mused at their intimacy. How did they know each other?

As if reading her mind, Joseph spoke, "I was reading some rather dull accounts of the Byzantine empire this morning when Bridget came in looking for you. She remembered me from last time she was here and knew we were close friends so she solicited my advice. I hope you will not be offended, Antonia, that Bridget was quite candid and informed me about her reason for returning to the inn."

A terrible sensation engulfed Antonia's body and a knot began to form in the back of her throat. It was as if her sixth sense was telling her something bad was about to happen. Instead of responding, she glanced back and forth between Joseph and Bridget with wide, unblinking eyes.

"Antonia," Joseph began, after she remained quiet. "Bridget has something she wants to tell you that I imagine will be very difficult to hear."

"What is it?" Antonia blurted out finally. The tension was becoming powerful.

Joseph gave Bridget an encouraging nod and she turned toward Antonia. As she spoke, she refused to make eye contact. "I'm your sister."

"What?" Antonia couldn't process the words Bridget was saying. "What do you mean?"

"I mean, we have the same father . . ." Bridget's voice trailed off and again she glanced over at Joseph.

"I don't understand."

"I have proof," Bridget said. There was a manila folder on the coffee table that Antonia had not even noticed. Bridget pushed it toward her. Antonia picked it up and scanned the pages. The pages in the folder were notarized and stamped and appeared completely legitimate. But how could this be? Her father had an affair? She couldn't imagine. Her father had been madly in love with her mother. According to the document in front of her, Bridget was twenty-five years old. That would mean that her father had cheated on her mother when Antonia was eleven? She tried to think back to that time. She didn't remember any sign of conflict between her parents. What did she remember about being eleven? She remembered that for her birthday she had received a purple sweatshirt with the number eleven printed in white. She wore it for the entire year, until it was completely threadbare and her mother was finally able to dispose of it. She had requested roast beef, potato pancakes, asparagus with hollandaise sauce, and angel food cake with hot fudge for her birthday dinner and had celebrated with extended family. The rest of the year was sort of a blur . . . she was sure she had rented horror movies with her best friend, Paige. She had been interested in a boy named Jesse. But what did she remember about her parents? Not much.

"I can't process these pages . . . my head is spinning."

"I'm sorry, Antonia, this must be a terrible shock," Joseph said as he patted her hand softly. "I know how much you revered your father and mother. One of the most challenging aspects of growing up is to learn the foibles of our parents; it is very difficult to see them as human. But I think if you listen to Bridget, you will perhaps gain some clarity. And as traumatic as this is for you, it is also very hard for her."

Antonia felt her eyes well with tears. A few streamed down her face, and she brushed them away angrily. She didn't want to cry. She felt furious at her father and stunned by the revelation; the last thing she wanted to feel was sadness. It would be too overwhelming.

"I'm sorry, Antonia. I realize that you had no idea that I even existed."

Antonia shook her head.

Bridget nodded. "I understand that . . . I wasn't supposed to exist."

"I just can't understand it. I always thought my parents had the perfect marriage. This is such a shock. Did my mother know?"

"I don't think so," Bridget said.

"That's good. I'm glad she didn't know."

"Look, I know I have totally rocked your world and you must feel awful. And I can say from the bottom of my heart, I am sorry. I'm sure you have an image of your father and the idea that he had an affair with my mother, well, I can't imagine that it's a good revelation."

"How did it happen?"

"My mother is actually quite awful. I'm sorry to say that. Of course I love her, she's my mother, but she enticed your father. My mother was—is, to a certain extent—a predator. She does not care if a man is married or not. She wants what she wants. She's very beautiful and very manipulative. And she met Dad—your father—at work. She was a temp at his office. And they went to drinks, and all I am sure of is that it was a one-night stand that Alan was very remorseful about . . ."

"Wait a minute, you *knew* him?"

"He would visit from time to time. He wanted to make sure I was okay. I know, I know, this sounds bad. But the fact was, he knew my mother was nuts. She got him drunk, got pregnant on a one-night stand, then lorded it over him. She was no different from Glenn Close's character in *Fatal Attraction*. She has done this repeatedly over the years; I also have three half-brothers, so I have a clear sense of who she is. Dad, um, Alan, begged my mother not to tell you and your mom. Remarkably, she never did, although I know a few times he had to stop her. It was only when she turned her attention to another man that your father was finally liberated from her craziness."

"Why didn't my dad tell me? He lived ten years after my mom died. He could have said something . . ."

"I think he felt terrible," Bridget said. "He didn't want to betray you."

Antonia shrugged. "That's almost harder to hear . . . that he felt like he had to keep you a secret."

"Your father loved you dearly," Joseph murmured.

"I wish he had told me . . ."

Bridget continued. "The last thing I wanted was to hurt you and bring this up. In fact, I debated whether or not I should even come . . ."

"Tell her," Joseph prompted.

"Tell me what? There's more?" Antonia asked.

"Unfortunately. Look, I didn't grow up near you, I actually grew up in San Luis Obispo. I knew nothing about you or your mother, and after our Dad . . . Alan . . . died, I never thought to investigate. I went to college in San Francisco and have been working there for some time in fashion as a freelance stylist. I work with magazines and local clients. I meet a lot of people. About a year and a half ago, I was at a bar in the Mission and I met a man. He was older, but very handsome and charming. We started dating. It was great at first, but he became increasingly controlling and aggressive. I thought of breaking it off, but he also made me paranoid and was able to manipulate me. Every time I was done with him, he would become very sweet and tender and apologize. He spoke about his evil ex-wife who had destroyed his life and his professional career and then left him to move to the Hamptons and open an inn . . ."

Antonia gasped. "Philip."

Bridget nodded. "Somehow, no doubt through his police connections, your ex-husband Philip had discovered my existence. He played me from the very beginning. It was all about revenge toward you. I was so naive at first, I believed everything he said. He was the one who sent me here a few months ago to 'spy' on you. He had convinced me that you were planning on some new way to ruin his life. That's why I came and was so strange. When I returned to California he was even more jumpy and frantic than usual. Not to mention violent. I finally had the wits to get out of there. I filed a restraining order and took off. The reason I came here this time was not to hurt you, Antonia, but to warn you. Even my mother told me not to do it—it's like that saying, crazy knows crazy. That's why she was calling to find me and stop me . . ."

"The woman on the phone," Antonia said softly.

"Yes. I know she was worried and wanted me to walk away from all this. And I suppose I could have done that and sent you a warning letter without revealing myself, but it seems like if Philip could find out that we're half-sisters, he can find out anything else. Someone is helping him. And I want you to be careful."

Antonia felt an accelerated sense of dread coupled with remorse. It was inevitable that Philip would insinuate himself back into Antonia's life—it was too much to ask that she would be totally free of him. He had once said they were inexorably linked. She was foolish to believe that she could escape him. What terrified Antonia now was that he had done his research. Usually his brutality was abrupt and harsh. He was thorough in his efforts to ensure her misery, but he was not fastidious or calculated about constructing the circumstances. At least she had always assumed that much. Now she wasn't so sure. Strange, because when they were married, Philip often distinguished between criminals whose murders were premeditated and those who committed crimes of passion. He aligned himself with the latter group and even expressed some admiration for those who "love too hard and are forced to do something about it when their heart is broken." But now, it turns out, he was in the former group. All of his evil acts were premeditated. And now it appeared that some more were coming her way.

"I'm really sorry that happened to you," Antonia said, extending her hand and patting Bridget's. "I'm sorry I've been unable to stop Philip and now he has attempted to ruin another life."

"Antonia, don't be crazy! It's not your fault."

"I know it's not my fault. But I won't put up with it anymore. I'm going to figure out a way to get him and put him away forever."

"I'm not sure it can be done," Bridget said glumly.

Antonia glanced up and stared at Bridget's face. From the

moment Antonia had met her, Bridget had felt familiar. Now she knew why. Antonia's emotions were running rampant. She was disappointed and angry at her father for betraying her mother. She was sad that their marriage wasn't the storybook marriage she had envisioned. It would be so hard for her to sift through her memories and reconstruct them. It was also a shame her father had never introduced Bridget into her life. But there was a small kernel of joy that would take some time to get used to. She had a sister.

29

After Bridget left Antonia's emotions were all over the map, as if she was on the biggest hormone roller coaster of her life. Her world had just been rocked to the core and she had no idea how to digest it. So she did what she always did when she was emotional: she marched into the kitchen and opened the large double-wide refrigerator. Her eyes immediately went to the bowl of glazed strawberries marinating in twenty-year-old aged balsamic vinegar. She retrieved the bowl as well as a large jar of fluffy white whipped cream and wordlessly walked over to the counter where racks of sugar-coated biscuits were cooling. She took a plate and covered it with biscuits, whipped cream, and a generous portion of strawberries. Soyla and Kendra eyed her strangely—she had not responded to their salutations when she entered the room, which was totally uncharacteristic of her.

"Antonia, you gonna work today?" Marty asked in a teasing tone.

"Not sure."

"But it's Friday. We're swamped."

"You'll be fine."

She grabbed a knife from the drawer then made her way to her apartment with her feast, leaving her staff staring at her incredulously.

Antonia used food in many different ways. She ate when she was sad; she ate when she was happy. If something bad happened, she used food as a treat to cajole herself out of her funk. If something good happened, she used food as a reward or to celebrate. Now, she sank herself into her sofa and began shoving forkfuls of strawberry shortcake into her mouth. It didn't taste as good as it normally did. She kept thinking each bite would have a healing effect, but in fact, the sticky sweetness made her feel worse. Antonia put the plate down on the coffee table, curled herself into the fetal position, covered herself with her furry pink throw blanket, and cried.

Antonia cried for her mother, who had been betrayed. She cried for her father, who was no longer the paragon of a faithful husband that she had thought he was. She cried for human weakness. She cried for the evil that Philip still wanted to inflict on her. She cried for Bridget, because it must have been lonely to grow up without a father and with a crazy mother. As she was on a hard-core crying jag, she decided to widen the periphery and extend it to others, so she cried for Susie, whose promising life had been extinguished at such a young age. She cried for Susie's family and friends—even though she had no idea if any of them were guilty. It was only when Antonia found a small reason to cry for Larry Lipper that she stopped. Lucidity came to her. Sometimes you have to draw a line, and Larry Lipper was that line. After that, Antonia fell into a deep sleep, devoid of dreams.

* * * * *

"Jesus, Bingham, what the hell happened to your face? Did someone suckerpunch you? Your eyes are so pink and puffy you look like a prizefighter that's gone twenty rounds."

Antonia sat up. Larry Lipper was standing over her. Darkness crept in through the window and Antonia felt totally disoriented.

"What time is it?"

"Relax, it's six o'clock."

"Shoot, dinner service time."

Larry flopped down in the chair across from her. He held a giant Starbucks cup in his hand and took a swig.

"I think by now we both know that your staff can deal without you."

"The sad thing is that's absolutely true. Although maybe not sad, but sad for me that I'm redundant."

"Why are you so down in the dumps?"

"Larry, what are you doing here? How did you get in?"

"Joseph let me in. I told him it was urgent and I promised not to violate you. He's a pretty good gatekeeper, I might add. But somehow he softened, even said it might do me good to talk to you. What happened, did you and Old Joe get into a fight?"

Antonia rubbed her eyes. "It's nothing of the sort."

"Jokes aside, Bingham. I can be a good listener."

"I don't want to get into it now."

"If someone is messing with you, they have me to deal with. I may be small, but I'm tough. And I fight dirty—lots of biting and kicking in the groin."

Antonia smiled. "Thank you. I'll be fine. Just tell me, what happened at Scott's?"

"Couldn't find him."

"What do you mean you couldn't find him?"

"Wasn't home."

"Are you sure it was the right address? Genevieve said Talmadge Lane."

"Yes, I'm sure. He was AWOL. The blinds were drawn. No car in the driveway. I asked the neighbor and she said she saw him and his gal pal pack up their car and take off early this morning."

"Did she happen to notice if the car was totaled?"

"She said it looked fine to her. But that's because it was a rental."

This spurred Antonia's attention. "What do you mean?"

Larry smiled gleefully. "I mean what I said, Bingham. You still asleep? The old broad said Scott showed up in a rental car this morning. She could tell by the plates. Then he packed up and took off."

"Where do you think his real car is?"

"He's either hiding it somewhere or it's in a junkyard. No doubt it's got serious damage from crashing into Dougie Marshall's Mercedes. I asked my buddy at the police station, but he didn't have any report of Scott Stewart's car being stolen."

"Oh my gosh, this is crazy! So we think Scott crashed into Dougie to keep him from talking and then took off with Holly somewhere?"

"Bingo, Bingham. Takes you awhile, doesn't it?"

"Did you tell the cops you suspected Scott?"

"Sorta," Larry said. He took the lid off his coffee cup and began licking the milky layer of froth with his tongue. "I don't want to hand this to the cops, I still need to be the one to solve the case for the book deal, but I told them he was a person of interest."

"Larry! He could be in a homicidal rage. You have to tell the cops."

"I will, I will. I first asked my buddy to find out anything else they might have on Scott. You know, past arrests. When he gives me that intel, I'll give him mine."

"Risky."

"You know I like to live on the edge."

"I should head to the kitchen."

She stood up and stretched. So it was Scott, he was the killer. Of course she wasn't sure *why* Scott would have killed Susie, but sometimes motive remained elusive.

Larry gave her a compassionate look. "Take care of yourself, Bingham. You're a good egg. You deserve to be happy."

* * * * *

Antonia was subdued for most of dinner service. Marty and Kendra could sense her mood and toned down their teasing. When orders had died down a bit, she made her way to the dining room to do a sweep and greet her guests. She found Len Powers and his wife, Sylvia, sitting in the corner, nursing coffees and sharing a crème brûlée.

"Delicious as always, Antonia!" Sylvia beamed.

"It's very hard to stick to my diet!" Len grumbled. "We agreed to share a dessert, but I'm already regretting it."

Both Len and Sylvia were what could be described as large or "big boned" people. Their bodies as well as their facial features were thick, and everything from Sylvia's blond bouffant to Len's Santa Claus stomach were robust.

"Life is too short."

"Amen," Sylvia agreed whilst scooping another large bite of the creamy confection into her mouth. "And I adore this crunchy sugar crust. One of the Lord's greatest creations."

Len took a sip of his coffee, dabbed his mouth with a napkin, and glanced up at Antonia.

"So Dougie Marshall, huh?"

"Any update on how he's doing?"

"The president of the club said he's banged up and will be for a while, lotta broken ribs and lacerations, but he's going to be okay," Len said.

"I can't believe it! Right outside the inn, Antonia," said Sylvia. "And I thought you had put the curse of the inn behind you."

"Wow, so did I. I didn't even think of it that way."

"Sylvia, don't get her all riled up," Len admonished.

"Did Dougie say if he saw the person who did it?"

Len shook his head. "If he did, he isn't talking. I heard he's totally spooked. Now this doesn't have anything to do with your discussion with him does it?"

Antonia gulped. "I hope not," she fibbed.

Len cocked his head to the side. "Because I caught wind that you were looking into the Susie Whitaker murder. I think it's a shame to bring that all up. No good can come of it."

"I'm learning that the hard way."

"I mean, you got Dougie getting hit by a car, and my brother Kevin has taken off—it's like you unleashed Pandora's box."

She was taken off guard. "Wait, what do you mean Kevin has taken off?"

Sylvia answered for Len. "I know, very strange, it being the busy season and all, but he called last night and said he had to head out of town. I was a little nervous . . . you know, because of his past troubles and all, so I pressed him to see if everything was okay. He mentioned that Susie's death had come up again and no good would come of him getting involved so he decided to take an extended vacation."

"Where did he go?"

"He wouldn't say," said Sylvia.

"Look, Antonia, sometimes you have to let sleeping dogs lie," counseled Len. "I'm not trying to tell you what to do, and damn if I don't want to find out who killed Susie. That was a terrible tragedy and no one should get away with it. But there are consequences. A lot of people involved were troubled back then or became troubled after."

"Like Kevin and his girlfriend Kimberly?" interjected Antonia.

Len sighed. "Yes. That was terrible. I can't defend that."

"We didn't speak to him for years," Sylvia chimed in. "But he kept begging our forgiveness so we talked to our priest and he said we had to open our hearts to him."

"Kevin running away doesn't look too good, especially after what happened to Dougie. It could make it seem like Kevin caused the accident," Antonia said.

"Oh, dear, no," Sylvia said with a shake of the head. "Kevin wouldn't do that. I really think he's turned over a new leaf. And he was genuinely scared when I talked to him. I think someone had warned him or threatened him . . ."

"Why didn't he go to the police?" asked Antonia.

Len gave her a look. "You mean with his history? When you've been arrested you steer clear of the cops."

"You're right."

"I hope you can solve this murder, Antonia," Sylvia said. "It's time to catch a killer and have everyone who was caught in the fray move on with their lives."

* * * * *

That night Antonia read over Susie Whitaker's diary again. Antonia was Catholic and tried to attend church as much as possible. She respected the beliefs of her church. She also chose to believe that the dead could send signs to the people they loved, or the people they needed to connect with. This belief made it easier to reconcile the loss of her parents. As she held

Susie's diary in her hand, she felt a burning sense that Susie was trying to send her a message. It was as if she was telling Antonia that she was so close to finding the killer that she had to stay the course. Antonia wanted Susie Whitaker to rest in peace. But it was clear that Antonia would have to uncover her murderer in order for Susie to do so.

And it appeared now that it was not such a sure thing that Scott Stewart had killed Susie. The range of suspects had again reopened with Scott and Kevin both on the run. Antonia felt that she was unable to clear anyone in the case as of yet. Agatha Christie's detective Hercule Poirot always said to look at the victim in order to solve the crime. Was that wishful thinking? Especially when the victim was a teenaged girl—not the most reliable narrator of her own life. There was one passage that Antonia had noted, but thought she was just being optimistic. On July 17 Susie wrote:

I know secrets. I am good at keeping them. But sometimes when something is really bad, you can't keep your mouth shut.

What had she meant by that? What was she referring to? Antonia wanted to know. Oh, Susie! Antonia wanted to return back in time and help her out. She wished she had been there to advise her. There were some secrets that were better off remaining secrets, and others that demanded discovery. With Susie's case, as well as the revelation that Bridget was her half-sister, Antonia was confronted on all sides by an insistence for the truth, no matter how harsh and brutal it was. It was strange to Antonia that these long-ago decisions made by others were profoundly affecting her now. In one case, the murder of a young girl, and in the other case, the birth of one. Life was strangely cyclical. Not to mention unexpected. Antonia had been thrown some curve balls in life, and she'd had to call upon her inner strength to deal with them. As bitter as it was, she had to accept Bridget and not blame her. She could sort through her new sour feelings for her father later on. As for Susie, Antonia needed to bring her justice.

30

It rained the following morning. Not torrential, but crying jags of hard pellets interspersed with small sprinkles of drizzle. For various reasons Antonia was not a fan of rain on summer days, especially Saturdays. First, it made the guests cranky. They had planned their vacations and paid a lot of money to come and stay in East Hampton so they could enjoy the beautiful award-winning beaches. They were frustrated and angry when their plans were thwarted. Coupled with that, in rainy weather, the guests often didn't have anywhere to go so they ended up hanging around all the public rooms, grumpy and bored. Town was always a mob scene on rainy days, and as East Hampton had the largest movie theater on the East End (the only other theater being the slightly smaller one in Southampton) there were long lines and sold-out shows on days with inclement weather. The fact of the matter was that a cozy inn was not so cozy on a wet summer day.

Antonia and Soyla baked extra batches of fruity muffins and scones for the morning breakfast service as well as several frittatas with feta, spinach, and tomatoes. When there was little to do, people tended to graze on food all day. Despite the wet weather outside, the inn had the aroma of freshly brewed coffee, bacon, and a hint of cinnamon buns. Jonathan had lit a fire in the parlor and purchased extra copies of the newspapers at Scoop Du Jour in an effort to avoid a showdown between guests over the various sections that were most often in demand. The parlor was buzzing with the hum of morning conversation and the clink of cutlery.

"How are you doing this morning?" Joseph asked somewhat sheepishly as he zipped up to the buffet table. Antonia had been rearranging the breadbasket, adding warm popovers and replenishing the scones.

"I'm okay."

"I'm sorry about what happened yesterday. We didn't mean to ambush you with that information."

Antonia leaned down and hugged him. "I know you always have my back, Joseph. And I'm glad you were there. It was so much to take in . . ."

"I can't even imagine. But before you do anything, I think it's of the utmost importance that you talk to your friend, Officer Flanagan, and let him know what's going on with your ex-husband. He should have Philip on his radar at the very least. I think it's crucial that he has the information about your past and alerts his colleagues to be on the lookout."

"That's not a bad idea," conceded Antonia. "I hate the fact

that I have to tell everyone here about my messy past, but I agree that, with Philip, safety is an issue."

"Paramount."

"I also need to check in with him about Dougie Marshall. I hope he's on the mend. In addition, Scott Stewart and Kevin Powers have both made a hasty exit out of town. I want to make sure the police are aware of that."

"I think it's prudent to keep them involved. You need them, Antonia. Be careful."

There was worry in his eyes. Antonia patted his hand.

"I'm going to be okay."

"I know."

"Really," she insisted.

He nodded, still pensive. "I know this part is delicate, but how do you want to proceed with Bridget? She is staying with a friend in town until tomorrow. Do you wish to see her again?"

"I suppose I should. I'm still processing the fact that she exists. It's so bizarre."

"I can imagine."

"I never thought of myself as the typical only child and always wanted a sister or brother. Maybe it will all work out."

"I hope so."

* * * * *

Officer Flanagan was in his office but led Antonia into a conference room where he closed the door. She loathed police stations, for a multitude of reasons, and had forgotten how tense they made her. The garish lighting, the blank walls, the ominous energy that permeated the hallways—there was no place she would less rather be. There were people reporting for parole at the desk when she arrived and she conjectured that they shared a similar anxious reaction to the location. She internally commiserated with them and promised herself to avoid any more murder expeditions that would bring her into contact with the law.

After pleasantries, Antonia cut to the chase and filled in Officer Flanagan about her ex-husband, Philip, and the recent revelation that he was meticulously plotting some sort of revenge. Officer Flanagan listened carefully and took copious notes before briefly leaving the room to alert his colleagues. Antonia was grateful to have that part of the conversation over and done with. She was still unable to reconcile the part of herself who had married a maniac, and although she knew she had nothing to be ashamed of, it offended her sense of self that she had to continually revisit the situation. When Officer Flanagan returned he held two mugs of coffee bearing the logo of the police department and set one in front of her before sitting down.

"I am sure you are also here for another reason," he said. His face remained stern but his eyes showed a trace of . . . humanity? Amusement?

"You know me too well."

"What's up?"

"Both Scott Stewart and Kevin Powers left town abruptly. I think it has to do with the Susie Whitaker murder. I'm not sure if either of them is the killer or if they feel threatened. In fact, I'm not sure what to think. But after Dougie Marshall was hit, something changed. People are scared. When I interviewed Alida Jenkins she was very forthcoming until she received a text and then she totally clammed up. I'm not sure what to make of Pauline Framingham. Is she a sociopath? A psychopath? I'm actually not sure of the difference. But her friends have suggested she is playing me and this is all a game."

Officer Flanagan let Antonia ramble without interruption. When she was done he nodded.

"I was planning on paying you a visit today, so it's fortuitous that you came to see me first. Here's the problem, Antonia. I received a call from a friend at the courthouse. It seems that there has been a petition submitted for an order of protection against you . . ."

"*Against* me?!" exclaimed Antonia. "Who did that?"

"It was on behalf of Pauline Framingham, Russell Framingham, Scott Stewart, Alida Jenkins, and Kevin Powers . . ."

The blood rushed to Antonia's head and she felt dizzy. "I'm speechless. Are you sure? Is this true?"

He continued. "Unfortunately, yes. They have to prove reason to the court as to why they need this protection, and if it's approved, a sheriff will serve you notice . . ."

"I feel faint," mumbled Antonia.

"I understand. Look, I know you, Antonia. And I told my friend at the courthouse that this was a bunch of junk, that you had been hired to look into the Susie Whitaker murder and then Pauline Framingham had a change of heart. But the fact remains that she had a change of heart. I am not sure this order of protection will be approved, but my advice to you is to walk away from this case. No good will come of it, and you could lose everything."

"You're right. You're totally right," Antonia agreed. "Do you really think the order won't go through? It would be *horrible* if it did. My business would suffer, my reputation . . ."

"I'll do the best I can. But it will help your cause if you firmly agree to drop everything."

"I promise. It's not worth it anymore."

"That's right. It's not worth it anymore."

"I feel bad for Susie . . ."

"I understand. It's hard not to commiserate with the victims. Occupational hazard."

"Maybe you can look into it?"

He sighed. "I'll see what I can do if you stay out of it."

"I promise."

"Smart lady."

* * * * *

Antonia drove back home along the wet roads, embarrassed, scared, and demoralized. Officer Flanagan was right, she had to walk away. She said a few prayers on her way home—to her mother to keep her safe and out of jail; to God to solve the murder of Susie Whitaker so that Susie might rest in peace; and to Susie for forgiveness for abandoning her case. There were forces far too powerful at play for Antonia to compete against.

Attempting to put a cheerful spin on the situation, Antonia took a critical look at her inn as she pulled her car into the driveway and couldn't deny that she was lucky. A successful inn, a well-respected restaurant, good friends like Joseph and Genevieve were truly all she needed. She had to stop dabbling in these murder investigations. People relied on her. What would she tell Marty, Kendra, Soyla, Hector, Jonathan, and all the others if she had to close the business because she was just too damn nosy? It would be pathetic.

The inn was noisy and alive when she strode through the front hall. She shook the raindrops out of her hair and placed her umbrella in the stand by the front door.

"Antonia!"

Giorgio Leguzzi lifted his hat toward her as he made his way to the front door.

"How are you, Mr. Leguzzi?"

"I'ma okay."

"Are you heading out to Cittanuova?"

"I am. But I am sad to inform you that the time has soon come for me to depart. I am needed back home and must leave Tuesday. It will be difficult to depart, but I must."

"I'm sorry to hear that. I'm almost afraid to ask, but any progress with Elizabeth?"

"Unfortunately, my love eludes me. I am living in a tragedy where the lovers are star-crossed. Alas, it is no doubt my destiny."

"Oh, don't say that! Maybe you can come back and try again?"

"I would like that very much, but I no longer possess the optimism."

"Well I possess it! Please return. Perhaps if I have more time I can assist you. We can really dig deep, put an ad in the paper, reach out to people. You know they even run local ads at the movie theater . . ."

"You are very kind, Miss Bingham." He took her hand and kissed it. There was a sweet sadness in his face, and Antonia's heart broke for him. "I thank you for everything."

"I'll pray for you!" Antonia blurted out.

He bowed before selecting one of the inn's long green umbrellas out of the stand and venturing out into the rain. Antonia watched as the funny little man walked down the steps toward the path to town. She hoped he would be successful in his quest for love.

"Antonia, you're needed in the kitchen," Jonathan said as he whizzed past her in the hall.

"I know, I know. And today, Jonathan, I'm not going anywhere else. I am planting myself in the kitchen until the end of dinner service."

He gave her a quizzical look before responding with an encouraging, "Brilliant."

31

There had been so much going on that Antonia had almost forgotten about her dinner engagement with Nick Darrow. Almost. She had no reason to call it a date, it was just friends breaking bread together. Yeah, right. She couldn't lie to herself. In her pathetic mind, it was a date. But she knew that in his mind it wasn't. Oh, how the heart can play tricks on you!

They had agreed that he would pick her up Sunday evening and they would drive together to the restaurant, Inlet Seafood, as it was near the tip of Montauk and a good thirty minutes away. No use spending the car ride alone when they could talk in private, Nick had said, and Antonia readily agreed. She felt as if she was embarking on an adventure, and the fact that they were visiting a place removed from the hum of her current world emphasized that. That evening, she took time selecting her outfit and donned the casual but beautiful ruby-colored dress that Genevieve had given her for Christmas the previous year from Ralph's resort collection. She took time with her hair and makeup and slipped her feet into low heels. She admired herself in the mirror and was actually quite pleased. She didn't dress up often, but when she did, she felt well rewarded. That was what always frustrated Genevieve about Antonia: when she made the effort to use makeup and slip on a nice dress, she looked "stunning" in Genevieve's words.

Antonia had devoted the entire Sunday to the inn instead of her murder investigation. Larry had called her several times, but she didn't take his calls. The Windmill Inn needed her attention, and she was not going to dip her toe into anything that could land her in jail. She felt like one of those teenagers who had dabbled in drugs and then was brought into a prison and lectured by hardened, tattooed prisoners and ultimately "scared straight." No more crime for her.

"You look great," Nick said as he held the car door for her. His face bore a reverent look and he couldn't take his eyes off her.

"Thanks," she said with fake nonchalance.

When he walked around to the driver's side, she quickly ran her finger over her teeth to make sure there was no sticky lipstick smeared across them. She remembered she had been on a date once and was drinking this sickly Georgian red wine (hey, it was cheap) and toward the end of the evening she went to the ladies' room and her mouth looked like a cherry bomb had blown up all over it. She was mortified.

The car ride went smoothly; they both kept the conversation casual and talked more about local events and current affairs. Nick kept stealing glances at her and a half-smile played on his face the whole time. The topic of Nick's wife and what the heck Antonia was doing in his car was not addressed at all. *That's good*, Antonia told herself. *Keep it lighthearted.* Sometimes the fact that she was able to elicit personal information from people with almost no effort worked against her. There had been times when people had confided in her and the next time they saw her they were embarrassed, so they avoided her like the plague. She had no desire for that to happen with Nick.

Inlet Seafood was owned by six local fishermen and served the freshest fish on Long Island, almost all of it hauled in that day. It was sustainable, local, and ocean to table before those buzzwords and phrases were scrawled all over chalkboards in Brooklyn.

"This is my favorite place," confided Nick before quickly adding, "after the Windmill Inn, of course."

The restaurant was housed on the second floor and had panoramic views of the Long Island Sound. The décor was casual as there was no need for any flourishes with a vista like that.

Antonia noticed again that when a celebrity entered a room there was an almost magnetic force that swept around every corner and changed the energy in the room. People noticed Nick, some greeted him, while others pretended he was invisible—regardless, he electrified the place. Celebrity was such a strange phenomenon. Antonia wasn't quite sure what to make of it, but Nick wore it with total nonchalance.

"This is perfect," Nick said as the waitress led them to the corner table and handed them the plastic-coated menus.

"It is," Antonia agreed. She glanced around the room and then froze. In the opposite corner, seated with her family, was none other than Alida Jenkins. Antonia's first impulse was to stand up and run as fast as possible out of the restaurant. No way in hell did she want Alida to think that she was stalking her. How mortifying would it be for Alida to stand up and point and scream "Arrest her!" in front of Nick?

"Everything okay?" Nick asked, reading the worry on her face.

"Yes, sure."

"Are you sure? 'Cause you look like you just saw a ghost."

"No, I'm fine. Just someone I'd rather not see."

He looked in the direction she was staring. "Alida Jenkins?"

"Yes, do you know her?"

"Of course I know her. We're both celebrities."

"Oh, of course."

He gave her a crazy look. "I'm kidding. Not all celebrities know each other."

"Oh, right."

"Antonia, what's going on? Do you have a problem with Alida? Did she beat you out for a cover of *Vogue*?"

"No, I'm fine."

"Antonia, look. I am an actor, which means I essentially lie for a living. I can tell when someone is a bad actor, and no offense, but tonight you're not winning any Oscars. What's going on with you and Alida?"

She sighed deeply and apprised him of her business with Pauline Framingham. The conversation lasted from edamame to the sushi rolls and through a shared brownie sundae dessert. The food was spectacular—Antonia particularly adored the Blackbird rolls which had the freshest tuna wrapped around shrimp tempura. She had a very hard time restraining herself from throwing them all down her throat at once. Nick was an incredible audience, firing questions at her, offering his own theories, and forcing her to reanalyze every clue she had uncovered. They spoke at length about Susie and Antonia had the feeling that she was describing a friend she had known well. She hadn't realized how much Susie had attached herself to her soul and how protective she had become of her. She described Susie's hopes and dreams to Nick in great detail, as if Susie had shared them personally with Antonia. She felt a sense of sorrow.

"You can relax now," Nick said as he swirled sugar into his coffee. "She's gone."

Antonia turned and saw the busboy clearing the table where Alida had sat.

"Yes. I don't know if she saw me, but I didn't make any eye contact."

"That's good."

"And if you'll excuse me, I will head to the ladies' room."

Antonia had been dying to use the ladies' room since the second glass of wine but had held off for fear of detection from Miss Jenkins. She walked down the stairs and peered around the corner, ascertaining that Alida was no longer on the premises. She went to the ladies' room and used the facilities. When she was washing her hands, Alida Jenkins swung open the door and entered. Antonia was so startled that she panicked. She dashed to the stall and quickly slammed the door. After sliding the bolt through the lock she slammed down the toilet seat and squatted on top, silently praying for powers of invisibility.

"Antonia?" Alida asked through the door.

Antonia didn't respond. If she held her breath long enough, perhaps Alida would think she had been hallucinating, like maybe she'd had a bad clam and it was causing blurred vision.

"I know you're in there."

"It's not Antonia," Antonia said in a high-pitched British accent.

"Okay, you're being really strange. What's going on?"

Antonia's pulse was racing. She didn't want to say anything. What the hell did Alida mean, "What's going on?" She was filing court orders against Antonia for harassment, of course Antonia was not going to run into her arms and propose they do Jaeger shots at the bar.

"Go away."

"I need to talk to you!"

"I love my freedom! I want liberty!"

"What?"

"I can't afford to be hauled off to court."

"What are you talking about?"

"The restraining order."

"Antonia, open the door. I promise I won't have you arrested."

Antonia held her breath. This wasn't happening.

"Please, Antonia. I swear."

She was cornered. There was nowhere else to run. She

glanced up to see if the ladies' room contained one of those small windows that characters in movies always seemed to find conveniently located when they were ready to make their escape, but it did not. Reluctantly, Antonia dropped down from the toilet seat and allowed her feet to hit the tiled floor with a thud. She opened the door with shaking hands and glanced up at the tall supermodel with fear.

"First off, I want to say I had no idea that you were going to be at this restaurant tonight. No idea. I didn't even know I was coming here until I got in the car. I mean, I knew I was coming here, but to Montauk, not here, here. It wasn't my choice. I wasn't like, 'Hey, let's go to Inlet.' And you can ask Nick Darrow, he will vouch for me. And he's equally famous as you, so there is that famous person code."

"I didn't think you were stalking me."

"Then why the restraining order?"

"It wasn't my idea. The Framinghams are very persuasive . . ."

"You know, I keep hearing about how powerful the Framinghams are. I'm kind of sick of it. Did you ever hear of free will? Not everyone has to do what they say just because they're billionaires or own a lot of stuff. You're famous enough that I'm sure you don't need that fragrance contract anymore. If you and all your friends banded together rather than running scared, I'm sure you could take them down. It's getting kind of pathetic."

Alida smiled, despite the dressing down. "You're right. But it's not as easy as it sounds."

"I don't see why the hell not."

"They've had power over all of us since we were very young . . . it's hard to change the way you regard someone."

"What do they have over you?"

"They know I was there the day Susie died."

"Did you kill her?"

Alida shook her head. "No."

"Then what were you doing there and why does it matter?"

"Maybe it doesn't matter . . . it seemed to be such a big deal at the time and I lied and the lies kept perpetuating the next lies. I went there to meet Russell."

"Russell? I thought he wasn't even there."

"Well, it turns out he wasn't there. But he told me he would be."

"Why?"

"He called me that morning and asked me to meet him at the house. Russell is very odd . . . but there is something refreshing in his honesty. He always told me how beautiful I was and that I should be the face of their fragrance. He was quite insistent on that. Pauline was less than supportive, needless to say. We were best friends, but there was always an undercurrent of rivalry. Maybe it was because it was Russell's idea, I'm not sure, but she would shoot him down every time he mentioned it. I had a friend from work drop me off at Georgica Beach and walked over to the Framinghams' . . ."

"Why didn't you just have a friend drop you at the house?"

"I worked at a camp for inner-city and underprivileged kids. Many of the counselors were graduates of the camp. For some of them, it was their first time out of the city. I thought it would blow their minds if I were to invite them to the Framinghams'. I tried to be very lowkey at the camp and not let anyone know I was from a fancy background."

"I see."

"So I went through the street entrance rather than from the beach because the plan was to meet Russell near the guesthouse. I wanted to avoid Pauline. I had no idea she and Susie would be playing tennis; we were all so lazy that summer. Luckily she'd gone to fetch lemonade. Susie was in a bit of a tizzy when I saw her. She was upset because she and Pauline had been fighting and Pauline had asked her to leave."

"Really? Why?"

"Susie said that Pauline was becoming tired of her and 'wanted her own space.' Susie even made the air quotations when she said it. She was upset because she knew she had gone too far and overstepped her bounds as a guest, but she really didn't want to go back to Connecticut for the rest of the summer. It was way more fun in East Hampton."

"How did Susie overstep her bounds?"

"She said she had told Pauline's mom something. And her mom got really mad."

"Her mom, not her dad?"

"That's what she said."

"But I thought the parents were traveling."

"I don't know . . . it's hard to remember now. They were always in and out . . . maybe it was when they called?"

"Could be. What did she tell Pauline's mom?"

"I don't know. She wouldn't say, she was too upset. She regretted it. It was a bad decision, and Pauline wanted her gone. She was somewhat hysterical."

"Why did you leave?"

"I didn't have a lot of time . . . I had to be back at Boys Harbor for the awards ceremony. My friend had dropped me for a half hour while he went to get Chinese food in Wainscott—there used to be a place there, and he was craving it. I didn't want him to wait for me, so as soon as Susie said Russell wasn't around, I split—I ran back to Georgica Beach to wait for my ride back to camp. I know it sounds bad now, but I had no idea that she'd be murdered. She was always so dramatic and her feelings were constantly hurt so I thought her blathering was nothing. Obviously I would have stayed if I had any idea her life was in danger . . ."

"Did you see anyone lurking around? Is that why you told me and Larry that you believed the murderer was someone from the street?"

"No. But I thought if I could slip in there undetected then someone else could have. And that's what I still think. Someone came in off the street and killed Susie."

"A stranger?"

"I suppose that's wishful thinking. But I don't know."

"Why did Scott and Kevin take off? Has anyone threatened you?"

Alida shook her head. "No one threatened me, I don't know about them. I received an email from Russell asking me to stop communicating with you about the murder. Antonia, I think you should know . . ."

"What?"

Alida hesitated. "You're not the first . . . I mean, Pauline goes on tangents every few years and stirs this up . . . It's like picking a scab for her. She riles everyone up, makes us all stressed out, and then it's over and she rewards us with something."

"I know there were other private investigators."

"Not only private investigators. She's asked all sorts of people to do what you're doing. Most are not as . . . thorough as you and abandon it. But a few years ago there was a guy asking around."

"Really?"

"Yes. Just know that it's not worth it. You have a life, don't ruin it."

*   *   *   *   *

Antonia was distracted during the car ride home. She had apprised Nick of her interaction with Alida and they had continued discussing the investigation. By the time they reached the inn, Antonia realized they had not even touched on Nick's personal life or marital status at all.

"I'm sorry we didn't have a chance to talk about you. I pretty much dominated the conversation," she admitted.

"It was great. It was so nice not to talk about me or think about my life. I loved the distraction."

"I'm glad to be of help."

"You are a great help," he said. He put his hand on top of hers and pressed.

She smiled at him, wondering if she should invite him in

for a nightcap. *Too forward?* Making it too much like a date and not friends on a night out? Before she could say anything, he spoke.

"My life is complicated and I wish it wasn't."

"You're just going through a rough patch. It will get better."

"I'm meeting up with Melanie tomorrow to discuss everything, so you won't see me on the beach in the morning."

Antonia was disappointed but tried not to show it. "That's great. I hope you're able to work things out. I didn't realize she was back in town."

"She flew in yesterday. The truth is, Antonia, I'm not sure we should work things out. I mean, I never wanted Finn to be a child of divorce. That would crush him. But Melanie and I don't bring out the best in each other. We fight like hell. And can that be a good thing for a child?"

"I can't answer that, I'm sorry . . ."

"You're right," he said cutting her off. "It's unfair of me to put you in this position. But you know what it is?" He looked at her with that intensity that made her melt.

"What?"

"I don't realize how bad it is until I'm with you."

"Uh, yikes . . ."

"I don't mean that in a bad way, sorry, that came out wrong. I meant that when I'm with you, we talk about interesting things—other than Hollywood. There's no artifice. We are relaxed and happy. No drama. We're good friends. I'm not friends with Melanie."

Antonia wasn't sure what he was saying, should she read

into it? Was he saying that he wanted more than friendship?

"They say that's crucial to most relationships."

"What about you? Are you still seeing that guy, the chef?"

"Sam?" Antonia's face reddened. "No. That ended."

Nick nodded. He stared down at the steering wheel. "Are you upset about it?"

Antonia shifted her weight in her seat. She didn't love talking about past relationships. "I mishandled it. I'm pretty bad at relationships."

Nick smiled. "So am I."

"I guess we have that in common."

"I guess we do."

Something passed between them and they both felt it. Nick looked as if he was about to say or do something but then suddenly stopped himself.

"I need to figure this out. I don't want to bring you into my drama."

"I understand completely. I should head in, I have to be up early tomorrow."

"Okay. Well, wish me luck tomorrow. I hope I make it out of my meeting with Melanie alive."

"Good luck, Nick."

"Thanks so much again for being a terrific sounding board."

"No problem."

He leaned in and gave her a peck on the cheek. *That's all folks*, she thought as she walked up the path to the inn. *That's a wrap.*

32

Antonia was about to open the door of the Windmill Inn when a figure in the shadows moved toward her. She almost jumped out of her skin. It was Officer Flanagan.

"I swear I had absolutely no idea she was there! I tried to run away from her but she pursued me! I can prove it."

"Hang on a second, who are you talking about?"

"Alida Jenkins. She was at the restaurant I was at tonight. But I promise you I didn't know she was going to be there. And then she followed me into the bathroom. In fact, maybe I should be going to court and filing a restraining order against her!"

"I believe you, Antonia, and that's not why I'm here."

"It isn't?"

"No."

"Oh, okay." Antonia felt her entire body relax. "What are you doing here?"

"I came with bad news."

"Uh-oh."

"Yes. Dougie Marshall is dead."

"Dead?" Antonia felt a wave of fear course through her entire body. "How? Murdered?"

Officer Flanagan shook his head. "No. He abruptly left the hospital without being discharged, got in a rental car, drove down to the beach, and turned the gas on. He's dead, Antonia."

"Oh, no! I don't understand . . . do they know why?"

"Maybe the accident did something to his head . . . we're not sure. He had a visitor and was very agitated after that. The nurses sedated him, but in the middle of the night he checked out."

"Who was the visitor?"

"They don't know. Couldn't even tell if it was male or female. The nurse only saw the visitor from the back and he or she wore a baseball cap."

"How did he get a rental car?"

"It was in the parking lot. It had been rented in his name, and he had the keys."

"That's so strange, when would he have had time to do that?"

"We're still working that out. The point is, Antonia, I came here as a friend to reiterate to you how dangerous this whole thing is. Don't get wrapped up in it anymore. Stay away."

"Scout's honor!" she said, although she had never been a scout. She made some sort of sign of the cross on her chest—she had no idea what she was supposed to do—but she wanted Officer Flanagan to understand her sincerity.

"Good. Take care of yourself."

"Will do."

* * * * *

Antonia eschewed her Monday-morning walk and spent the time with Hector in the garden instead. There had been some unwanted visitors in the vegetable patch who were feasting on all of the carrots and lettuce. At first it all seemed Disney adorable, but now Antonia and Hector were running out of patience. The challenge was that the source of entry remained elusive. The patch was wired and fenced and had basically a military gate around it, but still the pesky rabbit/mole/vole had been able to breach their security.

Antonia was pulling out half-eaten arugula and chewed up celery and dumping them into a pail when Hector called out to her.

"What?" Antonia asked.

He motioned her over to the far side of the garden. "All along I think the animal was coming from the east side, because they eat the vegetables there. But I thought to myself, maybe they come from the other side and walk across? And look."

He pointed proudly at an almost invisible hole in the fencing.

"Well, I'll be damned," Antonia said. "I think we've found ourselves the interloper's access. Sorry, Fantastic Mister Fox. You'll have to head over to the neighbors' to feed."

"Yes. Sometimes you have to look at things from a different angle. It's not always what you think at first."

"Sound advice."

After finishing up in the garden, Antonia returned to the inn. She placed her gardening gloves and boots in the mudroom and washed her hands in the sink. She took a stroll through the kitchen and made her way into the parlor. There was a stack of newspapers strewn all over the sofa in the far corner that Antonia began to refold and place neatly on the coffee table. When she had completed her task she turned around and gasped.

Pauline Framingham was sitting in the armchair watching her.

"What are you doing here?" Antonia exclaimed.

"Dougie is dead," Pauline said flatly. Although her tone was calm and neutral, her face appeared anguished.

"I know."

"Because of me."

"You killed him?"

"Of course not. But I'm the reason he's dead."

Antonia walked closer to her and sat down on the edge of the coffee table. "Why do you say that?"

There were tears in Pauline's eyes. "I'm jinxed. Everyone around me dies. It's my penance. I'm not allowed to love anyone else or have anyone else close to me."

"Who doesn't allow you?"

"It's my destiny."

"Pauline, is someone threatening you? Are you in danger?"

"I *am* danger, Antonia."

"I don't follow. Do you know who killed Susie? Did you kill Susie? Who killed Dougie? Maybe if you tell me, this can be stopped."

Pauline stood up abruptly. "Nothing can be stopped. And what does it matter anymore, they're dead."

"But maybe we can stop more people from dying?"

Pauline didn't answer as she strode to the door. Then she turned around. Her face was no longer sad; it was now enraged. "We can't stop anyone from dying, Antonia. We're all going to die."

"I don't understand . . . why did you come here?"

Pauline composed herself and smiled. "I'm throwing the memorial service. I want it to be here next Thursday. Make sure it's nice. Tea sandwiches and lots of booze."

Antonia was rattled the rest of the day. When she was at the front desk with Connie, she was completely unable to answer any of the guests' queries as to where the best beaches were or what restaurants to check out. Those were normally answers that Antonia could recite in her sleep. She dropped a pot of chilled cucumber soup on the floor in the kitchen and she accidentally hung up on someone booking a private party in October. Jonathan gently persuaded her that maybe she should take a break in her apartment until she felt like herself again. She had to laugh, because when would that happen?

Of course the first thing she did when she walked into her apartment was knock her pocketbook over and spill everything out on the floor. Lipsticks ricocheted under chairs; her keys were flung into the soil of her potted fig tree and a tangled mass of receipts spread out on the carpet like ticker tape. Antonia got down on her hands and knees and began crawling around the floor retrieving items. Perhaps this was a prudent time to weed through the garbage that had accumulated.

Antonia pulled the trash can closer and began throwing out candy wrappers (it wasn't her fault that they kept a dish of bite-sized morsel at the checkout counter at The Salon in Amagansett) and bank deposit statements. There were some old felt-tip pens that no longer worked that she chucked in the garbage. Not to mention a ton of business cards—how did she accumulate that many? She began making neat little stacks of cards that she would keep and those she would throw out. She held up Giorgio Leguzzi's card and felt a wave of sadness. She hoped he would find his love. The next card belonged to Elizabeth Howard, decorator. *Now, who was that*, Antonia mused. Oh yes, the woman who had bumped into her car. Antonia was about to replace it in the pile when she froze. She picked up Giorgio's card and Elizabeth's card and put them in each hand and held them together. Could it be? Could the Elizabeth who he was searching for be the one who had crashed into her?

Antonia immediately retrieved her phone and dialed. Her heart quickened and she prayed that she was right.

* * * * *

"Mr. Leguzzi!"

"Giorgio," he replied, turning and bowing to Antonia.

Antonia had been waiting for hours for him to return to the inn. She had called Cittanuova, but they said he was not there. She knew he was planning on leaving soon, and she had little time.

"I've been looking all over for you," she said. "Where were you?"

"I went to look at the Madoo Conservancy before I departed. Very beautiful."

"That's great," Antonia said, taking him by the arm. She dragged him into the parlor. "I have someone I want you to see."

The man was confused but went along with Antonia to the parlor. She flung open the doors.

"Ta da!"

Elizabeth Howard, who had been waiting patiently but had been somewhat startled by Antonia's revelation that the nice man she had met last fall had come back to America to win her heart, stood up and smiled shyly. Antonia turned and glanced at Giorgio Leguzzi's face. At first she felt as if she had done something terribly wrong. His face appeared stunned and confused. But almost immediately he broke into the biggest smile she had ever seen and wore a mask of ecstasy.

"Elizabeth!" he said. He opened his arms wide and ran to her.

Elizabeth's face broke out into a hot flush. "Giorgio."

They embraced. Antonia was on cloud nine as she watched them. *What are the odds that they found each other*, mused Antonia. Was it fate? Destiny? She thought of herself and Nick Darrow. How had they found each other? Walking on the beach every morning. For a split second Antonia was lost in reverie, imagining Nick crossing an ocean to find her. It would be too good to be true. She was so happy that Giorgio and Elizabeth had discovered one another, though. Someone had a happy ending. Finally, Jonathan tapped her on the shoulder and motioned for her to leave. Probably best not to interfere in their reunion.

"He's so lucky that you found her," said Jonathan.

"I think he's so lucky that *he* found her. I love true love."

"Don't we all."

* * * * *

The matchmaking buzz was a healthier high than the being-in-love buzz, Antonia concluded. There was no downside; it was all about happy endings. When you set someone up successfully, it was as if you were living in a Technicolor Hollywood movie where the prince and princess ride off into the sunset and live happily ever after. There is no morning after where they have stinky breath and realize that they don't like sharing a bathroom because there are all these mysterious hairs around the sink. The fact was, you had to look for love in unexpected places.

Antonia wasn't sure why, but that made her think of Bridget. Maybe since she was in a happy mood—she'd been mentally high-fiving herself and doling out internal hugs all day— she decided to spread the love. She placed a call to Bridget and asked her to lunch the following day before she left town. Of course Joseph was now her family, but it was exciting to have a blood relative alive to share things with. Ironic that it took someone as evil as Philip to send some joy her way.

33

Three giant buzzkills popped Antonia's emotional high that afternoon, and they were all revelations about the Framingham case. The information wasn't necessarily bad, but it was enticing enough to draw Antonia back into the fold. Despite being determined—no, hell-bent—on not pursuing the investigation any farther, the gods were clearly conspiring against her and kept presenting evidence that would be difficult for even the least nosy/most emotionally unaffected/inhuman person to ignore.

Example one: at three o'clock, Genevieve showed up at the inn, slightly frantic. She found Antonia in the kitchen and pulled her into the mudroom.

"Remember I said I would look through my diary and see what I had written about Susie's death around that time?"

"Yes, Gen, I do, but frankly, I don't really want to hear it. In fact, I can't hear it . . ."

"You have to! This is major."

"I could end up dead if you bestow this information upon me."

"Too bad."

"Seriously, I'm not listening."

Antonia put her hands over her ears and began to sing to drown out Genevieve's words. It was a move Genevieve would have made, and Antonia felt like she had gained a checkmate against a great opponent. But Genevieve just stared at her skeptically and waited for her to finish. It didn't take long and Antonia was annoyed with herself for giving in so easily.

"All right, what is it?"

"You know, you are too easy," Genevieve said. "I like it, but wow."

"Just tell me."

"Okay, I wrote about when Susie died, and I will read you the passage."

Genevieve whipped open a pink-striped diary. It was thick and had a puffy cover that she had coated in Wacky Pack stickers.

"Dear Diary, Today a girl was murdered in town. She was friends with Holly. Holly said she hated her. Holly asked if I remembered the dolls she had shown me. The voodoo dolls that she made? That was one of the girls. I hope she doesn't make a voodoo doll of me!"

Genevieve put down the diary. "Holly had made voodoo dolls of Susie, Pauline, and Alida. I remember clearly now. She was showing them to Victoria, and I came in the room and they hid them, but then they told me. Holly said she hated these three girls, they were mean girls and she wished them all evil so she was pricking them with pins in their hearts and eyes so they would be in pain."

"That's sick."

"I know. But now I wonder, what if it worked? Or what if Holly had something to do with Susie dying?"

"There's a big difference between making a voodoo doll and killing someone."

"Is there?"

"Yes."

"But it shows homicidal intent."

"Sort of."

"I think it's important," Genevieve said defiantly.

"It could be. Why don't you tell the police?"

"I'm not going to tell the police, they'll laugh at me."

"But if you think it's important . . ."

"Antonia, I am giving you this clue so *you* can solve the crime."

"I'm retired."

"Come on."

"You know who you should tell? Larry Lipper. I bet he's in his office now."

"I don't know . . ."

"Trust me. He would love this."

* * * * *

Example two: Antonia was able to push the investigation out of her mind after Genevieve departed but then Joseph came by the kitchen and asked to see her.

"Geez, Antonia, no one wants to let you work today," Marty teased. "Seems like it's becoming a habit."

"Good thing I have you to hold down the fort," Antonia said, before she excused herself and followed Joseph to the library.

"I'm sorry to bother you, but I think I solved the question about why Russell was paying Scott and Holly."

"To cover up the murder?"

"It's actually not that sexy and really quite obvious. Scott was teaching him tennis on his private court."

"How do you know?"

"I was on line at the hardware store and there was a tall man talking quite loudly in front of me to his companion. She was much younger and let's just say could have been wearing a little more yardage of fabric on her body. He was lamenting that his tennis teacher had taken off and then when he charged his purchase to his house account and said his name, I put two and two together."

"That's certainly less sinister than I had imagined."

"Agreed. I fear our minds are jumping to the most macabre conclusions when perhaps a simple explanation would suffice."

"True. And I can see why Holly was so agitated and didn't want Scott teaching Russell anymore. It's best to avoid the Framinghams at all cost."

"Indeed it would appear so."

* * * * *

Example three: Larry Lipper showed up not even fifteen minutes after Joseph left and demanded to speak to Antonia.

Marty and Kendra just rolled their eyes. Antonia led Larry into her office.

"Did Genevieve find you?"

"Who?"

"My friend Genevieve. She wanted to show you something."

"No, I was out doing important things."

"Like what?"

"This."

Larry slapped a pile of glossy photographs on her desk. Antonia glanced down and her heart skipped a beat. They were the crime scene photos from the day of the murder. Antonia thought she had a clear vision of Susie dead but she realized that it had been only in her imagination, she had never actually seen any photos. Until now. There were stills of Susie from various angles but in all of them she lay on the ground on her side, the back of her head a bloody mess and her hair tangled in gore.

"This is awful."

"I know."

Antonia sunk into her chair. "I wish I had never seen this."

"I hear you."

"Then why did you show me?" she asked, peering up at him with an accusatory look on her face.

"Because I need you to see something. Look, here is the picture of the court."

Larry pointed to a panoramic shot of the tennis court. There was a policeman in the corner and Susie's body lay in a heap by the gate near the fence. Antonia shuddered. It was so eerie to think that she had stood where Susie had died. How was it possible that Russell and Pauline were able to play tennis on that court? If it had been her house, and she had their money, she would have demolished it or moved away. And even if she didn't have their money, there was no way she could play there. It was sacred ground as far as she was concerned.

"Okay, what are you inferring?" Antonia asked.

He slid his finger from the gate where Antonia had entered the court all the way across to the one next to where Susie's body was found.

"I think her body was moved to make it look like she was at that gate near the back."

"I'm sure the police would have noticed that."

"They never mentioned it."

"Okay, well, even if that's the case, what does it matter?"

"I think it matters because it mattered to the killer . . ."

"Larry."

"Come on, bear with me. I figured two heads were better than one on this. Why would the killer care where the body was found? What difference did it make?"

Antonia stared at the pictures as if they would give her the answer. "Maybe they wanted that intruder theory to be put forth."

Something Hector had said about the intruder in the garden sprang into her mind. You had to look at it from a different angle . . .

Larry nodded. "I thought that. But I actually think, maybe

Susie did see something and they wanted her as far away as possible."

"You mean . . . what do you mean?"

"I don't know. But I thought maybe you and I could go back to the court and have a look around . . ."

"Uh-huh," Antonia said, shaking her head. "No way. I'm off this case."

"Antonia, we are so close."

"You are. You can be. I can't."

"Some detective you are! They really have you scared."

"I admit I'm scared. Know thyself. If I don't know who I am at this age, I will never know."

"I love all the kumbaya self-awareness, but spare me. This isn't a self-help group meeting. Get your pocketbook or the lady stuff you roll with and let's go."

"I can't."

"You can't? Antonia Bingham, that's pathetic. Look at this girl."

Larry held up a close-up photograph of Susie Whitaker. Her eyes were open and unblinking. They appeared to be staring at Antonia and Larry.

"This girl is asking for your help. You need to finish what you started and help her."

34

"I can't believe you talked me into this. We are insane."

"We are not insane. We are vigilantes," Larry replied.

They had parked in the Georgica Beach parking lot and were making the short walk on Lily Pond Lane to turn left onto West End Road. Antonia had insisted on donning jogging apparel ("You own that crap?" Larry had said when he saw it) so that in case they were detected they could plead that they were on an innocent power walk. It didn't matter that Larry was wearing loafers and khakis, Antonia was indifferent to the possibility that he might be arrested and only cared that she might.

They strode past Grey Gardens, which was completely devoid of activity and stood in front of the Framinghams' driveway.

"I'm nervous," she confessed.

"Don't be. You have your sneakers on; you can do an Olympic dash if we're spotted."

"Can we just walk past the property once so I can try and see if anyone's home."

"How are you going to see? There's a full hedge and the house is two acres away."

"Humor me."

They walked slowly past the house and, indeed, it was impossible to decipher any movement through the sparse holes in the dense foliage. Antonia was nervous, and casing the joint was only making her more tense.

"Okay, can we sneak in now?" Larry whined.

"Give me a second."

They had pivoted around and were lingering in front of the hedge to the house. She tried to peep through but she could only see flickers of the fence that surrounded the tennis court.

"Maybe if we go over here?"

Antonia crossed the street with Larry trotting along behind her and turned around to see if the view improved. Not really, she had to admit. She was wishing for some sort of super power that would allow her to see through foliage and fencing, but as hard as she tried, it was impossible. Suddenly a dark car turned down the street and was driving toward them. Antonia didn't recognize the car, but squinted to see if she could make out the person driving it. As he approached slowly she had a feeling that he looked vaguely familiar.

"Quick!" Antonia bent down to pretend to tie her shoe and pulled Larry down next to her.

"Antonia, what the hell? Here?"

"I don't want anyone to see us."

The car drove past them and turned quickly into the neighbor's house. Antonia sighed with relief and stood up.

"False alarm," Larry said.

"That was close."

"What are you talking about? You are making us suspicious by your wacky behavior. Seriously, Antonia. This is creepy. Look, there's a mail truck down the road, should we load our guns? Is the mailman after us? He's a federal employee, maybe he'll arrest us."

"I'm sorry, I thought it might be Pauline."

"Geez, really. It's only a next-door neighbor and I'm sure he didn't even notice us, or hadn't, until you made that bizarre jerky move. He's on his merry way home, not paying attention to anyone else. He probably thinks we're now fornicating . . ."

Antonia tuned Larry out. Her mind began spinning. It was something that Larry said . . . and suddenly a flood of memories came rushing back to her. All of the pieces of the puzzle suddenly fell into place.

Chester Saunders said: "I to this day don't know how they got her lawyer there that fast, but he was there by the time I was."

Pauline said: "I have a lawyer for every possible need."

Dougie said: "She loves her lawyer; the guy is like her best friend."

Eddie the gardener said: "In my opinion, it was Pauline's fellow that did it. I used to hear them arguing when I was clipping the front hedges. They'd be up in that guesthouse going at it really hard. Screaming and yelling. Those two just love a good fight. I imagine they still go at it. Saw him storm out of there two days ago."

Larry said: "I actually think, maybe Susie did see something and they wanted her as far away as possible . . . I think her body was moved to make it look like she was at that gate near the back . . . It mattered to the killer."

It mattered to the killer where she was found . . . because he didn't want her near his house.

* * * * *

"Larry, I know who did it."

Larry was brushing grass off his shirt. "What do you mean? Who?"

"Follow me."

Antonia charged across the street. Larry trotted after her. "Where are you going? Who did it?"

Antonia kept up her brisk pace. Instead of veering left toward the Framingham house, she marched into the neighboring property and began walking up the stone driveway toward the enormous modern white house that sat on the cusp of the dune. As she strode toward the manor she passed a guesthouse on her left that abutted the Framinghams' property.

"Antonia, where are we going? Whose house is this?"

"I'm pretty sure it belongs to Tom Schultz."

"Tom Schultz, Tom Schultz, that name is familiar."

"Pauline's lawyer. The Framingham family's lawyer who pulled the plug on our investigation."

"Are you sure you want to go here? Isn't he the guy filing restraining orders against you? One second you're all paranoid and the next you're a badass Nancy Drew. I can't follow your journey."

Larry was out of breath keeping up with her so his words came out between heaving gasps. Antonia didn't answer. Her heart was beating quickly, but adrenaline was pumping wildly throughout her body. As she approached the house she spied two dark sedans parked in front. A glance to her right revealed a three-car garage. She would bet her life that inside was the car that had been used to sideline Dougie Marshall.

Antonia climbed the steep slate steps and pressed on the bell firmly. Two large glass windows flanked the door and Antonia peered inside. There was a cold marble floor and a large white canvas on the wall featuring several black blobs that Antonia was certain cost a fortune. She never could understand modern art. She turned and surveyed the grounds from her aerie. A thin lap pool was tucked into the far side of the property, and a flower garden further beyond. The front door swung open and Antonia spun around. Pauline Framingham was standing on the threshold, dressed somewhat formally as if she were preparing to head to the city. A small smile curled around her lips when she saw who had arrived.

"What the hell!" Larry said. "I thought you lived over there."

Pauline ignored him. "Hello, Antonia."

"Hello, Pauline."

"Won't you come in? I was wondering how long it would take you to find us."

She led them in silence through the cold hall to the cavernous living room that was awash in light. One wall made entirely of glass offered an incredible view of the crashing waves and surf. The brightness of the ocean was reflected by the whiteness of the house, rendering the few colors almost psychedelic. Antonia had assumed she preferred old houses but now she thought there might be something to be said about trading teardowns for modern. Why look through itty bitty little window panes when you could have an entire wall of view? Although there was something antiseptic and noxious about the place, Antonia recognized. Probably due to the people who lived there. On a large low-slung white sofa that wrapped around half the room sat Pauline Framingham's lawyer, Tom Schultz. He didn't bother to stand up when they entered.

"Antonia, Larry, why don't you sit over there? Tom and I were having a chat." Pauline gestured to the seating area.

Antonia's heart was pounding with the surge of confidence she felt now that she had pieced it all together. She was not willing to let Pauline have the upper hand. But she was what they call "a man without a plan" and was scrambling to figure out what her next move would be. In the meantime, she perched herself in a modern black leather chair while Larry was swallowed up by the alternative seating option: a giant bubble swing that hung from the ceiling. He was so short his legs hung off the end.

Tom Schultz appeared tense and drawn. Crinkly dark bags hung sloppily under his eyes and his jaw was set in a defensive lock. He wore a monochrome suit and no tie and looked out of place in the surroundings. In one hand he clasped a cocktail and made no movement other than to divert his eyes to Pauline's to give her a gloomy stare.

"Well, Tom, it appears the cat is out of the bag," Pauline

said merrily. She sat down on the other edge of the sofa and picked up her wineglass. "Cheers!" she said, before draining it.

Tom shot her an irritated look. "Pauline, shut up."

"Can someone fill me in?" Larry begged, slowly starting to pump his swing back and forth. "I'd like to know what we are celebrating."

"Tom Schultz and Pauline are lovers. They have been for decades," Antonia said with certainty.

"Bravo," Pauline said.

"This is true?" asked Larry. "How did you figure it out?"

"Yes, Antonia, do tell us," Pauline commanded.

"Honestly, I'm surprised it took me so long. Everyone was dropping clues all along—about how important your lawyer was to you, how your lawyer was your best friend, your lawyer was here immediately to defend you as soon as Susie was killed. I was distracted by 'the lawyer.' I thought of the profession—and honestly, I thought of a team of lawyers all in one amalgamation. Maybe if someone had called him by name it would have come to me earlier. If they had all said 'Tom was there' or 'Tom is her best friend.' But they didn't. He was just a nameless, faceless person. And it would have been easier if I knew he was your next-door neighbor. But I was too busy wasting my time investigating the list of people that you asked me to talk to . . ."

"It's always fun to keep my friends in line," Pauline said.

"First of all, that's sick, Pauline," Larry said with disgust. "And second of all, do they all know? Alida? Scott? Did Dougie and Susie know?"

"I think everyone else knew they were together or suspected but they had all been given things and threatened over the years so they were too scared to say anything. Am I right?" Antonia asked Pauline.

"More or less."

"And Susie?" Larry asked.

"Susie knew and didn't approve," Pauline admitted between sips of her drinks. "Susie should have just stayed out of it. She infuriated Tom! Of course he didn't need to kill her . . ."

"Do you even hear yourself?" Antonia asked. "Susie was your best friend. She knew you were in over your head. She was acting in your best interests, Pauline. And this is how you repay her?"

"*I* didn't do anything!" Pauline snapped.

"You're right. You didn't do anything. And she was killed," Antonia reprimanded. "And you've covered it up for years."

It enraged Antonia to think of Susie being killed for being a good friend.

"Why did you kill her?" Larry asked Tom. "Was that really necessary?"

"She was a brat. She wouldn't listen to me. I told her to stay out of it, I threatened her, but she ran to the Ambassador and told him everything! I had to do damage control," Tom said flatly, and without remorse. He was too caught up in the indignity that he suffered to realize how insane he sounded.

"But the Ambassador already suspected the truth," Antonia interjected. "That's why he forbade Pauline and Susie from attending the firework party—*the Schultz firework party*. Susie wrote about it in her journal. She said when she went, she saw the Ambassador having a heated conversation with a woman at the party and I conjecture that it was with Tom's wife, who was, no doubt, as distraught about the affair as he was."

"You're married?" Larry asked.

Tom glared at him. "Of course. I love my wife very much."

Antonia walked over and picked up a silver-framed picture that was on a side table. It was of Tom and a woman beaming from a yacht. Antonia squinted and looked at it closely. A flash of recognition sparked in her brain. It was the woman jogger who Antonia had met on the beach. "Your wife tried to warn me about Pauline."

"Leave my wife out of this," demanded Tom.

Pauline's face contorted with rage and she spat, "Your wife has always been in this, Tom! If you would just leave her we could move forward! I'm tired of being second fiddle, you have manipulated me for too long! Telling me you'll leave her, begging me to remain with you, then jerking me around."

"Pauline, calm down. Let's stop this," Tom said.

Pauline ignored him. "Go on, Antonia, I'm loving this."

"I think the Ambassador warned Pauline and Tom to end it. He left for Europe. When they called home to check in, Susie told Pauline's mother that the relationship was still on. Tom was enraged and murdered Susie. When the Ambassador returned, he couldn't dismiss Tom as his lawyer because Tom convinced him that Pauline had murdered her best friend and he and only he could save her."

"Yes, Tom is quite the manipulator," conceded Pauline.

"For a brief time I thought it was your father who had killed Susie, having returned from Europe. But that was because Holly had said she heard 'them' in his office. But it wasn't 'them' she heard. She saw Tom come over and assumed he was meeting with the Ambassador. But he was meeting with you in the office."

"Very good," Pauline prompted.

"You know, I couldn't understand how a woman as attractive and smart as you had remained single all these years," Antonia admitted to Pauline. "But now it makes sense. You were seeing Tom. And every time you become tired of Tom not leaving his wife you make up a little diversion to rattle him."

"I need to keep him in line."

"But how do you know it was Tom and not Pauline who murdered Susie?" asked Larry.

"It was a violent crime. I remember what Kevin Powers said: 'I never thought Pauline would be so aggressive and bash her best friend's head in.' This from a guy who has a record of aggression. I guess it takes one to know one."

"It's true. I would never do that," Pauline said.

"I wasn't completely sure until now. I know that Tom hit her until she died. But you are just as complicit, Pauline. You are as guilty as if you had done it yourself. How could you do that to your best friend? How could you let Susie die? And never even tell who did it?"

"It wasn't my fault," Pauline responded. "Tom has always been obsessed with me. He will do anything for me, to have my love. Anything but leave his wife and marry me."

"Don't you feel shame?" Larry asked. "This guy is a monster."

"And now he also killed Dougie . . ." Antonia added.

Tom began clapping slowly but forcefully. "Enough of this. Well done, Miss Bingham. You cracked the case."

"I wish I could say thank you, but I feel no joy in this resolution. I wish I could bring Susie back."

"You found the answer and now off you go!" he sneered.

"I think you mean, off *you* go," said Larry.

"No, I don't think so."

Tom stood up, knocking over his cocktail so that the glass goblet shattered all over the cold stone floor. In his hand he held a gun, which he aimed at Antonia. He turned and glared at Larry. "Get over there next to her."

Larry stopped pumping his swing and put his hands up, trying to extricate himself from the bubble. "Now, now, we can talk this through . . ."

"Shut up!" Tom commanded.

"Tom, this is so boring, what are you going to do, kill them?" Pauline said drily, as if she were asking him the most mundane question in the world.

"Yes, I am. And I'm also going to kill you."

Pauline laughed a wicked laugh. She took another sip of her drink. "Oh, please, Tom . . ."

Before she could finish the gun exploded. Antonia dropped to the floor her hands covering her head. Larry cowered beside her.

"I told you to shut up!"

Antonia peeked up and spied Tom, his face enraged and

sweaty. She snuck a look to her right and saw Pauline lying on the floor. Blood was trickling from her shoulder. Antonia braced herself, her entire being consumed with fear. She had to do something, think fast, Antonia. Tom began walking toward her, she could hear his footsteps on the floor as if they were blasting bombs. Was he going to shoot her execution style? How had it come to this?

"You're next, bitch!"

She felt the cold nozzle press against her head. Then there was a loud explosion, almost like a superhuman roar. Antonia waited. Was she dead? She didn't feel pain. She glanced up. Light was streaming through the windows. Heaven? No. Larry had taken a swan dive into Tom, knocking the gun out of his hand and was now wrestling him on the floor.

"Larry!"

"The gun, Bingham. Grab the gun!"

Antonia slid herself along the floor and clasped her hands around the heavy metal gun. She had never held one before and her hands were shaking. She aimed the gun at Tom.

"Okay, Larry, I got it."

In an expert move, Larry whipped off his belt and spun Tom onto his stomach on the floor. He dug his knee into him as he tied Tom's hands together with his belt. When he was finished he jumped up and took the gun from Antonia's wobbly hands.

Antonia rushed over to Pauline, who was gasping for air. She grabbed a throw blanket that was on the sofa and pressed it against her shoulder, where the bullet had landed. Pauline was trying to say something to her, and Antonia could barely make it out. She leaned closer. Maybe she would hear some words of remorse from Pauline, for all of the death and destruction that she had unleashed. Maybe Pauline would finally acknowledge how bitterly she had betrayed her friend Susie and then retreated back into her vast wealth and all the armor that came with it in her personal fortress.

"Pauline, what are you trying to say?"

Antonia leaned closer.

"He doesn't deserve me," she finally choked out, before losing consciousness.

35

The police arrested Tom Schultz and he was charged with two murders: Susie Whitaker's and Dougie Marshall's. Officer Flanagan told Antonia he was pretty certain they'd nail him on Dougie's but Susie's would be harder to prove. Antonia dearly hoped that Schultz would be brought to justice and convicted of her death so Susie could finally rest in peace. It wasn't a lot to ask.

Pauline recovered, was eviscerated in the press, and took off for Europe. Antonia wasn't sure she would ever see her again, and was happy if that was the case. She did receive a check from the Framingham family trust asking her to cover the cost of Dougie's memorial service. Antonia hoped that somewhere in the bowels of Pauline's polluted heart she had a conscience.

Kevin Powers, Scott Stewart, and Holly Wender crawled out of hiding and returned to their lives in East Hampton, as did Alida. All of the people that Pauline had cast a shadow over with her reckless and selfish ways were happy to have her gone. Despite the intense interest by the press, none of them chose to comment on the story. They were finally free of a decades-old burden and able to lift themselves out of the tragedy.

Larry glued himself to his computer and began writing his account of the investigation with himself as the sole investigator. (Antonia asked him to leave her out of it, and he readily agreed.) Genevieve returned to her dating scene and Joseph returned to the library.

Antonia returned her focus to the inn and the restaurant but had some loose ends to tie up before she could be completely focused. The first was her lunch with Bridget, an engagement that they were both tentative about. Antonia decided to keep it casual, and made up some Pierre Robert cheese and tomato tarragon sandwiches and packed a Greek salad and brownies and they met on the beach for a picnic. They were both hesitant and kept the conversation lighthearted. Antonia was not ready to ask Bridget any questions about her experiences with their father, a sentiment Bridget seemed to intuit. But they actually liked each other, and promised to stay in touch and try to build a relationship. In fact, they had plans for a call later in the week to discuss what to do about Philip when Bridget returned home.

Dougie Marshall's memorial service at the inn was a depressing affair. With Pauline out of the country, the lone person Antonia knew was Alida, who made a brief cameo. The crowd was preppy and the only insight Antonia had into them was that they were heavy drinkers as it was the highest daytime bar bill she had ever seen. She felt guilty about Dougie, as if she had caused his death, which she inadvertently had. It would take her a while to reconcile that fact. The sad truth Antonia had learned in the past year was that the fallout from murder was more death.

Antonia kept her word and accompanied Kendra to the Instagram ceremony at Wölffer. She saw Sam from a distance and was surprised that she had forgotten how good-looking he was. She was about to approach him when a young blond came over and entwined her arm with his. It was clear they were a couple. Always the chicken, Antonia ended up waving at him and keeping her distance on the other side of the tent. She could have sworn she saw Sam watching her out of the corner of her eye several times, but she left before they ever had a chance to interact. She felt a tinge of sadness that their relationship had been fleeting.

Nick Darrow stopped by the inn a few days after their dinner and surprised Antonia in her office as she was doing some long overdue paperwork.

"I hope I'm not bothering you."

Antonia glanced up from her desk. She put down her pen atop the check she was signing and motioned for him to sit down. "Not at all."

"I heard about Pauline Framingham and the lawyer. Good job solving another crime."

"I can't take credit for that . . ."

"You're too modest."

"Okay, I'll take some. But it was a boiling kettle. Only a

matter of time before it exploded. Pauline wanted everyone to know, she'd had enough of her twisted relationship with Tom Schultz."

"I can relate."

Antonia cocked her head to the side. "How are things with Melanie?"

"Not good. It's not going to work."

"I'm sorry."

He shrugged. "It is what it is. Meanwhile, we have to really put on our best acting because we have to return to Australia tomorrow to finish the movie. It's going to be very difficult pretending to be in love with her for the big screen."

"That's why you get paid the big bucks."

"True." He ran his hand through his thick hair. "Listen, Antonia. I'm gone a few weeks, then I need to head to L.A. to do another film, but not for too long. Hopefully I'll be in a better place when I'm back."

"I hope so too."

"And I want to stay in touch. Can we email? I know you're a bit of a Luddite. Or maybe we can write letters?"

"Let's do that. I have a box full of stationery that I am desperate to use."

"Sounds good."

He stood up and walked to the door. Antonia felt as if he was dragging her heart with him. He slowly turned around and stared at her.

"When I'm back, maybe . . . maybe things can be different. Between us, you know."

She knew what he meant and felt herself melting. "Sounds good," she said.

"Yeah?"

"Yeah."

Before she could suppress the sad emotions that his departure was conjuring up in her soul, he had crossed the room and come around behind her desk. She stood and his arms were around her, tightly enfolding her into his body. He pressed her toward him and kissed her, gently at first, and then with increasingly firm intensity that caused all of the blood to drain from her body and left her weak and dizzy. There was an urgency in his gesture that evoked sensations she had never felt before. It was a dream-come-true kiss, one that she had only dared to envision in her most hopeful and unrealistic fantasies where she felt like a heroine swooped in on by the hero. And yet it was happening. The kiss escalated, and she felt herself leaning further and further into him, until he finally broke away.

He stared at her for a beat before he spoke.

"Wait for me," he commanded.

He was out the door before a dazed Antonia could respond. She flopped down into her desk chair for what seemed like hours, staring into space. *I will.*

* * * * *

"This is how I like it," Antonia sighed one evening a week later as she settled in for a nightcap with Joseph in the library at the inn. "No drama."

They had driven to Connecticut via the ferries that morning

to place a bouquet of daisies on Susie Whitaker's grave. Alida had told Antonia that those were Susie's favorite, and Antonia agreed that Susie seemed like a daisy sort of person: cheerful, simple, and forever young. Susie was buried in a field next to her parents in a small country cemetery. Under her name it said "Beloved Daughter, Beloved Friend." Antonia thought of Pauline's earlier comment that the dates on a gravestone marking birth and death were ultimately the least relevant dates of your life. She agreed that it was true. It was all the days in between that mattered and it was those days that she wanted Susie to be remembered for. She deserved at least that. As Antonia and Joseph were leaving a breeze blew up and spread the flowers all across the plot. Antonia took it as a sign that Susie knew they were there and was just maybe thanking them.

The days in East Hampton were becoming shorter and a chill had settled into the night air. The end of summer was on the horizon and Antonia knew that the quieter fall was soon to come.

Antonia smiled at Joseph over the rim of her glass then spoke. "Guess what? I received an email from Giorgio Leguzzi. He and Elizabeth are having a fantastic time in Italy."

She didn't mention that she had also received a letter from Nick Darrow, full of funny observations about his film set and including his latest rantings on the world at large. She had reread it over and over until the paper was worn. She would wait for him. She was waiting for him. Was it possible a new life would start for them? She couldn't even imagine. But that kiss was keeping her going; it was the fuel that charged her every waking moment.

"Lovely to hear, my dear."

"You know, I think I might switch to matchmaking rather than crime solving. It's so much more pleasant, don't you think?"

"I think that's a wonderful idea!"

"Yes, I agree. I'm officially retired from sleuthing. Give me love over death any day!"

"I'll drink to that, my dear," agreed Joseph, gently clinking his glass against hers.

THE END

ABOUT THE AUTHOR

Carrie Doyle is a best-selling author who lives in New York City
and East Hampton with her husband and two sons.

Visit Carrie's author site at **WWW.CARRIEKARASYOV.COM**
or learn more about Carrie (and Antonia and the Hamptons!) on
WWW.DUNEMEREBOOKS.COM.

ALSO BY CARRIE DOYLE (WRITING AS CARRIE KARASYOV):

The Infidelity Pact

WRITING AS CARRIE KARASYOV WITH JILL KARGMAN:

The Right Address
Wolves in Chic Clothing
Bittersweet Sixteen
Summer Intern
Jet Set

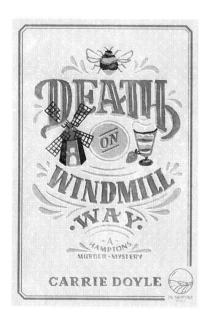 

DUNEMERE

Books

WWW.DUNEMEREBOOKS.COM

CPSIA information can be obtained
at www.ICGtesting.com
Printed in the USA
LVOW11s0902110617
537714LV00002B/508/P